Mrs. S

Mrs. S

K Patrick

4th ESTATE • *London*

4th Estate
An imprint of HarperCollins*Publishers*
1 London Bridge Street
London SE1 9GF

www.4thestate.co.uk

HarperCollins*Publishers*
Macken House, 39/40 Mayor Street Upper
Dublin 1, D01 C9W8, Ireland

First published in Great Britain in 2023 by 4th Estate

1

A catalogue record for this book is
available from the British Library

ISBN 978-0-00-856099-7 (hardback)
ISBN 978-0-00-856100-0 (trade paperback)

Typeset in Stempel Garamond
Printed and bound in the UK using 100%
renewable electricity at CPI Group (UK) Ltd

MIX
Paper | Supporting
responsible forestry
FSC
www.fsc.org
FSC™ C007454

You are clear
O rose, cut in rock,
hard as the descent of hail.

I could scrape the colour
from the petals
like spilt dye from a rock.

If I could break you
I could break a tree.

If I could stir
I could break a tree –
I could break you.

H.D., 'Garden'

You are not made by yourself,
but by the thing that you want.

Fanny Howe, 'Catholic'

She argues with the gardener. Her voice is not raised. I stop to watch them. Stood opposite one another in her grand driveway, branches from a dark-green shrub in his wheelbarrow. He does not know he is being argued with, he does not know how to read the angles of her body. One foot taking aim, the other carefully sets her balance. Chin, skyward, it rips through the overhead pine tree. Her hand – I want more detail, I can't have it – throws his gaze towards the flower beds. He lifts his shirt almost to his nipples to wipe his face. Thinks he is putting his masculinity to good use. Flashing his hard work. His bellybutton too. The size of a fingertip, refusing to be eclipsed by muscle. An unregulated softness. He is vulnerable. There is nothing he can do. Her energy is concentrated and precise, light through a magnifying glass. Left standing with his shirt balled into his fist. He pushes the wheelbarrow away, back into the garden, to face his mistake. Oh, she is vigilant, she knows she is not alone. I am discovered, I burn. Like her I stand my ground. Dare her to wave, to give that hand to me.

Miss Miss Miss. What else could I ask them to call me? Matron is the job title. Strange as it is, that might sound better, a nice word to wear. At least I could taste a little butch in it, a pair of crossed arms, a dramatic mole, a stiff back. No, Miss instead. The Girls repeat it all day long. They flirt with me, with each other, with the reverend who blushes in his long black robes. I don't remember possessing this adolescent power. They make eye contact and hold it steady.

A bust of the dead author sits cold on a plinth. As The Girls walk in from church they dart to kiss her head, to tap her nose, to tickle her chin. The Housemistress does nothing, I do nothing. The ritual feels hard-earned. Especially in this weather. Spring flowers rotting in the cold snap. Clouds pinned to our shoulders. The Girls press chilled mouths, chilled fingertips, to the marble. I blow into my hands. When one Girl traces the dead author's lips with her tongue, I interrupt weakly. Hey, hey. Don't do that. Recently I've learned not to say please.

She emerges from her office. Mrs S, the headmaster's wife. She prefers luxurious fabrics. Today, in honour of the unexpected frost, a cashmere polo neck. As she sees The Girls she smiles and tugs on her sleeves. Her nails are painted maroon. Last week they were bright red. Fingers have the poise of a conductor's. Morning Ladies. Good morning, they echo. Each shifts quickly away from the dead author's head. The Girls respect Mrs S's beauty. She is tall. From a few feet, the closest we have been, I notice I am taller. Only just. Her face tricks me into familiarity, lifted from a painting, a feminine ideal. Cheekbones that stun. She knows it. Smiling, pulling them tighter. Surely rich like the rest of them. Her job is vague, a counsellor of sorts. She has a large office in which The Girls are invited to drink tea and talk through their weeks. I have never been inside.

The Girls shake off their blazers, the same style for over two hundred years. Rain drips onto the worn red tiles. The whole uniform is done in an awful blue. A cheapened summer sky. Tights, shirts, tie, hair ribbons, pleated heavy skirt, all blue blue blue. Mrs S stops to chat with The Girls. I catch her eye. She looks at me briefly, expectantly. Luckily a Girl needs her attention and I am freed.

The school is haunted by the smell of breakfast. I used to love breakfast. Now it has been intensified beyond pleasure. A tray of scrambled eggs leaking water. Bacon with shimmering, rubberized fat. Damp toast. Soft apples. Pears with snakeskin. I slip a banana in my pocket and leave the dining room quickly. In the staffroom I am eyed up, then largely ignored. Each year a new version of me enters the school, sent over from Australia, spoken to only when

3

needed. What was promised to me? A visa, a true English experience, a dead author.

I surprise myself by liking the headmaster. Mr S, her husband. This morning he sweeps in, wearing that strange cloak clipped around his neck. Another bizarre tradition. Large hands, large neck. Large thighs too, I assume, if I could make them out beneath the thick pinstripe trousers. The charm of unworried men. He is taller than all of us. Mrs S, I imagine, likes this about him especially. His height he keeps friendly, stooping as he greets people. For a few seconds he stands close to me. His clothes smell clean. On his skin there is cinnamon, something woody and sweet. That big body, so well taken care of.

The women talk with him, most of the men nod. Months later and I have still not talked to many of the staff. A few were interested in my accent, in the parts of Australia I know well, which are parts they don't know at all. Some have cousins, an aunt, an uncle living in the big cities. Their disappointment visible when I don't recognize the streets, the surnames. The Housemistress I like enough. Like me, not often seen in the staffroom, her body stiffening whenever required to meet with another teacher. She creates a tension she does not want. The other teachers wary, unable to place her. I wait in case she appears. Sometimes after breakfast, to deliver information about The Girls who are ill, who will be spending the day in bed. Today the door is not swung open with her usual force. I am disappointed.

The bell rings. I have nowhere to be. During the week

my job centres on what I have been asked to help with. A class here, an outing, a sports match. My only preoccupation is The Girls. Waking them up, moving them to school, to breakfast, to prep, to dinner, to bed. The middle of the day wanes. I sip my coffee and read the papers on other people's desks. Marking. A holiday permission form. Two shopping lists done in sloppy handwriting. Teaching is a job I have considered. On the history teacher's desk is a stack of thin exercise books. I open the first. Inside, one of The Girls has written answers to questions on the First World War. Number one is a list of battles and dates. Number two is a few short sentences on the perils of trench life. She overuses the word very. The conditions were very harsh, the mud very thick, the food very bad, the rats very prominent. Nostalgia confused with meaning. He has not yet given her a mark.

Over the chair is his jacket. A smell of past rain and tobacco. I hear footsteps in the corridor and step away. They fade, a door opens, and the person is released outside. I slip a hand into his pockets and find a pipe, a wallet, even a hip flask. Rain starts up again. Driving into the windows. I want to open the wallet and find what clubs he is a member of, how many bank cards, I want to see the image of his younger face on a driver's licence. My boredom is unusual in its current cruelty. I didn't use to be like this, I don't think. I don't think I used to be like this. Wind applies pressure to the building. Something is blown over on the path, skittering across the gravel. Spring's sudden violence. I

The school pretends to be a town. Within the grounds are two shops. One labelled a tuck shop that sells emergency pieces of uniform, stationery and sweets from enormous jars. The other is only books. They sit side by side, cheap units in front of the older buildings, shamed by their movability. Both are open only in the mornings. I walk across the tarmac, the weather possibly improving, momentarily calm. Heat has been promised with great anticipation. The daily forecasts have become a thrill. A temperature, a sun, a cloud, a raindrop drawn on the large chalkboard that hangs in the corridor.

Lessons are happening all around me. In the main building each grand window shows a desk, or blackboard, they still use chalk. In a third mobile unit, alongside the shops, is Home Economics. The lower windows are more revealing. Pictures of the uniforms across the past one hundred years line the walls. Proudly positioned. Skirts at the ankles, the knees, back at the ankles. Straw boaters and red-piped blazers largely unchanged. The Girls sit at sewing machines, fiddling with thread, flicking little levers. A woman's voice is loud through the open windows. She holds up a diagram.

They will be making teddy bears. The Girls are an older class, I recognize a few faces. Fifteen, maybe sixteen years old. Too old, surely, for teddy bears. I think the teacher catches me watching her. I don't move. The Girl nearest the window turns now and I involve her in my look too. A bell sounds. Class is dismissed. I leave the scene, noticing last minute the pieces of teddy bear across each desk, readied for the machines. Torsos, legs and arms in neat arrangements. Round plastic eyes. See-through bags of stuffing.

Above, the clouds begin to move fast. More rain is visible over the hills. Despite working at the school for months I have not yet visited the bookshop. The sign was obviously done by a student from years ago, the colours faded and water-stained in places. Childish drawings of books, some with faces, some in flight, pages opened as wings. Pens and pencils with large, bespectacled eyes. A display sits by the entranceway. On the table is a lace tablecloth, too large, dropping almost to the grey carpet tiles. Three books have been selected. Each covered in dust, each written by, or at least about, the dead author. The editions are not special. Two covers show a famous portrait, cheaply cropped at the chest so you cannot see her clasped hands, the odd way her fingertips press into knuckles. The other is a local scene. Grey skies, a storm whipped up by oil paint, green tremors and whorls across a fell. A biography. I flip it over and read the author's information. She attended the school from 1981 to 1987. I imagine her work details the place in more pleasing terms than the dead author ever did.

Hi. A Girl is behind the counter. In their final year they must take turns running the shop in between study. I have little to do with them. Hi. She is hunched over a thick textbook. Looks fun. Oh it isn't. In the margins she makes quick marks with a pencil. It is too hot, a smell of damp. In the corner an electric heater burns furiously. Postcards are for sale. More green scenery. Cardboard curled slightly. One shows a bust of the dead author's head, the same from the hall. The photo's contrast is too high. The wood panelling is turned almost orange, shadows built menacingly beneath her brow and chin. Can I help you at all? The Girl puts the pencil between her teeth. No, just looking. On the back wall are mostly textbooks. Maths, Physics, Biology. All the guides promise straightforward help with the more serious exams. English Literature is covered on the shelves adjacent to the counter. The Girl keeps the pencil between her teeth, not quite biting but rolling it back and forth. I pull down Shelley, Keats, Wordsworth. So you're the latest Matron? Stupidly I feel my cheeks flush. Yes. The one from Australia? That's me.

She imitates an Australian accent as she says Australia, dragging the vowels. It is surprisingly accurate. Not bad. Thank you. The Girl closes her book, tucking her pencil within its spine. So what are you doing here? She leans across the counter. Working. Yeh, but why? I have family nearby. This is a sudden, strange lie. Oh right. But its quick dullness works. Her line of questioning comes to a halt. Yeh still you must miss the weather. The pencil is picked up again. And the beaches oh I can't even imagine the beaches. Ah well I lived inland, not many beaches, a lake maybe. Maybe? I mean yes, a lake.

The book is opened again. Well, I'd like to visit one day who knows, could even be next year. I am still holding the Wordsworth. You should, it's a nice place, Australia. Did you want to get that? I put the book back on the shelf. No, thanks, no. OK. She takes up her mark-making again, the margin filling sporadically. Hello, hello, isn't it busy, rush hour. Mrs S shakes rain from an umbrella. Yes. The Girl stands suddenly. I feel my own back straighten. She nods at me. A handsome coat. Ghastly, that weather comes out of nowhere. Rain has curled, then glossed, the fine hair at her temples. I imagine her, suddenly, as a very serious child. I look down, embarrassed for her, for me.

Neither I nor The Girl offer a response. Mrs S does not seem to expect one. I believe you have a book for me. Oh? The Girl is panicked briefly, searching under and around the counter. This! She is triumphant. Indeed. It is a large package. Hardback, too big, too ostentatious for fiction. Thank you. In front of us both she unwraps it. She is not careful. The painted fingernails don't seek the folded edge but instead tear straight through the middle. Wonderful, yes, this is the one. It is a book on roses. Second-hand, the cover image a garish trellis.

I am disappointed, had found myself hoping for something that might give more of her away. Not a gardener, then? I have let my disappointment show. Her eyes are on me, body adjusted slightly, elbows sharp. I could be, I want to say, I could be a gardener. Instead, I shrug my shoulders. No not really. The shrug is wrong, indifferent. I feel as though she looks at my throat, just where it leaves the collarbone, ridge into tendon. My fingers find the source and I touch a mound of bone as if it were the knot of a tie. I suppose it isn't for everyone, gardening. She doesn't smile.

And how about you? She moves away from my throat. The Girl doesn't shrug. I haven't tried, not properly, I helped my mum plant some herbs last year but they all died. Well that's a shame, perhaps not enough sun. She tucks the book under that sharp elbow. Thank you. She casts the farewell into the shop. I wait as long as I can bear. A few more books picked up and put down. The Wordsworth once more, daffodils on daffodils. You sure I can't help you with something mate? The teasing is harsher. No, thank you, I'm all good. No problem.

The Girl doesn't look up as I leave. The weather is changed again. Sun hits the back of my neck. Wet tarmac releases its scent like a flower. Mrs S walks slowly, back straight. She is always like this. Her elegance is second nature. She follows the wide path past the science block, the main building to her left. Below is the crooked B-road that runs past the school's entrance to the few farms scattered in the fells' cradle. Clouds now thinned across the roofs, tree-tops. I follow her. A spy. She has already opened the book, turning pages, looking up intermittently to stay her course. There she is, a child again.

Ahead is the church, then the path that leads past her residence, over the river, towards the boarding houses. Not once does her stride break over the uneven surface. As she reaches the church she slows. A miniature twist of her neck. Does she know she is being followed? I can't believe I am following her. I can't turn around. I can't believe I am following her. If I turn around, if I go back to the school, then she will know my intention.

I keep walking, faster now, building into a story of heading back to my own room. In the distance the school bell sounds again. Now she turns around. In the middle of the road she faces me. Shocked into silence I stare. Did I forget something? Pardon? In the shop, did I leave something in the shop. Oh, no, I'm just going back to my room. I point, with a slight shake, at the church, trying to indicate a beyond. Well then. The book remains open, pressed against her hip, pinned by her forearm. Well then, walk with me. OK. We move into the sun. Here, take this for a sec. She hands me the book and removes her jacket. Each sleeve is folded over. On one wrist is a simple silver bracelet. I look further. Two rings. One a plain gold wedding band, the other an engagement ring, sapphires. She strides. I match her pace, continuing to hold the book. How are you finding it here? Oh you know, nice, everyone is very nice. Nice? I can't read her steadiness. I can't read her at all. That is, I realize, the point.

Yes, nice. I hope nice isn't the best we can do. The we is the school, the setting, each building, every girl, all teachers, the dead author. Nice is fine! Oh, now fine? Finally, she laughs. This is me, but you already know that. We stop at the long driveway. The Old Vicarage is positioned to best enjoy the river. From the entrance it is not visible, but audible, speeding up before the descent under the bridge. Must be a nice view, not nice, I mean soothing. I point at the top left window, which would look down onto it. It is, very soothing. I hand her the book. Oh, yes, the damn roses. Her manner seems purposefully old-fashioned. An old accent is faint in the background of certain words. She continues. The house, this place, it has a great collection of roses, and I don't know the first thing about roses, well I'm learning. She lifts the book and it slides from her grasp, spread open against the wet cobblestones. I try and fail to understand how I've managed to catch her off guard. She bends her knees to pick it up, bracelet slipping. Gardening, gardening I know. But roses? Roses are so. I catch her arm to steady her. Nice, I finish. Exactly. There is dirt on her hand. Using her skirt she wipes it clean.

There is nothing to do. I take my second bath of the day. Since giving up smoking this is my only remaining pleasure. I shuffle waves around the tub. So few other things, maybe a long train journey, offer the comfort of a simultaneous activity and passivity. Sex too, occasionally. Late-afternoon light is slender through the window. I can turn in a shoulder, a cheek. Maybe I will masturbate. My fingers move to and fro through the gloss.

My annexe, attached to one of the sixth-form boarding houses, is adjacent to the woman who runs the sanatorium, a nurse, The Nurse. Our living mirrored across two floors. An old, tiny house split down the middle. She is strict, painfully religious. The Girls have reported her, I've been told, for telling them period pain is a myth. I wonder if she interprets the twist, the hot knife in the guts, as a kind of holy suffering. We share a bathroom wall. In her half of the building little crosses are mounted in the kitchen, lounge, hallway, one even overlooking the toilet. Once, as she prepared too-sugary tea, I slipped into her bedroom. Beside her bed is another cross, this one larger, a Jesus at the centre with his intimately carved six-pack. Her water glass with its etched Christian fish. The Bible lives in a top drawer, nestled amongst foils of yellow antihistamine pills.

She complains about my excessive water usage. I tell her I won't flush the toilet more than once a day, or shower for the rest of the week. She is furious but ultimately powerless. I imagine her, at night, sending prayers my way, so sweet as to be malicious. In each of our interactions there is always the feeling that I would do better under her God. I don't mind her God, so tangible. The sexy Jesus in her bedroom. His body I too would die to have. Not just the chest but the legs, a footballer's legs, complex with muscle. Even those sad, raised palms. Brazen in their injuries. Such glamour.

I pick up the dead author's second most famous novel. The same copy I had at school. My name, twelve years old, in try-hard cursive inside the front cover. Somewhere in the later chapters is an erotic scene. I look for it half-heartedly. Gothic. All stone, rain. One long mood. My old notes appear every few pages. PATHETIC FALLACY alongside an underlined description of yet another storm. METAPHOR? SIMILE? Panicking over a particular, surely meaningful, detail of landscape. Reading it is distracting. I don't remember this twelve-year-old. At that point, in that English class, we strived only for a well-known sameness. Inventively, without being able to find the erotic scene in the novel, I imagine fucking the dead author. Not dead, but alive, hair pinned back, femme-ness deceived only by a hard mouth. She was miserable here. Otherwise not much is known about her. Within that misery, within that absence of historical fact, is a potential gayness. I take it. We fuck the old-fashioned way. Heavy petting in a stolen, shadowy corner. Upper-class. Maybe a private library, an enclave in a large garden of a country estate. A couple of chaste fingers. The endless, busy sound of fabric.

From beside the bath I pick up the dildo. A relic from a past relationship. This one flesh-coloured. Two more lie hidden at the bottom of my laundry basket. A large silicone vein runs the shaft. An accuracy I learned to love. First only the tip, then the gradual rest. Above, the base of my hand, the base of her hand, moves fast. My ex's face. Improbably, The Nurse's. The dead author's knuckles, terse, lifted from the famous portrait. On purpose I don't think about her, I don't think about her ridiculous roses. Too risky in its predictability, in its proximity to my reality. I need distance, I need not to hope. Otherwise fantasy could quickly lose its function.

Mrs S arrives last. The Girls try not to care. Look at her quickly, flicking from her shoes to her hair, they like to see how she dresses. The library is warm. She stands by the door and removes her jumper, green. We all watch, we all want to be the only one watching. She recognizes her audience. Smiles. Their unofficial welfare officer. Involved in the intimate aspects of their lives, out of choice, not duty, it seems to me. The Girls are spread across the room. Leaning on bookcases, sitting cross-legged on the patterned carpet. Some have dared to loosen their ties, undo a top button. The Nurse is impatient. As if she has been waiting a century to speak. She stands in front of them all. Her hands move in and out of fists, heavy at her sides. Taps her foot. Mrs S apologizes for her lateness, though it's only by a few minutes. The Nurse forces an enormous smile. Right. She claps her hands. Right, enough chitter-chatter, listen up Girls, or should I say Ladies? They do not know it is meant as a question. The Nurse presses her lips together. Hmmmmmm? Now they understand. Ladies, The Girls respond softly, reluctantly.

Mrs S moves through the room. Knots the green jumper around her shoulders. An example. Finds me at the far wall.

Decides to stand as I do, tilted forward, lower back pressed against stone. She whispers something I can't catch. I should whisper too, ask her to repeat what she said. I can't. I will spend a lifetime wondering. Another smile. The Nurse goes on. Ladies, as we all know, your first social is upon us. The Girls bite the insides of their cheeks. They do not want to give away their excitement, not to her. I could learn from their determination. Mrs S, her bare forearm, only a centimetre from mine. I'd like her to realize. She doesn't. The Nurse is not awkward. Power comes naturally to her, she seeks it out. There are, of course, a few things worth bearing in mind, the same things I've told the Ladies before you, and the Ladies before them. The Girls release their cheeks. First, the rules, no skirts above the knees. One of The Girls can't help it. She groans, other heads whip to find her. The Nurse's hand, no longer a fist, hits the skin above her heart. The Girls closest flinch. Any more outbursts like that and I shall make sure none of you go, do you hear? Mrs S turns to me, raises her eyebrows so only I will notice. Where did she grow up? Has she broken any bones? The impulse to know all of her, the idea that I could, the accidental promise of her raised eyebrows. Shameful, how easily I am trapped. The Nurse is relentless. I tune back in. Any skirts above the knee and you'll be sent back to your dorms, when dancing you shall be at least a foot apart, I won't bring my ruler because I shan't need it. Her tongue clacks. You're dealing with boys, they age differently, good manners do not occur to boys. The Girls look through her. Focus on the wall behind, I can feel their thinking: what does she know about these boys, their boys? You must be in charge, they don't think with their heads. The Nurse pauses for effect. It works. Shame settles on The Girls like snow, they blink, a few scrunch their eyes. Beside me Mrs S shifts, places her hands between the small of her back and the wall. The Nurse senses her win, the success of her applied pressure. So, you must do the thinking for them. She paces out of pleasure. Three steps to the left, to the right. You will remain where you can be seen, you may not leave the building until the lights are up, teachers shall be stationed at the doors, I expect you to be sensible, Ladies, to not let the side down, can I count on you? This time The Girls know to answer. Yes, they draw out the s. But it is not enough, The Nurse needs them to nod, to sign her verbal contract with their bodies. Any idiocy shall ruin it for the rest, am I clear? Yes. They are louder, almost comical, heads bobbing. Jolly good, that's it, you're free to go.

They save their secrets, file out in silence. The boys will arrive from the nearest private school, in pressed shirts and ties, breath freshened, knees touching on the coaches that drive them down the country lanes. Ridiculous. And yet, it is all there is. Things start to make sense. This one event, the anticipation they must make last. The Girls understand how to propel themselves forward. I go to leave, I will have to walk them back to their dorms, to monitor them as they eat dinner, as they get ready for bed. Mrs S stays at my side.

I expect you find all of this quite strange. Me? Yes. I guess it's not what I'm used to. No, I don't imagine that it is. She stops before the door. I do the same. Must seem a rather extraordinary way to find a boyfriend, I expect you had simpler methods? Sure, something like that. I hold back, too exhilarated by the question, it could mean nothing. Not so old-fashioned where you're from. Maybe more than you think. Is that so? Yeh, it was conservative in its own way, there were dances, a bit like this, there were shorter skirts, though, definitely above the knee. I see myself at fourteen, legs bare, an outfit loaned to me by a girl I would do anything for.

The Nurse stands behind me and clears her throat. She needs to be noticed. Mrs S uses her first name, touches her arm, she stiffens under her grip. Thank you for doing that. Yes, good, some of it sank in, can't trust them at this age, all those hormones making them daft. Well, I'm sure they'll do their best. We'll see. Her drama, the reach of her sigh, her chest restrained by the starch of her uniform. She wants them to fail. She doesn't acknowledge me, I like to think I frighten her. Well, can't stand around all day, this won't do, I shall be seeing you. Screeches away, rubberized soles planted heavily on the wooden floor.

You know, she's not really the tyrant she seems. The Nurse, Mrs S wants me to forgive her. I'll take your word for it. I find myself echoing her speech, wanting to seem grander, wanting to seem worthy. Yes, you'll have to, I suppose you don't have a choice. Her final smile, her hand already on the door handle. She doesn't say goodbye. Unknots the green jumper. Slips it over her head. Corrects her hair, fixes the sleeves. Turns once as she walks down the corridor. Finds me exactly where she left me, as she knew she would.

After dinner, prep. Shorthand for a word I haven't learned. Preparation? Too embarrassing to ask. For two hours after eating, The Girls must finish their homework. I take the youngest, sit in a classroom, behind the teacher's desk. Look out at them. The classroom is used for Latin lessons. Lining the walls are pictures of Vesuvius, of cracked Roman busts, curled families preserved in volcanic ash. On the chalkboard behind, an exercise in a grammar of belonging, he or she or we or they, the types of bodies changing the next word. It looks difficult. Pointless. I did not know Latin could still be learned. The Girls arrange their possessions. Open exercise books. They are not to talk. They don't wear uniforms. A freedom they use against me. An arm is raised. Plastic bangles colliding. Yes, I say, yes. Look up from my book, reading the same line over and over again. Miss? Yes? Miss, is it true that in Australia dingoes eat babies? I don't know. You don't know? I am foggy with heat. The radiators cannot be turned off, even in the rising temperature outside. An old, heavy window is shoved up. Three of The Girls work as a team, squealing, worrying about their fingers, putting their heads into a breeze that does not exist. Sit down, guys, come on. Miss? She is patient, waiting for my reply. No, I mean, I don't know, you should get on with your work. I shift in my seat, cross my arms. How else to learn authority but to imitate it. Miss? The Girl puts her hand into the air once more for effect, unsatisfied. Miss? Yes. So you think she did it? The mother? She killed her baby? The rest of The Girls stop their writing. Listen with their elbows, their chins, their torsos, leaning forward only slightly, creating a specialist tension, letting their pens hover just above the page. I don't know. Miss, it's your country, you must know something. Probably, yeh, most likely she killed her baby. It's what they wanted. To have me release some murder into the air, to break the classroom's illusion. The Girl's face is happily scandalized. Eyes wide. She lowers her arm. Shakes her head. That's what I thought, so sad, isn't it Miss? Yeh, yes, it is. My face reddens, do they notice, of course they notice. I have lost and I hardly know how.

I did not see what happened, only the aftermath. One of The Girls punched one of the visiting boys in the nose. She has broken it. A clean break. Septum collapsed, a precious heap of small bones and cartilage, two black eyes. Her punishment, for starters, I'm told by another teacher, is that she must clean up her mess in the bright light of day. A phrase they love to say, as if this morning will be worth more than last night. I enjoyed their terror as they explained the scene to me. The blood! Oh the blood, just unbelievable, the blood. Inside, the gym is only half-emptied of party paraphernalia. Long trestle tables line the far side. I see a few balloons caught against the ceiling. Empty glasses have been left balanced in secret places. Coupons are given to The Girls at these events, one watered-down wine each, red or white. Once, there was a counterfeit scheme, a teacher explained, a few of The Girls caught forging the coupons, the wine running out suspiciously quick.

A trail of blood begins in the middle of what was the dance floor. Only a few drops. He walked, maybe staggered, towards the toilets at the end of the enormous hall. The drops of blood increase, streaked by his shoes, or maybe by the shoes of those following him. I reach the door to the men's bathroom just as The Girl arrives. Her arms tight across her chest. It is unlikely she respects me. She doesn't say hello. Listen he deserved it. There is a wobble in her voice. She tries again. He deserved it. A sentence rehearsed on her walk here. I'm sure he did. There is blood across the white toilet door. On the metal handle it is less obvious. The sheen lost. She sees it now, the blood. I correct myself, I want to appear softer. I know he did, I know he deserved it. She looks at me, then back at the blood. Tries not to move her head so I won't register her interest. Her body locks and unlocks, arms unfolding and folding again. I pick through a selection of keys. Behind the stage, the teachers explained, is a tiny staffroom where I will find the cleaning products. She stares at the ceiling. Her parents have been called. Arguments over expulsion or suspension. I see her knuckles are swollen. A grand bruise threatens. Does that hurt? No. It might be broken you know. She doesn't reply, moves away from me. A necklace has turned the wrong way around. The pendant, a silver star, hangs at her nape. I wonder if she punched him twice.

Come on. We walk the length of the gym. I unlock the door. Here give me a hand. She takes only the mop. OK so boil the kettle, for the bucket. She winces as she grips the plastic handle, each knuckle extraordinarily close to the skin. Every movement purposefully slow. She exists in new anticipation of pain. You know where I'm from there's a nickname for that injury. I point at her hand. If you've broken it, I mean. What? A hard stare. The dickhead. What? The dickhead. I take the kettle from her and fill it with water. Her face slackens. Oh that's me. She offers a cautious smile. One hundred per cent that's me, you know dickhead isn't a swear word we use much here. Yeh? She struggles with the cap of the floor cleaner. Yeh. Finally it pops free. The bright-yellow liquid spatters the grey walls. Fuck. She looks at me. A particularly forbidden expletive. I notice now the firm beginnings of another bruise, this across her collarbone, partially hidden by her hair and t-shirt. Fuck, I repeat.

She pours the yellow liquid into the bucket. A third of the bottle disappears. Next time you only need a capful. Oh. She sneezes once, twice. The sensory shock of the chemical smell. It's strong, isn't it. In defiance she sniffs it deeply. Her head moves in a new sneeze, this one silenced, sucked back behind her eyes. My instructions are to sit and watch as she completes her punishment. I position myself awkwardly on a narrow gym bench. She walks the sprung floor, eyes searching for the beginning of the blood, struggling to remember where it was she punched him. Just there. Where? I get up and point. There. She shoves the bucket with her feet. Plunges the mop. Steam rises. She does not twist, does not remove the excess water, she has never mopped before. The chemical liquid slops towards the stage. She dashes backwards, not wanting to wet her feet. Fuck. This time she does not register the word's institutional power. It's OK. I take the mop and soak up the water. Come on, it's OK, just sit. She obeys. I finish the job. The trail of blood disappears into the mop's wig, briefly visible against the white.

The Girl's fingers go towards the bruise on her collarbone, then stop, eyes snapping open. She is exhausted. Thanks for that, for helping me. You're welcome. Outside, there are excited voices, The Girls walking back to their dorms from lunch. She tenses, looks towards the window. Wants to know what they are saying. Did something happen? Something else, I mean? She laughs. I am too sincere. Her laugh breaks against the walls. The room's own voice swells in the following silence, a clock ticking embarrassingly above our heads, the balloons nudging the ceiling. You can tell me. No offence Miss but what would you know about it. I don't need to ask her what she means. She is angry, I am sequestered by my lesbianism. She laughs again, harder. The teachers will want the opportunity to forgive her and this, I understand, is what she will refuse.

I look towards the bathrooms, sitting either side of the front entrance. Well. What Miss? She might like me to protest my alleged lesbianism, or scold her, make a confession of my own. I won't. This isn't it I'm afraid, there's more to be cleaned. In the men's Miss? I wait for a joke, some loaded gesture. Instead, she is engaged. Sitting upright, her hands pause above her knees. Yeh, the men's. She stares at the door, at the sign, at the small, sexless symbol of a man. I guess that's where he went afterwards, after it happened. Her voice, the tone, separates her body from the event itself.

Against the cheap white paint of the bathroom door the stains are more stubborn. She gives in, uses her injured hand, pinching a rag delicately between thumb and forefinger, her pinkie finger left floating. I work hard on the ghostly red fingerprints that wrap around the doorframe. Perhaps this is where he steadied himself, gently touching his face once, twice. Inside, the mess is not so terrible. There is only so much a single broken nose can produce. Fuck it stinks in here. She has established the fuck, using it on purpose, letting me pass her minor test when I say nothing. What do they do? Piss on the walls? Each stall is investigated. The bathroom doubles as a changing room. Belongings left by boys from last night, from plays, from other socials. She turns over the few items abandoned on pegs, checking a jumper for a name label, pulling a pair of sunglasses from a jacket pocket. She is careful with a pair of dress shoes. Strung up by their black laces. She touches a hand to the leather. Somebody went home barefoot I guess. Yeh. She places her unbruised hand inside the left shoe, moving her wrist back and forth, testing out the length, eventually fitting in half her forearm.

Blood is concentrated around the sinks. Toilet paper balled across the floor. The bloodiest evidence, colour as bright as when it left his body. We each put on oversized dish-washing gloves, hers leaving an inch of space between rubber and skin. That is gross. She tosses the toilet paper into a bin bag. So gross. On the wide mirror I notice red smears, almost reaching corner to corner. I imagine the boy leaning in to examine the damage, tap running, a few friends pacing in the background. He brings his fingers to his nose, collects more blood and drags it across the glass on purpose, pleased with the evidence, with the drama.

For a while she has not thought about the other injury. Now her shoulder rolls back, her neck strains. She resists the urge to touch it, not wanting to remind me of its presence. In the bathroom's artificial light I see the bruise is dark red. Already the edge has started to fade into green, the blood under the skin beginning to age. Does it hurt? It's fine. Is he your boyfriend? No way, never. I expect another laugh. Instead she turns to me, confusion apparent. What do you want me to say? I pause. A muscle flickers beside her ear. What do you want me to say? Without meaning to I have been asking for a confession. Hello? Miss? Nothing, I don't want you to say anything, you don't have to say anything.

We continue to clean in silence. The sound of somebody at the entrance carries back to us. A door pushed open suddenly, footsteps echoing through the gym. Hello? I recognize the voice. Hello? One sec. The Girl nods. I push open the bathroom door just as she readies herself to grab the handle and enter. We are face to face. Mrs S! The Girl calls out behind me. Hello hello. She pushes past me and goes straight to The Girl. Gently her arm goes around her shoulders. Now this won't do. With a bare hand she takes a bloody tissue from The Girl's gloved fingers and drops it back onto the floor. Immediately she registers the first bruise, then the second. Her gaze is subtler than mine. The Girl does not notice the fast movement of her eyes. Mrs S? The Girl's face softens. Mrs S touches her cheek briefly. It's not your job to clean. Selfishly I want her to look at me. She does not. You come with me, OK? Underneath the arms of Mrs S The Girl is ushered away. Only at the entrance does she release her, holding the door open wide, keeping it from touching her body. Finally she looks at me. Not quite indifferent, something I can't place. One second, two. And then they are gone.

I walk to the petrol station. Past the school, past the pub, at the road's curve. Unbranded, the opening hours are unpredictable. Today a picnic table has been moved into full sun to the left of the two pumps. Two men sit across from one another. As I cross the forecourt one gets up slowly, moving inside the shop and behind the till. I follow. The shop has random essentials. Each shelf heavy with Pot Noodles, toilet paper, batteries, bin bags, white bread, orange juice, plain flour, tins of peas. In a wicker basket are apples and blackening bananas. I pull out a pizza from the freezer, the topping indiscernible beneath the frosted clingfilm, and pause over the ice lollies.

Behind the counter the man sighs loudly. Don't leave that open too long yeh. I slide the freezer lid back across. Instead I peer through the glass. I take three of the cheapest. Neon liquid frozen in long plastic tubes. The kind that slices the corners of your mouth as you push and suck. That all? I nod. A cigarette is tucked behind his ear. His head has been recently shaved, hair now a handsome shadow, a mole visible after his forehead, another at his temple. I put the change in the charity box. Ta. No worries.

In no rush I move into the sunshine. Position myself in the opposite corner to the picnic table and bite open the first ice lolly. Lime, supposedly. Glowing green. He leaves the shop, I was the only customer, and rejoins the other man. Crackly music is played from a radio. The selected station is dedicated to hits from across the eighties. The opening bars of Bette Davis Eyes begin. The man with the shaved head leans back and closes his eyes. This song, fuck I love this song. The other man, with an ordinary haircut, looks down at his nails. He doesn't say anything. His friend keeps singing, wanting him to notice.

He tilts his face into the sun. I realize he works here too. Overalls rolled down to the waist. A pump attendant maybe. Or a mechanic. To the right of the shop is a garage. Enough room for one car at a time. Today it is empty. The song ends. An ad break offers insurance, mattresses, a day trip to a water park. The steady, soothing voice of the DJ promises an absolute classic, a stone-cold classic, he asks listeners to wind down their windows, to let the next one blast through the countryside. They both lean in to the radio. The man with the shaved head thoughtfully touches his cigarette but decides not to smoke it yet.

The song begins. Drums and piano. The man with the shaved head jumps up. This is it, this is the one, the one. His friend shakes his head. Don't know it. What? What do you mean? I mean I don't know it mate. The man with the shaved head sits back down. He pulls one leg up onto the bench. On his ankle is a little tattoo. Maybe a heart. How could you not know, are you joking me. The friend shrugs his shoulders. He looks across at me. Oi, oi, excuse me. Yeh? Do you know that song. The radio is lifted up above his head. He says he doesn't know this song, can you believe it, everyone knows this song. The name is there, on the tip of my tongue, then slips away suddenly.

Finally a voice sings. Bruce, it's Born in the USA, by Bruce Springsteen. Exactly! His friend looks blankly at me. What you still don't know? Not sure. Come on I don't believe it mate. Using only four fingers he touches his friend's wrist. As if realizing the strangeness of his gesture he lifts the four fingers and turns the touch into a slap. Come off it. His friend goes to move his hand. The slap switches to a grip. Admit you know this song! Mate come off it. Even she knows this song. His open palm sent in my direction. Yeh but I don't, you've got too much free time. The wrist is not released. The friend doesn't panic. It's Bruce fucking Springsteen! You don't need free time to know Bruce Springsteen! The man! The fucking legend!

With his free hand the friend reaches across and pinches underneath his armpit. Maybe pulling on his hair. Fuck ow fuck. Calm it down yeh. The next song plays, U2, one of my dad's favourites, loved with that same blunt passion. I'm not sure what to do. It's not my scene and yet I'm involved, smiling, letting them see me smile. I know I want certain parts, not even parts, just the fragments: an ankle tattoo, a wrist, the freckles, that touch turned to a slap. Things fading in and out, things from a distance, things that are fragile at the last minute. From the pocket of his shorts the man with the shaved head pulls out a lighter. Just feeling hyper. His friend yawns. You're always hyper. He inhales then offers it across the table, the other man, this friend, declines, shaking his head. My body is a temple. He coughs. They both laugh. I finish the last of the green ice lolly and pull the next from my plastic bag. A chemical blue. I taste blood from the corners of my mouth. Miniature cuts numbed by the cold.

The office is not as grand as I imagined. I have been summoned here. The furniture is cheap wood, made in the last ten or so years. Carpet too. Not the impressive dark wood of elsewhere in the main building. Her window looks out over the tennis courts. It is open. There is a repeated thwack of a ball followed by polite clapping from spectators. Every so often there is a sigh at a missed opportunity, a point ended. In one corner is a school photograph. Teachers and students, hands clasped, Mr and Mrs S stood in the centre. In the other is a plant stand featuring a heavily restrained monstera. A network of brown string guiding the thick stalks. Hello. Important not to let my heartbeat show. Hello. Apologies, another meeting ran over. That's fine. A silk t-shirt, high neck, light pink. The weather turned unseasonably warm. The country at last enjoying the long-promised rising plume of Spanish air. A heatwave imminent. She fans herself with a folder. Alright, well. She goes to speak then stops. Sorry, can I get you anything? Water? Tea? I'm fine thanks.

I wanted to talk. About The Girl? She is tense. Yes, about the incident on that Sunday afternoon. A flush at her neck, alive against the light-pink silk. Look I don't know much, just did what I was told. No, no I understand, I just. She trails off, twists her wedding ring. Who asked you to be there? There was a note on my shelf. A note? Yeh, in my cubbyhole. Shame sours my mouth, drying it out, I try to work up some saliva under my tongue. Who was it from? The teacher chaperoning, the head chaperone. Chaperone is not the right word, not the word used here, in this place. She doesn't write anything down. This is information she already has. The note is probably there, tucked into the folder. Didn't you talk to anyone? Yeh, yes, a few teachers were in the staffroom Sunday morning before I went to the gym. Right, right, they didn't have an issue with it? I don't think so. She has launched an investigation unprompted, I realize. There is no one for her to officially report to, only The Girl, only herself. Not her husband, otherwise I would be in his office.

It's obscene, that's all, antiquated. She mutters. The half-formed sentence is not meant for my ears. Wanting her to look at me I respond anyway. I agree. You agree? I give her a list of the teachers, the comments they made about the blood. Maybe there was something I could have done then, in the midst of their grouped fear, each person hoping to frighten the next. The Girls are not supposed to think of punching, let alone actually punch. I repeat this sentence, spoken by the history teacher in his tweed, to her. It's obscene, the whole thing. This time she speaks to me directly. I think about The Girl. Is she OK? Mrs S's fingers go back to her wedding ring. No, yes well, she has gone home for now.

Her parents? Yes, well they trust the school. She is overly polite. I can tell they have not been angry enough, the parents. Undoubtedly the mother, the father, are afraid of The Girl if the school is afraid of The Girl. Will she come back? Yes I believe so, in time for exams. The pragmatism is unbearable. I roll the sentence over before I say it to her. Once, twice. The pragmatism is unbearable. She stands and closes the window, keeping her back to me for a few extra seconds. I don't know about that. The room is quickly too warm. Somehow I have said the wrong thing.

And the boy? What do you think. She turns away from the window. Complaining daily about his nose, otherwise unscathed. On the walls are prints from various modern art museums. Exhibitions, famous artists. An Alexander Calder, a Matisse, a Georgia O'Keeffe. Each retrospective is dated within the last few years. I wonder if she likes these, feels for them, or if it is for The Girls who so often sit in this same chair. Perhaps they are even for people like me, a demonstration of taste. You like them? I blush. She has caught me out. Yes, no, maybe the O'Keeffe. From my husband, to brighten up the place. She doesn't care what I think either way. What I want is an opportunity to get to know her. To create an opportunity to get to know her. This might be impossible. How are the roses? I feel her smile. They continue to be very nice. The book is helping? Yes, somewhat. A sigh. Outside, the tennis ball is hit back and forth, a longer rally, a courteous tension building. She is on tiptoes, trying to see the match, opening the window wider. Her feet slip from the heels of her shoes. The movement feels familiar enough to make me brave. If you do ever need any help, I'm around. I look away, back at the O'Keeffe, letting my offer settle. Large white petals turn, moved by green. The folder is touched again. She returns to the desk. If you're not busy, you wouldn't mind? I copy her tone. No, I wouldn't mind at all.

Lunch. The chairs, the tables, rumoured to be from the dead author's time. Pretty spirals of woodworm have weakened a few of the legs. The Girls swap seats for fear of falling, for fear of the brief but acute public shame. Each teacher takes a turn as head of the main table. It is raised on a platform. Ten of The Girls are selected to eat here too, after good behaviour. The table is closest to the long windows, closest to the views, the fells fading backwards into sky. Today it is her, Mrs S. A high-waisted skirt, maybe wool, in grey. White shirt. A light gold chain visible just below the neck.

The job is to lead the rest of the school in prayer. Some recite what is already known. Others, like Mrs S, prefer something off the cuff. She looks around at the room rather than into her linked hands. After a difficult week, Lord, give us the strength to make good, positive decisions. She touches the light gold chain. The Girls exchange glances. I sit at the head of a table in the middle of the dining hall. To one side the kitchen continues to serve up the food onto steel platters, never pausing, not even during the prayer. The chaos of metal on metal. That permanent smell of meat, carried over from breakfast. Hundreds of years of meat, lingering in the wood, in the walls. Windows fog as steam releases from the large saucepans. Something is dropped. A clang, a muffled swear word.

Each week a menu is posted on the door of the dining room. Today, beef and mushroom stroganoff with boiled rice. For dessert, cherry clafoutis. What the fuck is a clafoutis? I have no one to ask. The Girls hardly speak to me. A couple of them whisper, shoulders conspiring. Are they glancing at me? Mrs S continues. In these decisions let us, may we, hold one another in grace. Her sentences are only the mildest of codes. I take pleasure in her lack of concealment, what she is saying now, how she says it, seeking out eye contact, in her cold voice. Not cold, stern. No earnestness. The Girls take the safer option, bent in prayer, eyes safely on their thumbs.

The entire school is aware of the incident. Collectively the teachers are suffering a mild hysteria, as if The Girls might now start punching at will. A letter of reassurance has gone out to each of the parents. I wonder if they, Mr and Mrs S, discussed the decision in private. I have not yet seen a copy of the letter but hope to. The possible wording, the possible position of each word. The repetition of incident. Mrs S ends with an Amen. She does not blink. The Girls echo dutifully, sending out a second Amen like a sigh.

A bell is rung, by hand, indicating the food can be collected from the pass. The Girl to my right gets up to retrieve it. This, I've only recently learned, is always the duty of The Girl to the right of the head of the table. She is younger, twelve or thirteen. Against the rule I get up with her. She doesn't protest as I help lift the heavy, hot dishes. First a sweaty stretch of rice, the grains bloated, over-cooked. Next the grey stroganoff. Slivers of onion. Strips of coiled beef. Food is served according to an old choreogra-phy. First me, the head of the table, then passed down one by one to my left. If the meal is good there is hardly any left by the time it reaches the final Girl. Often, I've noticed, this is also an opportunity for spite.

I could just serve her first, The Girl to my right, who will eat last. She is already holding her fork, worried. I plate my rice, then grey stroganoff, avoiding the beef. I could just serve her first. The Girls look at me patiently. My hand trapped around the spoon. The Girl to my left is waiting. She watches me. I have left it too long. Now they all watch. They can see my thinking. If I serve her first, what about The Girl afterwards, what about The Girl who will then be last in her place. I stand suddenly and briefly, spoon poised. Confusion begins to narrow their faces. No, no. There is no possible solution. I sit back down, defeated. The choreog-raphy begins.

I walk up the long driveway. The house emerges on the right-hand side. In front is a large garden set lower than the driveway, hidden from the main church path by an old hedgerow. Mrs S is at the centre. Everywhere she is attractive. Her in old jeans. Mud staining the hem, the backs of her calves. The gloves on her hands are slightly too large, maybe her husband's. The shirt too. Heavy cotton. Light-pink pinstripe. Today her hair is tied up. The little demon of her chin. Among the regulated wild flowers I am especially clumsy. A sharp grass catches my knee. Blood, even. The borders are purposefully overgrown. My ankles give out on unexpected edges as I try to follow the path. Behind it all is the house. The old vicarage, now too grand for a vicar. Limestone. Front door painted a tasteful pastel blue to match the uniforms, to match the school crest. Slow romance of yellow roses up the trellis. Why should this scene be so beautiful? The sky is wide open. She sees me and smiles. I am self-conscious in my old running shorts, old trainers. Sweat has already started across my forehead. The binder works hard underneath my t-shirt. I make it to the centre. The shirt is distracting. I wonder if her smell has already outweighed his. Each cotton fibre now adjusted to her skin. A shadow cast across her face by a large straw hat. I'd like to reach across and take it from her head.

Hello. She is formal. Hello, I return. I notice roses everywhere. Not just the trellis, but in curt circles surrounding us. In her hand is a pair of secateurs. Its sharp beak catches the sunlight. Her eyes are lost to shadow. I focus instead on her gloved fingers, restless with a torn belt loop. Thank you for coming. She places a hand between my shoulder blades. You'll be a great help. Gently she guides me towards a particular patch of roses, these a watery pink. At my feet are thorny limbs. Neatly cut by the secateurs. Here, we're making bunches. She inhales, maybe in thought, pulling back her lips. There are her teeth. Incisors, almost bared. She presses the left against her top lip as she crouches, leaving a dent. Like this. She selects a rose limb and opens the mouth of the secateurs. The angle is carefully chosen. Under her breath she counts the leaves that run the stem. At five she cuts. My hands, my thighs, my face are left open to scrapes. Already a thorn claws at my forearm.

Her hand returns to my back. I have spares. From a toolbox she produces another pair of gloves. If you need I can lend you a shirt. I think she is looking at my bare arms. Still I can't see her eyes. My back braces against the sun. At my feet she places a bucket filled with water. A few roses loll against the plastic. These are the colour of felt-tip pens. A cartoonish love-heart red. I know this colour. I know these roses. OK so let's aim for at least seven bunches? Finally she lifts the edge of her hat. Eyes blink then narrow. No mascara today. Irises blue, as indifferent as a watercolour. Can I get you a drink? No, I'm fine. What about that shirt? She removes a glove and grips my forearm, twisting to better see the scratch. Gardening is a dangerous sport. I laugh. Really, I'll be fine. With her free hand she pulls down her collar to reveal her neck. A raised cut. You're not the only one. Only now does she realize my arm is still in her hand, fingers tightening. Something passes between us. Breath across light. Or maybe more. More than breath, more than light. A glance like a cigarette burn. Nausea floods, then subsides. My arm is released. I put on the gloves and count the leaves. She watches. At five I cut. It is tougher than expected. The stem resists. When the secateur blades finally meet I recoil. The force is a surprise. My body tips forward. Tough stuff, roses. She smiles and pats my shoulder, maternal. Again I am clumsy. The smile, its type, is not what I wanted.

I'll get you that water. She walks towards the house newly authoritative. I watch her open the blue door and disappear inside. She reappears suddenly. Parading in and out of my mind. Here, please do borrow a shirt. She waves again. I see blood on my shorts. The cuts on my forearm, my thigh, are insistent. OK. She aims her torso at me: What? I call again dramatically. OK! This time I cup my hands around my mouth. She mimics falling backwards, as if the muscle of my voice has hit her squarely in the chest. I overdo my laughter so she will be able to hear. Stupid. The path towards the house offers more roses. An old bird bath almost falling off its plinth. Bees in the thicker flowers. As I walk they are caught in the breeze my body creates. Nudging my back, drifting around my neck, one considers the entrance to my ear.

The door has been left open. I notice the paint is peeling, showing another much older layer of lighter blue paint underneath. Above the door is the dead author's name again. Her surname, followed ceremoniously by Cottage, although this is surely a house. Each letter recently repainted in slick black. The school's endless theme: the dead author. Now she is delivered to this vicarage with its freshly painted attributes, with its charming yellow roses framing the windows.

Inside is pleasantly dark. The furniture too, dark. That handsome smell of wood. I remove the gloves and try to stuff them into my shorts. The pocket is too tight. Instead I leave them on an antique sideboard. A large mirror hangs on the wall. I pause, disappointed by the red in my cheeks. Down the corridor is a seat smooth with age, an intricate umbrella stand, a large portrait. This time not of the author but her father. Same thin lips. Hello, in here! I go towards the sound of a tap turned on and off. Here! I accidentally walk into a bathroom. The window done in stained glass, something something in Latin, what is it with Latin, an emblem of a blue fish, a red bird, both glowing with sun. No, here. Her laughter, patronizing, then her face. The kitchen is dated and spotless. A dishwasher churns in the

corner. It feels strange after the depth of the corridor. Huge
light swings in through two large windows behind the sink.
Out the back is even more garden. A hill sloping away from
the house and down to a curve of the river. In the middle of
the lawn is a table set with only two chairs, an abandoned
coffee cup, a plate. Maybe that is where she eats breakfast.
She catches my eye. It's enormous, isn't it. Yes. The furniture isn't mine, by the way, we had to move in as is. I notice
the mine, then the we. There is no ours. Although she tries
she can't quite push past him. The house, its occupants,
have always been a headmaster and his wife. A perk of the
job. Yes, everything in here is original. From when? From
the day it was first lived in, I suppose. A house with no
secrets, then. She looks at me. That unblinking, still blue.
What do you mean? I had wanted to sound clever. I mean
an entire history is on display, its entire history. Ah well not
quite, there's hardly anything of what's happened in
between, is there? A glass of water is placed in my hand. It
is a heavy crystal tumbler, better suited to whisky. There's a
short rip in the knee of her jeans, a second broken belt loop.
Again my eye is caught. Is it alien, to see me in jeans? A
little.

   She drinks out of an old tea mug. As decoration it bears
a cheap transfer of the school's crest. Dates too. A reunion
that happened ten years ago. Is that how long you've lived
here? No, no. I step backwards out of the window's sun.
We've hardly been here at all, two years, just over. I nod at
the mug. See? There is something of the 'in between' on

display, then. She is pleased. I suppose you're right, although this shitty mug is probably it. The word shitty is for me. A sleight of mimicry. She puts down the mug and investigates her hands. Soil under her fingernails. Another cut, smaller, at the base of her thumb. Ah, unavoidable damage! She brings her thumb to her mouth and sucks the injury. I look away. The damn roses. I want to offer her the same, some mimicry, a quick signal across the space between us. The damn rose book more like, useless thing. I imagine the headmasters' wives, each headmaster's wife, has left a successful legacy. Afternoons spent doing what we are doing, tossing roses into buckets.

Come on, up we go. She takes one last drink. I do the same. In the bedroom is the skin-and-breath odour of her sleep. She opens the window immediately, aware of the smell. A heavy woollen blanket on the bed despite the heat. A bathroom is off to one side, the door partially closed. I try to be more subtle in my gaze, moving only sideways and underneath, so she can't watch what I see. On her bedside table is a book. I would have to stare to make out the title. I move closer and feign a turn out the window. On the sweep I read the book's cover. It is in another language. There's the view. From here I can spy the roof of my room. The road too, one car speeding past, then another. She is above even the church's spire. Quite ostentatious, isn't it – even for a vicar? Very. Hung on the wall is a portrait of the three sisters, the dead author in the middle. This must be valuable. Oh yes, there was once talk of the entire house becoming a museum. I laugh, my turn to be cruel. She barely reacts.

The churchyard is visible too. Ten headstones wearing their yellow lichen. Each name and date is almost worn out. I see a few of The Girls sitting in the far corner, faces turned into the sun, tops rolled up, exercise books open and unread. I know they detour here. A gate opens directly into the churchyard from the path that goes to and from the main school. There's no need to engage with the church at all. At the end of the ten graves is a bright patch of grass. A few weary tulips. It is the sunniest place to be found within permissible limits. Once or twice I have taken a book to the same spot and left it closed on my lap, unable to keep my eyes open. She stands closer to me now. I hope I was seen. I hope I was seen by her. What was I wearing? If I called out now The Girls would hear me but not know where to look. Her head almost touches mine. Forever following my gaze. I feel it now, her eyes moving with mine. Ah yes, the tanning beds, the place to be. I want to ask if the nickname the tanning beds was created in my honour. But a phone rings. She moves away. Holds up one finger. Back in a sec. I am alone by the window. The rest of the room is unremarkable. Nothing that would give her away. Only the book and its title worth categorizing. I look for pyjamas across a chair. An abandoned pair of shoes. It seems she maintains her poise even in her own home. The curtains are neatly bunched. No reading glasses, no personal photographs, no dressing gown.

She returns and flings open the wardrobe, his side. Like the kitchen, it is a modern addition, quickly dated. New wood varnished to imitate the original. Grey and navy suits, a few untouched in their dry-cleaning packets. Camphor is suddenly strong. Ties hung on a special device. From a drawer she produces shirts, also pressed, but softer. One large crease through each torso. Here, choose. He won't mind? He won't notice. Each one is very good quality. Heavyweight cottons, most with a pastel pinstripe. I get a measure of his size. His shoulders draped across mine. That will do. I choose a light yellow. The fabric reaches the middle of my thigh. I roll back the cuffs until they pinch the skin of my forearm. No, no, the whole point is that they protect you from thorns. She comes close again. Pulls down the sleeves until they sit at the wrist. She is not gentle. The scratch burns. I catch her perfume. The camphor. Down below The Girls laugh suddenly. Each note carries into the room. We turn our heads at the same time.

Would you go back? She stays with their laughing. No longer touching me. You mean be their age again? I look at my wrists and adjust the cuffs, pulling them straight, wanting the shirt tighter around my shoulders. It wasn't so long ago for you, though, was it. The fabric snaps into place finally, hugging the edges of my bone, my skin. Her touch returns. Oh, it's perfect, look. She strokes the collar as if we are leaving for a party, one button done up, then undone. I return to our conversation. It was long enough ago, you know, I'm twenty-two. I hear myself, too indignant. The

48

Girls have fallen into a leisurely silence. Laughter replaced with sunlight. I imagine their eyes closing, heat taking over, necks slackening. Anyway I wouldn't do it, be their age again. She steps away. Takes me in from a short distance. No? No. Well I would, oh I would, you laugh, you cry, everything falling out of you all the time, you live a thousand lives a day. I stand tall for her, gripping the cuffs in my fingers, letting the shirt belong to me. Outside, the insects subside. I want to reply carefully, to not run too fast towards her disclosure. Something measured. It wasn't like that for me. Oh being a teenage girl is like that for everybody, surely. Not for me. I wait for her to ask why. She doesn't. If she is afraid to ask, she does not show it, not yet. I am taken in one last time, her eyes running along the shirt's seams. It's almost too nice for you to wear out there, you know, you should keep it, I'll find you another for our gardening.

No, no, I couldn't. You can and you should, please. Thanks, OK, thank you. What does she think she knows about me? She returns to the wardrobe and pulls another off a hanger. Similar, the fabric lighter again. This one blue striped with white. A top button missing. Here, now there's no need to sew on a new one. She throws it clumsily, we watch it land on the bed, one arm reaching for the floor. OK. A shyness returns. My unwillingness to agree with her observation of teenage girlhood leaves us in unfamiliar territory. I am left desperate to explain. I try, I will try and explain. It's just I had a hard time at school, that's all. I'm very sorry to hear that. She doesn't pry. I had been hoping for an opportunity to confess, to tell her who I am. She will not allow it. Perhaps that is what she fears. The conversation is abandoned as quickly as it began. There's a bathroom there, you can change, if you like. No final looks. We are strangers again. I will go outside, I will cut her roses, I will be careful.

I notice a small bunch of flowers on the only grave visible from the path. Just three or four stems. Picked from the lower section of the river, I think. Roots curled, still muddy, still wet, still as they would have been in the ground. I open the gate with its romantic creak. The small bunches have been left leaning against eight out of the ten headstones. Above the hills a pink is slowly revealed. Name, date, condition. Each girl killed by tuberculosis in the first years of the school's founding. Not uncommon, I know, for the era. Six girls were twelve years old, two only ten. The families could not afford to have the bodies moved closer to home. In the far corner of the low stone wall, beside the usually bright patch of grass, is a lone beer bottle. Behind, the church looms. Further away is her house. The grand bedroom and its view. From here her window is partially obscured by a beech, an oak, whatever the name of the large, old tree with soft broad leaves. The house is difficult to make out. Faintly I can hear the river's movements. The ripped-fabric sound of water. This scene, the flowers bunched together only by pure grip, the deaths, the possible outline of her through the window, the river carrying on. I look at the bottle again. Beer, a beer, would be good. I leave the graveyard and walk carefully along the main road. After a few minutes the pub is in view. It is even older than the school. A new, navy-blue sign hangs above the entrance, the name in cursive, a large English bird done in gold. Long, camp tail feathers. Short beak. There is no view of the river. Only one table out the front is busy, left on an angle, perhaps it was crammed into the last patch of sun.

Inside it is cool. The man working behind the bar rings his bell and announces last orders. There is no one else here. He looks directly at me. You work at the school? Yes. Not a student? No. I ask for a lager and he pauses. A lager? Yes. Tap? If possible, yes. He is a big man, his cream shirt puckered across his chest. I want him to like me. For there to be a mutual respect. A woman comes in from outside. Sunburn shines across her chest. She shivers. One strap of a floral vest top slips down her arm. Another please. Hope you're not driving. She winks. He puts down the pint glass he was yet to pour into. Turns his back to me and unscrews a bottle of white wine. He fills her glass comically high, all the way to the rim. One for the road. She looks at me now. Eyes soft with alcohol. Hi there you. I am taller than she is, in her flip-flops, a handbag in the crease of her arm, a pair of sunglasses balanced on her head. She reaches out and pulls on the waistband of my jeans. The man puts my beer down heavily. Thank you, thanks so much. At the sound of my voice she pulls back. Fucking hell I am drunk fuck. White wine spills onto my t-shirt. She flaps her hands. Sorry fuck.

In the doorway she takes one last look at me and shakes her head. Fuck. More wine spills.

The man is not afraid to stare. A coil of pleasure and shame, tight at the top of my throat, pulling like rope. Before picking up my beer I make a plan. I see a sign for a beer garden, out the back. The lager is cold, delicious. I try to look at him as I take a sip. Without warning I shiver. Could be the woman's shiver, adjusted. I did not bring a jumper. I lift the beer to him in thanks and head towards the slumped arrow indicating the way outside. In the garden are a few wooden tables, all empty. At the end of the garden is a cheap new fence and a few dying pine trees. The river is louder again. I drink half the beer in a few swallows. Behind me a pub window opens, then closes. The man, I suspect. I finish the beer without sitting down. A breeze picks up. Stars push forward.

I stand on a table and look over the cheap fence, hoping for the river. Instead I find somebody's backyard. Garden. Backyard. Two silhouettes visible in a kitchen. Another beer would be good. I am light-headed, disappeared slightly, I could fade back into the night if I tried hard enough. The man comes outside. I am still standing on the table. What're you doing, would you get off? He is more unsettled than before. Nothing. Get down from there. He is afraid of me. I will take it, in place of respect, why not. The moon is suddenly obvious. Not unlike the moon, desire punches through the present. It's a good line. Around here there will be nowhere else to get a beer. OK, OK. Could I ask could I bother you for another beer? If you get down from there. Sure sorry yes. I hope to hop effortlessly to the ground but lose my footing slightly on the landing. The grass is uneven. I am uneven. He leads me back inside.

Same again please sir. The sir hangs between us. Alright. He pulls it quickly this time. I overpay him hugely, misunderstanding the note, and tell him to keep the change. No funny stuff alright? He stares again now. I nod. No funny stuff. I wonder if he is referring to the woman from before. I twist on the stool and look out the window. She has left. The wine is only half-finished. The light too dim to see any lipstick mark on the glass. I can't think of anything to say to him. The funny stuff is me, all me, always funny stuff. He flicks on the bright clean-up lights and begins to wipe down the bar. Let me help. He looks across at me. With pity this time. That's not your job. No I guess not. I finish the beer as fast as the first.

Up the main road I go. There is just enough light left. My tolerance for alcohol has become very low. I am drunk. No cars come my way. The walk is silent. Past the church, I turn down the steep slope, the river finally reappearing. Too dark to see its course. I hang my head over the bridge. This is the area of the school most photographed. The dead author's original schoolhouse is now home to the younger boarders who sleep in large, cold dorms. For The Girls over the age of fifteen there are the smaller boarding houses, also old. Endless rumours of ghosts and disappearances. The imagined brutalities are always silent, always already happened. No screams. Instead, discoveries of oddly shaped bones they claim to be human but are likely sheep. Ordinary notches on the old stone that to them, to The Girls, are fingernail marks. Woodworm damages become names scratched into the timber. The lights are on in most windows. They are restless.

I stumble on the enormous cobblestones. In the warm air, on the warm air, the wild garlic is sickly. I press my mouth to the thorn scratch on my forearm. The new scab is crisp under my tongue. Is she awake, bristling, behind her curtains. Mrs S. I won't think about her. It is pitch black, stars now confident, as I look for my keys. This building is the smallest. My room smaller still. I have been told what it was before but have forgotten. Steadings? Stables? Are they the same thing? Somewhere, above the door, is a perfect carving of a horseshoe. I feel for it now.

My attempt at quiet is a slow comedy. Knocking a toe, an elbow, against the rough wall as I move inside, trying to step lightly, trying not to wake The Nurse through the thin partition. Finally, I find the light switch. I hear the creak of her bed, maybe feet. She knocks aggressively on the wall. I knock back. There is a surprised silence. Next she hits the floor. I hear the double smack of a furious slippered foot. Enough! I shout, lips touching plaster. I hit the wall with the flat of my palm. Enough.

The art centre has no trace of the dead author. Not even a view of her landscape. Commissioned by a progressive headmaster in the fifties or sixties: one large sloping roof, grand beams, an idea of light. The architecture has not been fully realized and so light has remained only an idea. Perhaps some budget cut before the final panes were added. Easels fill the far corner. There's no real ventilation system. None of these windows actually open. In the heatwave it is almost unbearable to stand in the swollen sunshine. I do it anyway, looking up, ghostly streaks of bird shit remain, the area obviously difficult to clean. Outside is reduced to block colours. Green, blue, blue, green.

The building is split into three large rooms. There is an astonishing amount of equipment. The Girls are offered the chance to try ceramics, even sculpture. I wander through, hoping for a blink of talent. The section dedicated to sculpture is dark. Bulbs fizz overhead. A shelf runs the whole room, lined, presumably, with objects meant to inspire. Feathers pinned under grey rocks. Large pieces of quartz. Sticks covered in lichen, colour still milky green, texture turned fragile. Bolts, a rusted chain, two antique keys. A set of miniature wooden bodies with movable parts. I pick one up and bend it back and forth. Someone has coloured in the torso with purple pen. In one corner, lying on the ground, is a large head. Papier mâché. A man's head. Eyebrows blistering. The paint dried in welts across the rough surface. I notice other outsized limbs tucked behind. A foot with perfectly square toenails. An arm patterned with moles.

Ceramics is equally windowless. It comes with another present scandal. Last week The Girls were provocative and made mugs with tits. Not their tits, maybe their mothers' tits. An aunty, a grandmother. The teacher did not know how to discipline their decision. For now the mugs remain partially hidden on the shelf amongst the poorly shaped pots, the chunky dishes no good for anything. I imagine the price of a kiln. Money can't forgive everything.

I go back into the main room, already stuffy. The Girls, inexplicably, are putting on one of Lorca's plays, The House of Bernarda Alba. Five sisters, I think, trapped under a tyrant matriarch in a poor Spanish town. I have been asked here to help complete the scenery by the art teacher, a woman I have never actually spoken to. Voices carry through from the corridor. I pull the t-shirt away from my body, trying to move air up my chest, up my neck. A few of The Girls pace into the room. Fuck me it's hot in here. One elbows another. Sorry Miss, didn't see you, we didn't see you there. No worries. Seriously Miss isn't this torture, to make us work in these conditions? They slump on the floor. It has to be illegal, doing this, on a Saturday even. Yeh totally illegal. I taste sweat on the edge of my lip. Not illegal, no. Can't you do something about it Miss. OK, OK, I can try.

I prop open the front doors, standing for a second in the fresh air. Hello, nice to see you. The voice. She is in the same shirt, the same jeans. The only difference is a leather belt. One extra hole punched through. Pulled tight across and over the torn loop. Brass buckle. Hi. Hands flat against her thighs. I'm afraid they've left me in charge of the painting. Oh? Yes, she's sick. Who? The art teacher. OK. And you, do you paint? No, never, not really, I just go where I'm told. She pauses, looks up. Well I used to paint, at university, another lifetime ago. I didn't know. Why would you? Now she moves her hands across her thighs, thumbs stroking, some bodily reassurance. So you don't garden and you don't paint. That's right. She waits for another answer, some detail I won't provide. My mystery is all I think I have. The thumbs move and move again. May I, then? What she wants is to go past me. I am still in the doorway. Sure, please, go ahead. The rest of The Girls appear. No uniforms on a Saturday. Instead matching denim shorts, t-shirts, trainers. The same plastic bracelets loose around their wrists. Hi Miss what are you the bouncer or something. Just attempting to get some airflow going. They ignore my answer, walking straight past, elbows brushing my side. I lift a broken piece of flagstone and lean it against the door.

Mrs S unfolds an enormous piece of muslin cloth. She arranges it carefully on the floor, floating about on her knees, instructing The Girls to bring her heavy items – a stool, a dense book on Rodin, a terracotta pot plant, an unopened paint tin – to pin down the four corners. This, this is what we have to paint. How? The Girls jut their hips. How can we even paint all that? That whole thing? Oh, easily. She doesn't break confidence. Hair let loose then scooped up again. A crow lands on the skylight. One of The Girls shrieks. They eat dead lamb eyeballs you know. That's rank. As if they do. I'm serious they do. All of them look up now at the sharp head, cocking left and right, an intake of breath when it takes off.

Well the picture has already been drawn out, all we have to do is fill in the gaps. Like a paint by numbers? On a grander scale, yes. She removes her shoes and walks across the cloth. Navy socks, worn at the heel. Is there a reference? Of course. A page from another dense book has been taped to the wall. Sliced not torn. Removed carefully with a ruler and a craft knife. Grey, white, black. Scraps of light. A horse opened by a scream. Picasso? Correct. She isn't impressed I know the reference. Guernica? Yes. Still not impressed. The Girls skid up to the image and take turns pressing their noses as close as possible. After a few seconds they walk backwards slowly, as if in some city gallery. Hands cup chins, heads tilt. That's intense. That's one word. Who chose this? Not me, Mrs S strokes her cheekbone, not me.

The decision seems extraordinary. I join her at the sink. Here. She drags her thumb through the bristles of a paint-brush. Old blues and yellows fade down the drain. Take one. I copy her technique. Isn't it a bit controversial, for a backdrop? Won't it cause trouble? Unlikely. Today she is not wearing earrings. No jewellery at all. It's Picasso for fuck's sake, nobody ever complains about Picasso. I delight in the swear word, a new fissure. She turns away. Not out of embarrassment but practicality. Come, girls, grab a brush. Using a screwdriver she prises open tins of paint. White, black. A Girl drops in her paintbrush and watches the liquid swallow it whole. That's weirdly satisfying. Yes. Mrs S nods. Painting is like that, weirdly satisfying. The Girl beams.

It is clear they want to impress her, The Girls. In each movement they imitate her seriousness. Flourishes are added to their steps, a slight twist on the heel, pouting their lips in concentration. Laughter is quickly and secretly forbidden. They already know something about the painting. Lorca too. The Spanish Civil War featured briefly in their history lessons. Just awful, what happened, isn't it. To Lorca as well, he didn't deserve that, no one deserves that. And so recently, when you think about it, when you really think about it. In front of Mrs S no one uses the word gay, no one uses the word ass. They want to add question marks, they want to draw her in. She is busy pulling out plastic trays. Paint is tipped into each one. She moves to and from the page pinned to the wall until finally she removes it entirely, taking it with her. Now she adds another colour in slow drips. Black dribbles into white.

The fact Mrs S does not quite wield her power only adds to it. We are all waiting to be noticed. The Girls follow her instructions with a nervous, happy energy. Paintbrushes pulled across the plastic and dabbed onto the fabric. The colours are good. Even the drawing is not bad, as already sketched out by the art teacher. Heads have been shaped by the same unnatural wind found in the original, sucked gracelessly between two worlds, or three, wherever you might find the last movement before death. Limbs all have their appropriate deadweight. Teeth and fingernails, unforgotten. Most impressive is the careful copy of the bull's dismay, the half-mouth, the tail, maybe burned, smoke unfurling in quick scratches. Painting, my painting especially, in some of the more detailed places, risks ruining the effect. It's not a bad imitation. She bends over me, then kneels, then slips sideways on the concrete floor. Definitely not bad. Her hand reaches out across the bull's back. I couldn't have done this, it must have taken her days. She presses her fingertips into the soon-to-be-black gape at the end of a severed neck. Do you hate Picasso? She smiles. No, well, I don't know, probably I do, cubism, it's just so, I don't know. The Girls watch us with squashed eyes. Men, maybe, the chunky way they think. Without knowing whether or not I am supposed to, I laugh. Chunky? Chunky. You know, they always think they've seen it all, from every angle. She blushes, I think she blushes. And you? Yes, at least I like this painting, I saw it in real life, recently, I was in Barcelona briefly, I mean Madrid, Madrid, before getting here. I feel childish. She shifts. I've seen it too. Listen I know it's ridiculous, to be doing it, to be recreating it, but here we are. I blink. It's not a problem, happy to help. Ah, the one thing I know about you, you are always happy to help. With her power also comes an ability to discredit. She gets up in one movement. I am left alone to paint. I begin with the places she has touched. The bull's back. The neck's gape. I take extra care, dramatizing my thought process, leaning forward and back, frowning, in the hope she is watching. If she's a painter I'm a painter.

The Girls take breaks to stretch their backs, rotate their arms. Not bad Miss. Two peer over my shoulder. As long as you think so. They're pleased, standing above me, authoritative. Didn't we need permission to do this? Finally, a question. Mrs S mixes more paint. Permission from who? From like Picasso? Another Girl pinches her waist. Picasso is dead you idiot. She panics. Isn't he? Isn't he dead? I believe so, very, in fact. Is it true you can only get rich from art once you're dead? Who said that? The art teacher, she lets us call her by her first name. Does she. Yes. The Girls inch forward. Mrs S bends over a section of painting. A streak of grey dries at her collarbone, more hardening on her fingernails. So do you think it's true? Why, do you want to be an artist? No, an actress. Well then. The Girl is discredited too, the conversation ended, wildly, on a private dream she didn't mean to disclose. Mrs S fills glasses with a concentrated orange juice. Biscuits are laid on a paper plate. Let's take a break, outside, shall we go outside? She rescues the mood. She controls the mood.

The Girls drag a paint-stained tarp onto the grass slope, they lie down, close their eyes. I sit on the sandstone steps, she sits a few beats away. Each forearm is turned over, as if she is experiencing the sun for the first time. This weather, it's going to waste. I suppose it is. Listen you don't garden, you don't paint, but do you swim? Swim? Yes, swim. She smiles, closer to the kind I want. Her fingers move to her earlobe, pinching it briefly. These little things. Nerves cleave my stomach. Sure I swim. Good, there's a place, it might even make all this seem worthwhile. She turns her head at the fells rising behind the art centre. What's tomorrow, Sunday, yes Sunday, meet me in my driveway around eleven? More crows circle lazily overhead then land on the roof behind. Claws, then their yowl. OK, sure, sounds good. Another smile. Then I will see you there. She walks back inside.

I wait a few seconds before following. In fast succession I adjust my binder, my t-shirt, my shorts, double-checking The Girls have not moved from the tarp, not wanting them to see my display. They don't speak. They don't move. Limbs lolling outwards. Five more minutes, OK. One lifts a hand in acknowledgement. Not wanting to appear keen, I force myself to move slowly, towards her, back down the corridor. Paintings, awful paintings, line the dark walls. Each one is a watercolour, framed expensively, showing some sloppy detail of a farm, a slope, a sky, a sheep, a tree. In one the art centre itself has been reproduced. It is my favourite. The brash shape of the building. A wooden plaque, embossed with gold, lists the winners of an annual prize. I squint to see the signature of The Girl in the painting's corner but the letters are too thick to make out.

She is surveying our work so far. I pause in the doorway as she adjusts certain lines, certain curves. No one will miss this on stage will they. She jolts. Sneaking up on me? Hardly. No, it's quite something, they've, we've done a fine job, the art teacher will be happy. The Girls clatter in. They crush the plastic cups and place them in the bin. Miss do you want the last biscuit? No thanks. She eats half and throws the rest away. Mrs S bends and sharpens the pale flames above the door, around the lightbulb. Look. She points out the too-soft peaks. It runs the risk of looking like a cartoon, like a caricature of pain. Her hand advances, planning her strokes before committing. Only half the painting has been completed. A ghostly patchwork. Come on guys, there's still plenty to do. I point at the paintbrushes abandoned in the sink. The Girls lean against the kitchen countertop. They look at Mrs S, not me. How much longer? Oh, hard to say.

The next portion of work is more subdued. Energy wanes. The Girls become careless, making purposeful mistakes, constantly requesting Mrs S with her dabs of white spirit. They giggle at the horse's head. One of The Girls adds the pupils, another makes the fat apostrophes of the nostrils. More giggles. He's sort of cute, look at those cute ears. She moves on to the mouth. The tongue, sharpened into a sound. Ribbed roof wrenched open. This bit, this is a freaky bit. Mrs S gently takes The Girl's hand in her own. Together they shade the jaw. Each tooth is finished. Fingertips guiding knuckles. There. Mrs S lets go. There. The other Girls examine their own knuckles. Subtly, or at least what they think is subtle, tightening and loosening their hands around their paintbrushes. Mrs S catches each motion. Yes, that's it, that's it. They cower, then confess, offering up their fingers. We don't know how, it's too hard, can you show us too?

One by one she takes each of their hands in her hand, painting small sections. The dead child's upturned nose, two jutted bottom lips, a lost hoof, a lost horseshoe. She arrives at my corner. And you? She hovers, examining the detail yet to be completed. Let's do this part, shall we? The Girls watch. The soft triangle of a knee. A shin. There is no hesitation. I brace myself to feel everything, to be able to re-examine her touch later, to be able to slow it down into some sort of understanding. Impossible. She moves at speed. I think, briefly, she slips her fingers between my knuckles. Maybe not, maybe she doesn't. Desire is still only a shape, an outline. Her hand switches, rolling underneath my palm. We paint along the leg as if it is a wave. At the foot she continues, adding lifelines with precise dashes, unbroken. Helpful? Yes, although now the rest of what I've done looks bad. Nonsense. She disappears to the middle of the room. Claps twice. Let's see what we can finish in the next hour, shall we? Yes, yes! The Girls are unashamed of their enthusiasm. I am envious.

Once again she wears a white shirt. This time hers, not his. I didn't know what to wear. In the end I pulled the crumpled shirt, his, from the bottom of my laundry basket. To smooth the creases I stood in the steam of the bathroom. The collar damp against my neck. She is too polite to say she recognizes it. Are you excited? Yeh. Good, I think you'll like it. The car is small, old. Red paint rusted over the tyres' curves. A crack in the windshield slowly growing larger. Inside it is spotless.

Her hand on the gear stick. No nail varnish, no bracelet. Earrings, gold studs. I notice a second hole, grown over. She touches her earlobe. Always on my lookout. Ah yes, from my younger days. When you were a painter? She laughs, avoids the question. Nothing is given away easily. She hands me a stout Ordnance Survey, a biro star, her biro star, drawn next to a particular square. OK, you need to read this, you're the co-pilot. Course, have you been before? Yes, but he drove us, Mr S drove. I let the air hang. Anyway it's there, you can see, where the river goes through the campsite. It is there, the thickened blue bend, a patch of criss-crossed green. I look again at her earlobe. She turns out of the driveway and onto the road. Goodness, what am I doing, the wrong way already. That sudden vulnerability. I want it to be me, to be my gaze, to be our gazes swapping in and out, one replacing the other. She takes the car up to the sports field. A large car park sits behind. The Girls wander about, holding hockey sticks, gum-shields plump behind their lips. She waves to a few. Screeches the tyres in a fast circle. She waves again in the rear-view mirror. They call after her.

You're so popular with them. Yes, only after a year of trying but never appearing to try. A minibus turns in beside us. The other team. She seems genuinely interested, craning her neck to see the uniforms, to guess the competing school. Did you want to stay and watch? No no. We drive away, past the pub, past the garage. I wind down the window. The tunnel whoosh. I lean out, my eyes watering, the hedgerow whipping close to my ear. We slow down at an enormous bridge. A long line of motorbikes is waiting to pull in. Ah, Devil's Bridge, have you seen? No. How have you missed so much? She indicates, following the motorbikes. There is no room for another car so she leaves the hazards on, blocking somebody else in. Quick hurry, before we get in trouble. In the middle of the bridge, the river wide and slow beneath, she shows me two round imprints sunk into the wall. The devil's hands? The devil's hands. So tiny. Not if you have hooves. She presses her knuckles into the dents. Stone worn smooth. Is it lucky? Probably not, probably the opposite.

I see now she is wearing men's swimming shorts. A faded pink. Also guaranteed to be partly his, like the car, like the trip. What's wrong? Nothing. Always nothing with you. Her tone is unexpected. A closeness we have not yet shared. She senses it too, shifting subject, putting her hands against the sky. Such a glorious day! A van sells bright-white ice creams. Bikers in their heavy leathers lean against the bridge, licking their wrists, catching the melt. Cones are tossed half-eaten into the rubbish. Wasps pearling in and out of the bin's mouth. Would you like one? Not yet, maybe later. I look too long at a group of young men, only in leather waist-coats, or shirtless entirely. Trouser buttons biting just below their bellybuttons. Want a picture? Come on then take a picture pussy! one of the men calls to me. She is already by the car, lifting her head to see, unable to hear. Squinting through the glare she waves me over. I look back at the man who has already forgotten me, now pushing a friend with a similarly beautiful chest. His arms around his middle, then his ribs. Soft punches thrown into each shoulder. I feel the itch of skin beneath my binder. Inevitable. I notice things I want to steal.

I go back to her. How would he be, sitting in this passenger seat, watching her hand on a gear stick, watching her hands against the sky, watching her hands made into hooves. He would have a beautiful chest. He would be less astonished. Everything OK? Always. I change tune for her. She raises that eyebrow. Well then let's get going. I hope there aren't crowds like this everywhere. Don't you worry, this is a secret spot. She taps the page open across my lap, finger just wide of her biro star. Well then, I say, parroting her catchphrase, I won't tell. Oh I see it's like that. Familiarity again. This time easier.

Sheep, fields, sheep. Slow pace of stone walls. Today the blue has heft, has a building heat. I didn't know you could have weather like this here, I didn't know. With one hand on the wheel she takes a pair of sunglasses from the door. Yes of course, honestly what do you think of us. Us. She never mentions a different home to this one. Wild flowers begin as we climb higher. The car struggles on the hill bends. Up, up, up. Tall weeds, but maybe not weeds, with starred white flowers. I am not concentrating on the map. Here! Ah, OK. She reverses down the narrow lane. A sign for the campground appears. She pulls into a passing place. I'm sure this counts as parking. From the boot she hands me a bag. Lunch! She puts on a green backpack, worn, straps frayed. Without worry she jumps up onto the low wall, spinning over her legs, landing safely on the other side. I follow, slower, more careful with my skin, not wanting a scrape, or nick.

Each movement she makes is positive, whole. This is a body at peace. She thinks of nobody else. Are we trespassing? Only sort of. To our right a few tents have been set up. In the distance is a line of caravans and an office. I see the tall not-weeds with white flowers up close. Don't touch, don't touch those. Hogweed, it will burn. I worry now, walking even slower, the space between us lengthening. We drop along a bank, following another wall, moving through a spot where the stones have been displaced. Downhill she marches towards a thin wood. Her calves are arrows through the grass.

In the broken shade she puts things in her mouth and calls out their names. Lovage, water mint. More, there's more, but she's too far ahead for me to hear. I round a corner and find her bent over a patch of pink faces, petals uptight. She frowns. This, I can't remember what it's called. Like the roses, the information is recently learned. There have been other books, other garish covers. This is one way of belonging. I understand. She struggles, combing through the images she's stored, books stacked somewhere in that grand house. No, I can't remember, how disappointing. A plane rips overhead. Seconds later an apocalyptic boom sounds off the rocks. We are in the middle of a valley. As if a glacier had only just finished moving through. She places her hands over her ears. There's another one. Sure enough another dot appears, expanding. Not a plane but a jet. Something harder, faster. The military prefer these secret corners of English countryside. The sound is dragged behind. I don't bring my hands to my ears. She watches. How can you stand it? I don't know, I don't mind.

We come out of the trees and stagger further down. The slope is steeper now. A sound of water increases. She crouches, picks a clover and bites behind its head. She doesn't offer, or ask, me to do the same. Instead the flavour is announced. Sweet, something like honey. Wonderful! she confirms. Her personalities catch, like loose thread on a branch. The old-fashioned headmaster's wife and this person, setting her teeth to a stem's nape. Stood tall in her pink shorts.

Almost there. Scree is loose under my feet. Water appears. A clear river. Heather makes soft mounds. She whips through the bracken. Points to a distant fell and suggests climbing it, not today, but one day. I am hopeful. We drop down onto a track. There is nothing but the rhythm of our shoes on the dusty surface. Birdsong. Breath, focused in the heat. I want to ask her how she, how they, found this place, but the quiet is too lovely. Familiarity, a new familiarity, this time bodily. Little clutches of fabric. The swipe of our thighs.

This is it! At first I can't see anything, only slabs of grey stone. She moves towards a copse of only five or six trees. Slender, silver bark. Green leaves. I watch her first, standing at an edge, peering down, pleased. It needed to be as good as she remembered. Without waiting for me she removes her white shirt. Each button a piece of my own spine, undone. Her swimming costume is an athlete's. Black, streamlined. I am surprised by her strength. She adjusts the fit, a finger slid underneath the short straps, then the place where the suit meets her hips. Catches me watching her, I blush. She calls to me. My anxiety has its own heartbeat. Desperate for the cool across my sticky face. I wear a sleeveless t-shirt, the binder hidden underneath. Underpants, too, the t-shirt's hem past my hips, stopping mid-thigh. You'll go in wearing that? Yeh, no costume, didn't bring one with me, never thought it would be warm enough to swim. Little did you know. She accepts my lie. My costume balled up in my underwear drawer. I no longer know how to wear it. I reach her at the edge. She has waited for my reaction. Below is a large waterfall. A pool eroded beneath it. Bigger than I imagined, enough to spend time swimming to either side. Jewelled surface. A fish, brown trout she explains, is visible deep on the stony bed. It's beautiful. It is. She clambers down and dives. Muscle, water. Her back is a swimmer's back. All arch and grace.

For a moment I can't move. She doesn't hurry me. Treads water, calm. I grip the edge with my toes. Promise myself I'll jump at the count of five. But only manage on ten, hopping forward, I can't make the same shape as her. Rush of rock at my back. Relief of vanishing beneath the bright surface. T-shirt ballooning around me. I open my mouth to drink, to taste the cold. Reappear to her face a few feet from mine. She smiles. There you are. We haul up to the water-fall. A large, flat rock partially submerged, able to be clambered onto. Matching flex of our forearms, she admires my brawn, I pretend not to hear. We sit side by side under-neath. She draws up her legs. The crease at her knee. Here she does not know, does not mind, what she gives away. Water hammering our heads, necks. Without warning she slips back in, completes a few lengths at speed. Front crawl. I float. If I could choose a different chest I would choose this water. If I could choose a different body I would choose this water. I say the last line aloud, river slipping on my tongue. What? She swims towards me. Slowly. Breaststroke now. What did you say? Nothing. But of course, nothing. She rolls her eyes. I roll mine back.

I'll buy us ice creams on the way home. Don't worry, your company is plenty. The line is well used, has been said to other people, she is sociable, she entertains. I want it for myself. It would be nice to be plenty. To be plenty the way she says it, the key change between the e and n. We eat. Olives, artichokes from the posh supermarket. She laughs when I call it that. Hummus, smoky crackers. Two kiwi fruit and two matching teaspoons. She pulls an artichoke heart from the jar and eats it whole. We swim again, rinsing the oil from the corners of our mouths, from our fingers. Afterwards we arrange our towels on the rocks and lie still. Birdsong. Insects, the river's full throat. A weightlessness arrives. I doze, waking up to her backpack zipping and unzipping. My God the time. What? The time, it's past five. Her watch left in the front pocket. Is there a rush? She sits next to me, cramping the left side of her body into mine. It is the most we have ever touched. I feel it, I feel the moment she realizes, a tightening of her torso. Too late to move away we are left in this encounter, unprepared. We inhale, we are drawn closer together. I try to control my breath.

After seconds, maybe ten, she stands and stretches. Now I'm all dried off I want to go back in. The temperature has not changed. If anything, a particular warmth now rises from the ground, the rocks. Even the trees radiate. Do it!

No, no, really I should be getting back. He needs his dinner? It is an unfair thing for me to say. She is gracious, letting it go, sticking to the facts. Yes actually, we have people coming over. What people, I don't ask. I picture it instead. Him, her, a second him, a second her. Something sophisticated, fish, a whole fish. A whole fish and its special matching cutlery.

Here, come here, check me for ticks. Ticks? Yes, ticks! I approach her back. She reaches around an arm, her arm, sharp elbow skywards, and stretches her fingers, indicating an area to be investigated. There's nothing. I look closely. Are you sure? A few moles. Those shoulder blades previously in flight through the water. She raises both arms. Shoulder blades in flight again. And here? She twists side to side. I am surprised by the dark hair of her armpits. Her smell. Nothing, there's nothing. Good. The shirt is pulled back over her head. It is over. Now you. I turn, reluctantly. Her hands pause. May I? Yes. She uses her fingers, reaching inside my t-shirt without lifting it, feeling along the curves of my armpits, double-checking the moles. The touch is practical, careful. I know she will look at herself again in the mirror, after her shower, making sure I did not mistake a freckle, did not mistake a well-known moment of skin, and leave behind a determined nymph, those tiny legs, those tiny heads. She swaps a forefinger for a thumb, sweeping it down my sides. I didn't understand I was supposed to use my hands. Now there will never be a second chance.

I have to see her the next day. And the next. Largely I am ignored. My skin hot. At one assembly, Monday morning, the teachers sitting in front of The Girls, there is maybe a sideways glance felt against my cheek. I turn slightly only to see her staring straight ahead, one smile for him as he addresses The Girls, then straight ahead again. In her outfit. Another silk top, this one designed with a small, lovely, hole at the back. Sunburn across her nose.

Muscle, water. That day is a parallel universe, set afloat upon my body. No longer in existence. She has created a lack so effortlessly. Is it knowingly, or unknowingly, done? I try to shift under her gaze in the corridor. She doesn't bend, only nods her head, walking past. The weather has not changed. There is a lethargy. Movement reduced, laughter dissolved into sighs. I am grateful for the melodrama. The lawns are permanently busy. Bikinis are not permitted so instead The Girls tuck their shirts in and up, socks and shoes removed.

On purpose I head to the graveyard and lie down with an interesting book, in case she should see me and ask what I'm reading. One, two, three days since our trip. I am ashamed to have nothing else to think about. The interesting book will never be read. Every other word I look up at her window. I am joined for half an hour by a few of The Girls. Propped up against the tombstones. They did not notice me when they first arrived and then felt too awkward to leave immediately. Were it not for the heat, melting us all, a tension would have been palpable.

If I had a car I would return to the swimming spot and confirm each step. Instead, I carry out other physical checks. In the bedroom mirror I hope for a tick, imitating her thumbs, her fingers. I drape the shirt across the back of the chair. Unwashed. My distress is a surprise. Before, I enjoyed a consistent, calculated nothingness. I had been liberated by that nothingness. Each day perfect, each day without a pulse. My immovable routines. For once I had been sleeping. Nine, ten, eleven hours. Now, in the middle of the night, her shoulder blades.

A week passes. On Friday I call my mother. I walk to the larger boarding house and use their payphone. All The Girls are at school so there is no queue. When I first arrived, at the bright airport, I bought a stack of plastic calling cards. Vague commitments, the only kind I've known. The phone is in its own room to give The Girls privacy. In here, too, are locked cupboards containing the sweet treats of each of the younger boarders. On the weekend they are granted access to their own stashes, issued by The Housemistress, their self-control not to be trusted. There are five separate keyholes. Each key lives on a smaller ring of other keys, one for each door in the building, worn by The Housemistress.

She walks with it on show, letting it hit against her thigh. Her pantsuits always navy, as if she is one of The Girls grown too large. A lack of glamour makes her age indistinguishable. Young compared to other staff. Though, I'd guess, she still has a few years on me. No make-up. Skin smooth everywhere except her forehead. Stern creases. Occasionally she looks at me. I sense the peculiar queerness between us. Not solidarity but something more, in the veins, in the blood, some mirrored mineral. I love her big walk, with the keys, when I don't think about what the keys are for. This tender marching out. A warding-off in advance.

Today I don't see her. I talk to my mother, half waiting for her, The Housemistress, to open the door. At home nothing has changed. There is some sort of trip planned to the coast. A very nice hotel has been booked. If she misses me it is in a warped way. Now I am no longer physically present she uses an outdated version. When we speak, it is five, ten years ago. I haven't come out yet. Her world is relatively undisturbed. The confession of my gayness left her permanently patronized, overly exposed. I introduced a subject she knew nothing about. Forced her into an ignorance she found frightening.

How are things there? She is tentative with the present tense. For a moment I consider telling her about my distress, if only for the shocked silence. It's good, hard work. Nothing wrong with that. No, nothing wrong with that. I imagine her with a sweet tea, mouthing silent sentences to whoever else came into the kitchen, repeating each detail. It is early morning in Australia. She will have plans later. The pub down the road, karaoke. Dad is there but will not speak to me. The absence is no longer dramatic. How is he, how is Dad? You know him, the very same, won't quit the cigs.

The door handle twists. She, The Housemistress, enters, all hips. I am sitting on the windowsill. A hand goes up in apology. Mum, I've got to go. OK love, speak soon. I put down the receiver, greasy from my ear. Sorry you didn't have to do that. It's fine there wasn't much left to say. I didn't know you were in here, thought you'd been and gone. She leans against the wall. The windowsill makes me bold. I blurt it out before I can change my mind. Fancy a beer? What? A beer. The Girls begin to appear across the car park, swinging their matching book bags. She grins. Thought you'd never ask.

On Fridays there are no prep sessions for us to run. The Girls have a sort of freedom. Mostly they watch TV, hooking their legs over the arms of the sofas, heads on each other's stomachs. In theory it is our time off, although this is unofficial. You ready now? Sure. Let's leave before they notice us and need something. Maybe she does not want to be seen alone with me. Bodies like ours are talked about with vicious glee. Two at once is pure defiance. She motions at the dining room door. I take intense pleasure in her fingers selecting the matching key first time.

She shushes me and giggles. It feels good. The empty dining hall is already laid for supper. This way. I brush past her as she lifts the hatch leading into the kitchen. At the exit she selects another key. It opens up to the rough road, right beside the river. The water's pace is slow. No rain for weeks. Where to from here? She points at the steep slope to one side. Can you handle it? Can you handle it? I point at her pantsuit. This? No problemo. She peels off her blazer and knots it around her neck. Tucks her trousers into each sock.

Odd, I notice now, one with a repeated pattern of a dog's face, the other plain white.

You first. Naturally. She charges up the bank. There is a path barely visible. At certain points her foot slips, a loose stone tumbling behind her. Sorry, she calls down, mind your head. At the top she waits, a hand outstretched. I can manage. Regardless she grabs my forearm and hoists me up. There you go. We follow a path between the few houses that have nothing to do with the school. The pub appears, garden first. I remember standing on the table. The man will no doubt be working. I try not to be embarrassed. At the door there is a mutual hesitation. Both of us make way for the other, hoping not to be the one to go inside first.

I give in and enter. At the bar I order two beers. She reads aloud each kind, then changes her mind, instead needing a gin and tonic. 'Tis the season. The man makes the drinks. He recognizes me then regrets it, turning his back, pulling sliced lime from a glass. Extra ice please. She places her elbows on the bar, unbothered. More. He shovels in cube after cube. Yeh perfect. He goes to add the tonic, unscrewing the lid of a plastic bottle already opened. Any chance of a fresh pour? I face the other way. Fleetingly I want to exit the conspiracy we have created. It's not cheap here you know. Her voice is a stage whisper. The man darkly retrieves a new bottle. At the hiss she makes a satisfied sound, a long ah. These are on me. Thanks.

I think of my mother. Yawning, her smoker's mouth, the large Alsatian walked around the block. You OK? I lift my glass to hers. The creases on her forehead multiply. Cheers, and it's sunny, who could want more! She leads us back outside. There are no tables available so we stand in between. She unknots the blazer and drops it to the ground. Sweat unbroken at both of our temples. So what should we bitch about first? The fact that there's no one around here to fuck? I reel, glad my face is protected by the sun's glare, the shock unable to be seen. She continues. I thought to myself, when I took the job, a school like this, sure to be full of dykes, well there's you at least, but no offence, you're hardly my type. Oh? Yeh no offence. None taken. This is only half-true. I am offended, had hoped for some flirtation, had enjoyed her unlocking doors, shushing me. So you think there's no one else? Who knows, I thought to myself, at least the PE department, some jolly-hockey-sticks PE teacher, but no, all married. Doesn't mean they're not gay. I want to talk endlessly about Mrs S. Say her name over and over again, force The Housemistress to consider her every detail. I manage to restrain myself. What else is there to say except her name? The Housemistress takes a large mouthful, sucking in an ice cube, knocking it against her teeth. Yeh, sure, but it's not like you can do anything about that, who has the energy. She swallows. Another long ah.

A panicked look is refreshing across her face. Shit I didn't even ask, just assumed. No, yeh, lesbian. I awkwardly give myself a thumbs up, then invert it, jabbing my chest. Forever in love with the word. Lesbian. The slow sexuality of it, a snake in the mouth. She looks around at the tables, peering over the top of her glass, a faux spy. All hets here methinks. I look now too. Tourists, mostly couples, with their sporty tan lines. Some in cycling gear, others straight off the fells in their zip-away trousers and expensive hiking boots.

I decide to enter into her game. Dunno, in outfits like that, all women look like queers. True, it's those cargo pant pockets, they do something to me. She slaps the section of her chest containing her heart. It feels good again, to be gay, to be standing in the sun, to drink a beer. What do you think hets keep in their pockets? Oh, easy, strong breath mints, factor-fifty sun cream. She pauses and stares without shame at a man's profile. He reaches into his trousers and produces a plain white handkerchief. He blows his nose. Proceeds to dab his brow. Oh my God! A hanky! She giggles. Do you think he's signalling? White, what does white mean? I'm not sure. She scratches her chin, an ancient philosopher, performing her thinking. Rimming? Sorry not sure. No, not rimming, it's orgies, one hundred per cent it's orgies. I laugh. Definitely orgies. Which pocket? What? Which pocket did he take it from? The right, no, the left. A top! She giggles again. Maybe he's my type after all. A few people look our way. Without turning their heads, afraid to let us see them seeing us, their eyes swerving.

The woman accompanying the man raises her hand and tugs apart the Velcro of a large square pocket. We both watch. She reveals a chunky camera. Should have seen that one coming! The woman switches it on, releasing a dramatic mechanical sound, the lens announcing itself. She shuffles in next to the man and tries to take a photograph of the two of them, faces ruddy. Each time she clicks the button there is another mechanical sound, the camera struggling to focus. She redirects the man, asking him to crane his neck to the left, to the right. Jesus this is painful to watch. The Housemistress hands me her gin. Here hold this. Confidently she approaches them and offers to take the picture.

They take her in, trying hard to be polite, the effort hardening their bodies. Afterwards the woman nods, overly formal. Thank you, that's very kind, thank you. You owe me a drink! The woman jumps. Oh, well, I mean. The Housemistress lifts up both hands. Only kidding! On her return the rest of the gin is downed. Bloody hets couldn't organize a piss-up in a brewery. She pats the keys, double-checking their presence. There is an anger, softened by time, now residual. I touch her arm. It was nice of you to take the photo. Well we would have been here all day listening to that sound. I don't immediately move my hand away. She allows this, remaining still, legs wide, patient as I finish my beer.

Another? Is the Pope a Catholic? This is her. Catchphrases swaggering across the hurt. As I walk across the grass she calls out. Heads turn. Make sure it's the fresh bottle of tonic yeh? Yeh. My eyes readjust to the dim interior. The man watches a TV behind the bar. He doesn't register me this time. Hi, same again. What was that then? A pint and a g and t. Right. He fills the glass with ice, a precarious tower, designed to unsettle me. The tonic bottle is lifted up unnecessarily high so I can see it's the one recently opened. I try to embody her imperious stance, looking at him, nodding. Chin running parallel to his chin.

Oh, summer is embarrassing. Already, it is embarrassing, to be a body on permanent display. The sun like eyes in a portrait, like a spotlight, I am followed everywhere. I cannot dress. What if I see her, how should I look? There is no answer. I am late. One t-shirt discarded, as if there might be a better option. The same t-shirt put back on again. The classroom has a shoddy fan. I put my face into the pathetic whir. No one has arrived to tell me what to do. The desks are pushed together to make one long line. Brown envelopes, a list of addresses, a stack of the new school prospectus. On the blackboard is a chalk drawing of a river's meander. The teacher's hand is rough, quick. Arrows added to assert a pressure at one bend. An oxbow lake labelled and aggressively underlined. Each impact of chalk has left white crumbs. I wait for an arrival. Nothing, nobody. It's a Saturday. The school is empty.

The task is obvious. The school is courting students by way of their rich parents. I pick up a prospectus. On the cover is a picture of the headmaster's lawn, four of The Girls lounge and laugh, told not to look at the camera. They must appear as if stumbled upon. A summer's day, of course, THE SKY IS THE LIMIT written along the bright blue. Footsteps. I look up at the door, I live in hope it is her, I live in fear it is her, it is never her. The cover promises that TOGETHER WE ARE BETTER. The Girls unwittingly part of a political campaign. The next page is the school as seen from above, the angle awkward. The Girls reduced to the size of insects, limbs barely discernible, as they move from the church to the main path. Stone burly, grey, each building enormous. Her house, Mrs S's house, you cannot see. Just out of the frame. This page promises tradition, promises excellence. The school's motto in cursive, ONE HEART, ONE PLACE. Next to the addresses are notes. Perhaps written by him, by Mr S. It is not something I am supposed to see. Dollar signs used to indicate money, those names with three in a row merit a clumsily drawn star. There are occasional, brief descriptions of a job, a personality, people he has met, things they like: Bordeaux, firm hand, red tie. A personal flourish will be added to his cover letter.

I turn over. There she is. Mrs S, sat in her office. A full page. The Georgia O'Keeffe past her shoulder. This is their contemporary touch. She too does not look at the camera but across the table, as if in deep discussion. But the person opposite has been cropped out, or was never there at all. Open on her desk is a notebook, the shapes of her handwriting. I lift the page closer to my face. As if I might be able to decipher something crucial, to look for some sign. She wears a blouse I have not yet seen. Perhaps already abandoned. It is green, almost see-through, it flows. Underneath, a white camisole. I take an inventory. One empty water glass, impossibly clean, her mouth has never touched the rim, one pen, something decent, a book open and face down, caught at a particular page. A clock, stern, alloy, not silver I don't think. Her hands are clasped in front of her face. She has been asked to perform too. Be serious, the photographer asked, act as if I'm not here at all, it's a normal day. She pretends to be self-conscious although she is not. It is more charming that way. Her understanding of the world, the way it works. I am doomed. Yes. I am doomed.

At first the screaming is faint. Animals, small animals, busy in the chalky summer night. My eyes open then close. Words carry further, a name, maybe the word help. A sharp release of adrenaline. I stand on my bed and heave open the skylight. Behind my room, behind the boarding house, is a brief section of woods. Otherwise it is only fields and fells. I remain standing, hoping to feel a direction. Impossible. Screams become shouts. I get dressed. I grope for a torch in a kitchen cupboard.

The shouts still, then liven. I walk along the river before turning up a slight hill into the woods. Trees are sparse. The river cuts down below, at its widest beside the large bank. Each voice becomes clearer now, The Girls, five of them, spread out across the stony swerve, calling into different parts of the night. What, what are you doing down there? They reform, pressing into one another, looking up at me. What the fuck? Miss! Miss! Miss, oh my God it's Miss. The slope is maybe twenty metres down. I can't see any faces, only the blankets draped around their shoulders. They came mildly prepared. Miss we're cold, we're cold and stuck can you take us home. Laughter. Strained octaves.

Yeh Miss come on come down have a drink. We're stuck, we're so stuck, oh my God.

What do you mean, stuck? We can't get back up, it's totally impossible. Miss we'll give you a drink if you help us. They call again now, help, help, help, cupping their hands around their mouths. How did you get down there? I flick the torch along the slope. Was it from here? Miss come on, hurry it's cold. Is anyone hurt? No, as if. Have you been drinking? Miss we would never, you won't tell anyway will you Miss. I make my way down. The slope is steeper than anticipated. I sit and slip forwards, imitating the pattern of their bodies, hooking my arms around the occasional sapling, tree, root. They call, keep cheering. Go for it Miss, go for it.

At the bottom I recognize each face. Four are fourteen, one fifteen. Wailing, their arms around my shoulders in a limp hug. Miss you rescued us. They pull away. On the bank is a thin pile of branches. Miss you're a big dyke why don't you light the fire. She smiles, The Girl speaking to me. Light the fire and hang out with us. I think we'd better get back. Miss where will you take us Miss. Back to your dorms. Let's go to your house Miss do you have anything to drink. How much have you had? A Girl lifts two empty bottles. Vodka maybe, probably. Look we couldn't light the fire. Two press their foreheads together, another swings her hands behind her back, the final pair clench each other's hands. Each self-aware in this mock innocence. I am terrified although glad it is not daylight, glad to be half shadow.

The smell is light, but there, cigarettes, the sweetening alcohol on the edge of every word. Miss you'll have to carry us back up there. One of them walks around me, reaching up, closing her elbow around my neck. A stage whisper. Only carry me back up there, leave them here. One jump, pulling me backwards, kicking her heels into my calves.

Hey, hey, come on, stop that. I pull her elbow away. We can walk, all of you, it's a five-minute walk from here. Miss no way Miss. Such serene faces. You know that, you know there's a path. No we don't Miss, we're not outdoorsy like you. Italics drop into their sentences. Listen bring the rubbish OK, bring the rubbish with you. The Girl holding the bottles puts them both to her mouth, tipping her head backwards. I see other supplies. A few unlit church candles, two lighters, one cracked, an empty packet of sweets pinned purposefully under a stone. This rebellion has also been careful. The blankets are the school's issue, a rough woollen tartan. Each boarder is required to purchase one to lay on top of their bedding. Red name tags stitched into the corners. Fuck this I want to stay here. Me too. Four of them sit, cross-legged, on the pebbles. Fuck this. The fifth stands next to me, a touch drunker, swaying, steadying herself against my arm.

Up, get up. No. What happens when you're hungry? Tired? Who cares who gives a shit. OK what happens when you're hung-over? Fuck you. Listen in a few hours you're going to feel terrible and wish you were near a bathroom. Fuck you fuck you fuck you, they call again, layering each voice over the next. Fine, whoever wants to stay can stay, I'm going back. I turn. Somewhere is the path, a lone rowan tree. I stumble forward. My torchlight pathetic. Just ahead the track emerges, swinging away from the river. Beyond will be a roughly made bridge across a narrow bend. I have been here before. A biology outing, The Girls dragging jars through the water, squealing at moss, threatening to taste it. Miss, Miss, Miss, Miss. Just before the bridge they appear. Miss you can't just leave us. I haven't have I, here we all are.

They belong in the larger boarding house, run by The Housemistress. The path follows the side of the building. One slaps her hand against the stone, home sweet home. Another slaps harder. Home sweet home, homo sweet homo. She presses a finger into my back. The other Girls splutter. At the front door I punch in the code. The hallway has held the day's heat. Wait here. But why? Just wait. I head up the stairs to find The Housemistress. I have never been to her room. Somewhere is a flat, an annexe, similar to mine. This one at the end of a corridor lined with dormitories. In the middle of the night, she has told me, The Girls will occasionally ring her doorbell repeatedly, feigning sleepwalking, arms outstretched, eyes rolled back. Each crime so discreet, so expertly done. On the second floor I find her already awake, disturbed by our noise. A flannel dressing gown. Barefoot. Jesus is everyone OK? Yeh, they're fine, just shit-faced. Just shitfaced? Who? Where did they even, where are they? Downstairs. OK, OK. She moves as if to run, then slows to a stride. Grips the banister. As if timing each step.

The Girls stand. Bodies more awkward indoors, under the lights. Well I can't, I can't begin. The dressing gown is worn around the thick collar. I can see the beginning and end of the thread, criss-crossing, fraying. In the entrance hall is a picture of the boarding house in black and white. Not one but two cheap prints of the dead author. She is young in both. Ordinary. The Girls are quieter in The Housemistress's presence. Two glance at her bare feet then at each other. Big toes flexed. We will deal with this in the morning you hear me. Yes Miss. They begin their procession up the stairs.

She sighs. Wait, hang on, with me. The Girls pause. Eyes glazed. We go through the dining room and into the kitchen. Here, come on. The Housemistress spoons instant coffee into five mugs. Boils milk on the enormous burner. Sugar, one tablespoon, another. She finds hot chocolate powder and stirs. The Girls watch, bewildered. Thanks Mum. One of them makes a mistake. The others look on in dismay, betrayed, wanting immediately to sever themselves from her. Not Mum, not Mum. It's OK. The Housemistress is forgiving, in her dressing gown, feet still bare against the linoleum. One slipper sticks out of each large pocket. It's OK. I want to twist a thumb through the worn hole at her collar. She rinses the mugs in the steel sink and refills each one. Drink, all of you, finish it alright. They do exactly as she says.

The church has lost an eye. One of the stained-glass windows has been broken. A rock thrown through at some point in the night, or the early hours of the morning, no one is sure. There are security cameras but they are fake, just plastic structures glued to the stone. The vicar tiptoes around the pieces. All dragged outside on tarpaulin, to be studied in the light, both of us awkward at the teamwork. He wears his robes even though there is no service today. All day he wears his robes, sweeping self-consciously through the school. He counts and counts again, announcing the number to me each time. I pretend to take note. The pencil only a stub, chewed. I have been tasked with helping him categorize the damage. At the school I am anybody's. Each fragment must be carefully boxed up, soon to be sent away to an expert who might be able to complete a repair.

It doesn't matter who has done this, what matters is that it is done. He wants to sound calm, forgiving. Instead he is fraught. Rubbing his hands, taking his glasses on and off to polish them. What matters is that it is done. I don't reply. He is not talking to me, but to himself, or God, long ago they coalesced, now he must bear witness to himself constantly. Right, well we ought to start boxing them up I suppose? He bends over the first fragment. Touches it cautiously. Indecisive about his grip, swapping thumb and forefinger. He investigates the details. A face revealed in the glass, eyes sloped in a type of grief. Or, I suppose, it might not be grief. The face most likely belongs to a saint. Fine scrapes of a fringe line his forehead. Symbols at his frilled collar, shells, stars, leaves, shapes too amorphous to tell. His stare is without direction, as if, unlike the rest, unlike the vicar, he has been able to look inward. There is not much opportunity for handsomeness. His eyes are too peculiar, his jawline too soft, his hair set sweetly in a medieval bob.

So it's true. Mrs S stands at the gate. My chest tightens. She looks almost admiringly at the damage. The vicar lifts both his hands. Ah, yes, I'm afraid, it's very true. Heels stun across the path. He shades his eyes to watch her. What a dreadful thing. She says one thing and feels another. I keep on with my task, checking the packing materials, set up in the shade of a pine. Side by side they regard the window. What will be more dreadful is the cost. He folds his arms. Yes, although you're not to worry about that, leave it to the others. She flaps her hand in the direction of the school, perched on its slope. The vicar grins weakly. Of course, of course, I just feel responsible. He cannot keep his body still. His weight shifts from one foot to the other. Oh, you aren't responsible, silly man, how could you be, unless it was your hand that threw the rock. She touches him now.

Her hand reaching out to his elbow, tapping it lightly. I am jealous. Forced to invent their history in order to recover myself. She thinks of him only as a brother, a younger brother, pathetic, alone. Oh thank you, yes. I watch him overthink. He decides, last minute, to touch her in return, accidentally glancing her waist on his way to her arm. They stand quietly for a moment. Both contemplate the window. Or at least they pretend to. The church demanding such moments of profundity.

It lasted hundreds of years, a reformation, an entire reformation, then it's destroyed just like that. He snaps his fingers. He loves her but we are not the same. I will have to join them, assert myself. She is in her formal wear. A ring is new on her pinkie finger. Silver, large. A crest. The school, this country, loves a crest. Farcical little identities. It looks wonderful on her. The knuckle swelling just before the curve. She turns her hand across her cheek. It feels as though everything new she does, this pinkie ring, is for me. Is it self-worth to hold my noticing in such high esteem? My noticing. Impossible to stop.

And what do you think? She turns to me. No hello, never a hello, what could be so obvious as a hello. Avoiding her eyes I look at the pinkie ring. About who did it? Yes, or maybe why, why someone would do this. Well, I guess it would be fun. Fun? The vicar wants to sound incredulous. His voice breaks. I am encouraged, I will be poetic. Yeh, to throw a rock straight through a window, moving like a meteorite, especially a window like that, it would be fun.

Oh no, there's something seriously wrong with you, if you find that fun, if you find such destruction fun. The vicar relishes his shock, hands flying to his narrow hips.

Mrs S, she is modelled on a saint, her life concealed. He waits for her to speak, I wait for her to speak. She takes her time. Oh I don't know, I think I can understand. She gently mocks him, the vicar. He doesn't realize. She picks her way forward, heel planting between each piece of glass, at any moment one could be cracked by the physics of her shoes, her body. He is confused. I go after her, she is looking for the offending rock. The vicar and I are not the same. I am fond, though, of his earnestness. His manhood aligned not with God, but with the pressures of being his proxy. He is left lamblike, bouncing, panicking.

We search together. He can only observe us. I allow myself glimpses of her as I crouch, checking along the building, in the neatened shrubs. Furtive, swatches of body, fabric, glass. The rock, most likely, was thrown from outside the building. We head inside, follow the trajectory. Inside, the damage has the unexpected shape of a puckered mouth, the lead bent rather than snapped at the point of impact. She calls out. It has been found underneath a pew. There is damage to the wood, the rock dropping, a chunk missing. Look at that. She puts a finger to it, tugs the splinter free. It peels further, clawing away more of the varnish, leaving a bleached streak. I am left to retrieve the stone. It is only half the size of my palm, worn down by water, lifted from the river.

Premeditated, do you think? Teasing, she takes it from my palm. Turns it over as if she might find some trace of the perpetrator. I guess so, I mean, I think someone at least went to the river, collected it, with the idea of coming back here. Yes, how strange. Again, she does not think it to be so strange, does not say what she really means. One of The Girls, perhaps, walking back to her dorm, it is late, she is furious or melancholic or wants to impress, she sees the church, it enlivens her. The Girl, this Girl, slides down to the river and returns with her perfect rock. In her hand the weight is a comfort. It has skin, this rock, tumbled smooth. Cold, heartless, she feels it warm up in her fist. An extension of her own hand. It is night, there are only night-time witnesses, they can never be sure and what do they know, anyway. The rock leaves her hand before she knows she has thrown it. The noise terrifies her. She would do it again.

Mrs S has thought it too. She closes her fingers around it, strokes a thumb across the dark-grey surface. I feel the heat of her thinking, how easily she can imagine it. I am not troubled but she is. She is reminded that such feelings, such teenage feelings, can manifest in this way. It had not occurred to her. She understood The Girl who punched the boy. Such violence has a logic that can be categorized. This, this is different. I stand beside her. It's not so strange, not really. She turns her face to me. No, I don't suppose it is. The vicar calls to us from the door. Mrs S lifts the stone. Look what we found. What? What is it? The weapon, what else. She brings it to him. You could dust it for fingerprints.

I could. He cannot think of anything witty to say, it is not his style. Well, good luck, be careful. Mrs S leaves us, he watches her leave, I am forced to rise above.

Let's crack on shall we. His lips are dry. He begins to count the pieces again. I go back to my shabby pine. She disappears down the path. The rest of the day will barely matter. Right. He claps his hands. Right, bring those over here, let's pack them up. I drag over the slim cardboard boxes, the ream of brown paper, the plastic bags filled with old newspaper. We cannot help but hold each piece to the light. The medieval colours. It feels good, to hold something that was not supposed to be held, not like this. Slowly I recognize the scene of Adam and Eve, the watchful saint cast to one side. This panel depicted the temptation, the snake's head a woman's, reaching out to Eve from the apple tree, an apple already in Eve's hand. The snake-woman's expression almost loving, accidentally empathetic. She knows what she sets in motion.

I wrap each piece in newspaper. Swaddle, swaddle, repeats the vicar. His authoritative language is the Bible's. He walks up to the gate to speak with a passer-by. A local, maybe, one of his flock, at church every Sunday to gobble up her communion. In the break I find the head of the snake-woman. Her profile trapped, the slope of her nose, the dark drape of her eyelid. Across her pale forehead a brush of light-green foliage. She looks at the apple in Eve's hand. The fruit now lost to another fragment. Her snake body too, gone. She floats free. I want it.

He talks, still he talks, the local touching her own face, she is pleased to be noticed by him, even he has his power. Beside me is a shrub. I lay the fragment behind it. Obscured by shadow, by clusters of leaves. I pad a wad of brown paper inside newspaper and use it as my replacement, laying it inside the box gently, as if it were glass. Good, good, getting there, aren't we? Yes, almost. Later I will collect it, later I might give it to Mrs S as a gift, a reminder, who knows. I could, I could do it. Easy as a rock through a window.

The Housemistress is at my door. She is in sports gear. Cheeks red, mud flicked up her legs. One hand presses into her hip as she steadies her breathing. I am still in my pyjamas. Lazybones you should come running with me. I try to smile mysteriously. It is quiet, birds fade in and out, not even a breeze. I think of her body moving up the hill behind the boarding houses. Her heavy breath, her watch glanced at, her triumph at reaching the top, the view across the fields, even the distant fells. How about a glass of water? Course. I leave her on the cobblestones and then think twice. Come in come in. Thought you'd never ask.

She is all fresh air and laundry powder. Today, as if marking her run, her moment of freedom, a single silver hoop in one earlobe. A private indication. The kitchen is minuscule. She fills the doorframe beautifully. I pour her a glass of water. That's the stuff. She spills down her chin, down her top. I pour her another. It's hot out there, wild, but I'm not complaining. Yeh don't scare it away. Teeth still unbrushed I speak on an angle. A piece of green, some plant, is caught in her shoelace. So I'm here for business not pleasure. Yeh? Nice PJs by the way. I look down at my top. An old one of my uncle's, advertising a pub, a local of his. A woman sits on a man's lap as they both drink from the same glass of beer. Thanks, not mine, well it is now, but I don't condone it.

Look I'll be straight with you, the only time I'll ever be straight, I'm not going to dob The Girls in. No? No, I've dealt with it in-house. She notices the piece of green and pulls it free with difficulty. The plant seems to be sticky, laid across each shoelace. Fucking thing. It sticks to her fingers, to the edge of the bin. So you've dealt with it in-house? Yes, I mean they know they've done wrong, they're not going to pull anything like this again. What was their punishment? A few different things, I got creative, no television, bathroom duty, and they're leading prayers at each meal, that might be the thing they hate the most, the prayers. Sounds like you've got it sorted. I do, yeh. She waits for my compliance. I'm not saying anything to anyone. Good, great. They're embarrassed enough. I get it, I guess we've all been there. Oh definitely, the places I've been shitfaced. Same. In the pause she sees something out the window, ducking and weaving her head to double-check. I try to look, try to see what she sees. Only a robin, hopping from the wall to the cracked, empty bird feeder.

Speaking of which, speaking of being shitfaced, what are you doing next weekend? She rubs her hands together. Nothing. An exeat will empty the school, The Girls, or at least most of them, will go home or elsewhere. I'd considered catching the long train to London but the fare was too expensive. OK I have a proposition. What's that? An offer you shouldn't refuse. She places the glass in the sink, reaching across me, more laundry powder. There's a bar, in town. What here? I gesture around the room, meaning the immediate surrounding houses, the main school, the pub, the petrol station. Yeh right. Where then? The big town. Oh, I've not been that far yet. How have you not gone insane? I shrug.

I want to say no. Leaving means being stranded somewhere else. Tell me about this bar. Fuck I don't know it's a gay bar what more do you want? Right. She is disappointed in me. Don't you feel like having a drink somewhere different? Don't you feel like just being somewhere different? I notice the leg hairs, faint but long, up her calves. Sure, yeh. This, to her, is confirmation. She shoots a thumbs up. Yes! OK! Next weekend? Otherwise we will be waiting until the next school holiday, you know? Fine, fine. Show some enthusiasm. I fire back a thumbs up. That's the attitude. Imagine, we might both get laid, laid, wouldn't that be something. She pats my cheek. Wouldn't that be something.

Mrs S has come to the staffroom. The large birdcage, where all the teachers become birds, with their fast eyes and fingers. At first her arrival initiates a thrilled silence. Then there he is, the history teacher, stood beside her, announcing himself awkwardly. The rose, a rose, by any other name, would be so sweet. He puts his thumb to his forehead and skims his hairline. Even in this heat he wears his tweed suit. Oh dear, what a shame, I've butchered it, who butchers Shakespeare, bloody long days at the moment aren't they, this weather addles my brain. I have my back to her. In the kitchenette, aimlessly boiling a kettle, washing the pile of coffee-stained mugs.

Anyway, this particular rose, so named for its colour, the colour of her complexion, apricot you see. Oh? Mrs S is polite, not that it would matter, his lecture has already begun. Yes, apricot, the blush of youth, well a sickly youth, the youth of this winter climate, you know, not quite pink, never quite made it to pink. He pauses, in need of her endorsement to continue. She smiles. Cornered into being encouraging. Certainly, I can picture it. Two plasters patch her forearm. You don't need to picture it, you can see it, there's a particularly fine portrait in your husband's office. His smell is strong enough that even the sound of his voice conjures it. Pipe smoke, a house in which no windows are opened, vinegary groin, vinegary armpits. I shall have to go and take another look. She passes through him like a ghost. He tries harder. I'm sure you could visit it whenever you want, you have your all-access pass. Is that what it is? He grins. In a manner of speaking, that's marriage isn't it. Her smile thins. I suppose that's one way of looking at it.

He hasn't quite finished. We arrive at his crescendo. I can bring you a cutting, of the rose, you could add it to the collection. Well, it's not my collection. No, of course, but isn't it important, a good idea, to add your own touch, a legacy. Perhaps. She lifts her head, gloriously, to me. A lightning manoeuvre. But I'm afraid I'm no expert in the garden. Her modesty is a game. He waves his arms about. No such thing, anyone can garden, it's a question of confidence and patience, if you ever need help, I've got these. He waggles his fingers in the space between them. Green fingers you see, my father was a great rose enthusiast. How wonderful for you. She stops him dead. It was, wonderful, a wonderful thing, he was a good man, my father. Well, thank you for the tip, I shall see what I can get hold of. She motions as if to leave. Good, yes, good. He is abandoned.

The drama teacher comes to talk with me. I anticipate a favour. Hello hello how are you? Fine thanks. Lovely. She pauses. Lovely, listen, I wonder if you might be available to assist me? Mrs S has been trapped by a group of science teachers. Me, assist? Yes, yes, with the play. She plants her face in front of mine, sensing my attention is elsewhere. Yeh, sorry, sure. The play, you know the play, I need an extra moment for them to connect. She bangs her fists together. The pouting tendons of her long neck. That bygone English quality, a neck that has genealogy, a neck included in lifetimes of portraits. Sure no worries. No worries, no worries, no worries, oh I do love that unique Aussie catchphrase, you are a nation of catchphrases. She touches it, her neck. All good. And there's another! All good, what a simple thing, to be all good. I suppose so. All good then, all good and no worries, I shall let you know when, please bring your finest Pepe el Romano. Before I can ask what the fuck she is talking about she has slipped gracefully from the conversation, already making her way out the door, neck first.

One of the science teachers, maybe biology, is suddenly animated, complaining, describing some event I can't hear. Mrs S nods along in consolation. Another joins in. His arms enacting a similar movement, creating a climax with his colleague. Her hand goes to her mouth, also in consolation. Everyone wants her husband. She is an intermediary. Most complain to her about The Girls. It is the common ground. This story I don't doubt is about some remark, some ongoing remarks. Perhaps these two, one with his oiled moustache and the other rumoured to have cracked two ribs while sneezing, have been victimized. I decide to stay for as long as she does.

From the staffroom it is impossible to know the weather outside. The light is rendered weak. Each pane of the tall windows has been covered with a cheap plastic decal. A pattern of linked flowers. This prevents The Girls from seeing in. The air of mystery is preferable to the reality. Inside is not what they want. They hunt relentlessly for valuable intimacies that might shift a power dynamic. A teacher's holiday photo, a holiday outfit. Perhaps some indication of lust: a letter, a Post-it note. Better still would be the discovery of a tryst, an indication of alliances. Who stands closest to who. Whom stands closest to whom. But there is nothing. If they were to finally make it inside, The Girls would be disappointed. Each desk is kept clear of personal detritus. Perhaps, most likely in fact, it is encouraged. Any secrets are carefully maintained. Teachers obey the bell just as The Girls must.

Across the room Mrs S is finally alone. She comes to the kitchenette, not looking at me until the last second, aiming instead for the kettle, wanting a cup of tea. Unable to resist I go to her first, whispering. What was the issue? With them? Oh, The Girls keep singeing things with the Bunsen burners. Her lips hint at laughter. What sort of things? Textbooks, ponytails, science goggles, whatever they can find, whatever they haven't burned before. How stressful for them, for the teachers. Yes quite. For a moment we stand in a blissful silence. One that I have not felt since the day we swam. The windows glower.

How are the roses? Terrible as usual. She offers me her

arm so I can better see the two plasters. And here, look. On the side of her pale-blue dress is a speck of blood. I dare to pinch the stain between my fingers. She glances at me, tilts her head. I let go. Brushes the dress with the flat of her hand. Everything I own is stained with my own blood, and I hate the smell, I never realized it before, but I hate the smell of roses. Me too. Really? Oh good, that makes me feel less alone. The kettle clicks. She picks it up. Lets her hand touch the steam then retracts it. You know of all the things I thought I would be doing here, gardening was not one of them, was not in the job description. You don't strike me as the gardening type. I don't? No. Although she does. She does strike me as the gardening type. I have seen it, I hold on to the image. Her body so picturesque amongst the flowers. Limbs, stems, limbs. An interchangeable elegance. What did you think you'd be doing here? Now there's a question. She pulls at the edge of a plaster then smooths it down. I don't ask again. She closes her eyes. Releases a long-held thought. You know, I should like to get rid of them all, the roses. She spreads her fingers across her forehead, massaging her temples. Now that would be a real legacy, how would you do it? Oh poison, a chainsaw, I don't care, although perhaps a chainsaw, just take off the heads en masse. She kisses the part of her hand she let burn briefly in the steam. All of them, gone. Sounds like a plan. Doesn't it? The bell rings. It affects neither of us. Suppose I ought to get on with my day. Sure. It was nice to see you. Sure. She lingers. There is more she wants to say. Her hands hover at her hips. She thinks better of it. Good, great. For a moment I think she might touch my side, finding a rib, or maybe my arm. She doesn't. It is unbearable.

Early evening, the car park outside the largest boarding house is peaceful. I sit on the kerb, the dead author's novel at my feet. This book, carted from home, what is home, to here, her country. Didn't I want to try out the rain? The job, an easy way onto a visa. I have always been in pursuit of something. A kind of survival. To think one step ahead. Inside, The Girls go through their giggling preparations for bed. Ants pace across the tarmac. My mother would stop me when I was a child, pointing out their cargo as it was passed from one set of pincers to the next. She admired their hard work. We trap each other, my mother and I. She keeps me there. And I do the same, my mother, the woman obsessed with hard work, with building an honest life. A dog barks, told off sharply by its owner, then barks again. Tucked into my binder is the paper-wrapped stained glass. The risk of sitting, of not taking it straight back to my room, the tip almost at my belly. What am I doing? Everything compresses. My entire chest becomes glass. Imagine, me, see-through, held up to the sun. An image of perfection. No one else is around. Away from the windows I lift the binder. Fresh air. I take out the piece carefully. The snake's expression removed from its context, free to seduce, no longer limited to Adam and Eve. I open my book and half-hide it inside. Against the pages it is just as irresistible, just as absurd.

Sunday. I see her. My body knocked loose. A wrap dress. Fine fabric. I sense her shoulder blades even though I cannot directly see them. Some of The Girls are lined up along the back wall of the church. They are in the choir. She waves at them, a secret wave. Over the top of the uniforms they wear heavy woollen robes. Once a bright red, now duller through use. A few mimic the secret wave in response. Mr and Mrs S sit on the pews nearest the back. Laid out in the choir's section, just behind the vicar, are the few songs The Girls will sing. All week they practise. At the heart of their seating is the grand organ. A woman from the village plays. She seems too young for such an instrument. As she thumps the opening bars her eyes squeeze in bliss.

We stand for the first hymn. Briefly I think I can smell Mrs S's perfume. Carried across the pews. None of the songs are familiar to me. I mouth the words as I read them. Lamb of God, lamb of God. I can hear Mr S sing, always. His voice is good enough. Loud, finding the notes, but only just. The organ keys clunk, the air shifting in each pipe, the metallic sighs. The woman's eyes are open now, leaning

forward on her stool to follow the music. The music director stands but does not sing. He looks at his feet then up at
the rafters. Once the hymn is finished, we sit back down.
He remains standing. Back hunched. The vicar shakes out a
few prayers. The Girls, the choir, sing the responses in
Latin. Mouths synchronized. The music director's palms
float up and down. The Girls fit their voices around him.
He strains against himself.

I feel Mrs S look at me. She finds the corner of my eye.
Nods as I turn my head. A slow nod, she luxuriates in my
glance, reaching inside my ribcage. I will try and talk to her
later. Each Amen, each Ave Maria, hangs between us. She
stops looking at me. I make it all up. I am making it all up.
There could be nothing. There is nothing. We have to stand
again. At least inside the church it is cool. The sun cannot
penetrate, not really, each piece of old stone permanently
cold. Now we sit. The vicar our lacklustre choreographer. I
turn towards her again, I cannot resist. She looks up at the
broken window, the damage barely contained by clumsy
planks of wood, fluttering tarpaulin. We find each other
again. A knowing look, shared. I watch as she searches the
congregation. Not looking for guilt, not looking for the
perpetrator, fascinated only by the possibility of this
person's existence.

The vicar asks that we pray. Some of the local women tip
forward onto their knees. Hitching their skirts. They take
the cross-stitched cushions from their hooks. As they find
the right position they grunt softly. A desire for God is the

most straightforward. No risk, only reward. The vicar spreads his hands across the lectern. He is most comfortable when all the eyes are closed. Before him, the congregation is at last as vulnerable as he feels. For effect The Girls also use their prayer cushions. Bent, napes of their necks displayed. His voice no longer quavers. I am too shy to use the prayer cushion. The one at my section of pew has a design of three lions, triangle heads, bewildered expressions. I don't pray, it has never occurred to me that I could.

What does Mrs S think about? I drag my eye as far as it can go to see her. She kneels. He kneels too. She doesn't hold her hands in a prayer position. Instead she is slumped over, as if asleep, head cradled by forearms. Hair fallen out of place. She does not move to fix it. Elsewhere she would. She rubs the edges of her longest fingers with her thumbs. There is a thought turned over and over. A comfort needed. It is me she thinks about. It is not me she thinks about. Her past, risen. The church is designed to evoke the before, to tend to history in the same specific motion of hands, of lyrics. I will her to open her eyes and see me again. I'll forgive, I can offer her whatever forgiveness she needs. Does she actually believe in God? One day I will ask her. She will laugh, she will not answer.

Above the choir stalls, carved into the oldest section of the church, are The Three Accidentals. I squint to see them. Named by The Girls, three pagan forms, limbs fat and short. Eyes and noses severe. If you look closely, difficult without a ladder, between each set of legs is a slit. For whatever reason they are women. The exact date of their creation unknown. The final prayer. It is almost over. The biggest prayer, the famous one. The Girls all know it by heart. Hallowed be thy name. I can hear her voice again, another vision of her as a child, murmuring, barely realizing she is speaking, the habit is so old. Amen, Amen, Amen. A tension fills the church. Everyone eager to leave. Sunday is finally open to pleasure. The Girls fidget. They try not to talk through their plans too loudly. Some might go to the river, try and find a spot still deep enough to swim. Pew by pew The Girls exit. I follow them outside. Blinking, yawning, as if moving out from a cave. I hover by the entrance. The Housemistress is already outside. She flirts unashamedly with one of the pastel women, who looks alarmed but still reaches across to touch The Housemistress's forearm. She catches my eye and winks.

Mrs S exits, joined by the vicar who speaks anxiously with her husband. They discuss some male philosopher. I catch snippets of the conversation as they pass by. A theologian, old-school, darker side of things and all that. Before I can speak she takes my elbow and sweeps me to one side. We stand underneath the old sundial. What do men know about ethics? Not much, if Abraham was anything to go by. Oh God, you actually listened. Hard not to. I suppose. She drifts for a moment, as if heading towards the same thought she had during prayer. Here we go, look, how they love him, they can't get enough. The women in pastel gather around her husband. The vicar slightly edged out. Does it bother you? She laughs.

The smallest thing spurs me on. He loves it too. Yes, he does, doesn't he. The old sundial casts two thin shadows. Come on, tell me your news. I don't have any news. How depressing, I don't have any news either, even more depressing, we ought to find something to do. I look at her for as long as I can without vanishing entirely. What sort of thing? Oh I don't know, tennis? Not sure about tennis. She laughs. Today she is in a mood I can't fathom. Perhaps she has argued with her husband, perhaps she has fucked her husband. Her energy cannot be contained. I am her outlet. I don't care. She drums her fingers against the stone. I know, do you smoke, let's smoke. Smoke what? A cigarette! What else? Right, sure, if you want. I do want. Her dress twists to the left and she adjusts it. The fabric yanked at the neckline, retied at the waist.

Are you done for the day? Yeh. The Girls would make their own way back to the boarding houses. Lunch would be served in a few hours. Sunday ends informally, food laid out, a cold buffet, The Girls able to come and go as they please. Well then, how about we make a getaway? Her husband is still surrounded by the pastel women. The vicar has now been engulfed by the group, talking earnestly, a severe look on his face. They listen to the vicar, the pastel women, but cast glances only at Mr S. The Girls have all but disappeared. The Housemistress too. Busy with something else. Often she waits for me. Not this morning. There must be another, more urgent activity. Perhaps the woman in pastel. Stay right here. Mrs S walks quickly to her husband. She reaches up and whispers in his ear. He turns briefly to look at me. I wave, embarrassed. Before she leaves he puts his hand on her buttock and squeezes, the dress riding up her thigh an inch. Done a hundred times. He does not realize, or does not care, that I can see. One of the pastel women tries to engage her and she instead steps backwards, shaking her head politely, indicating that she must be on her way.

Escaped, she makes a face, a face only for me. Forehead flattened out, eyes wide. Let's go then. Where? To buy cigarettes, unless you have some. No, I don't really smoke, not anymore. Not anymore? No. Aren't you rather young to have already had and abandoned a habit? The only personal question she has ever asked me. I panic. No, maybe. We follow the path out of the church, using the front entrance, avoiding the passageway that leads past the dead girls. Out on the road she walks even faster. I struggle to keep up. Are you OK? Me? Fine. You better buy them, the cigarettes, I shouldn't be seen I suppose, The Girls might, well, they might find it a little too encouraging. Sure. Here. She digs in her handbag and finds a note. Use this. It's fine. No, no, it's my terrible idea, come on, at least let me fund it. I have almost no money. I take hers. Shame will continue its reinventions. No matter what I do.

The garage is busier than usual. Three cars fill the space between the pumps. Customers in shorts and t-shirts, ready to be outdoors, desperate to get somewhere else. I recognize the mechanic, helping. He doesn't recognize me. Smell of petrol, the chemicals hard at work in a floor cleaner. The man behind the counter fiddles with his earring. He doesn't recognize me either. I am nervous. I choose us the same lurid ice lollies I ate before, both blue, and take them to the counter. And some cigarettes please. What kind? He nods at the selection behind him. I don't deliberate. That one. At random I select a gold packet. He frowns. I have revealed something in my choice. Have a good one. Yeh. He goes back to his earring. I am almost outside when I remember. Wait, a lighter, one lighter too. They're just there. Right. Quid yeh. OK. I drop the coin. He peers over the counter. There, it's there. I crawl towards the shelves stacked with tins. There, right there, by your leg. I pick it up and wipe it clean on my t-shirt. Thanks.

Mrs S waits on the forecourt where I left her, in full sun. The mechanic looks at her approvingly but she doesn't notice, or at least has learned how to disengage from such looks. Got them? I wave the packet. Oh good, great. And these. I rip open my ice lolly with my teeth and suck. Blue slick against my chin. For you? Oh. She holds it. Will you open it? I rip hers too. She pushes it up and out, letting pieces break and fall to the tarmac. Blue pooling stickily against the hot black. How disgusting. Still she eats it. Wipes the stain from her chin. Where shall we go? This way. I follow her around the back of the garage. Car parts scatter the grassy area. Two minibuses succumb to rust, jagged holes happening through the doors, over the wheels. She picks her way through the engines, the tyres. Beyond is one field, then another. She climbs over a stile and lands softly on the grass, barely green. We'll find a spot. My church clothes are stark. The collar of the polyester jacket rubbing raw against my neck. I fold it over my arm. She strides ahead, a picture, leading me once again into sky, into fell. Ahead suddenly she stops. Quick, quick, let's go back, back that way. Shimmering by the next wall is a group of people, maybe some of The Girls, also with their cigarettes.

She is shocked, laughing, making me run, pushing at the small of my back. I drop my jacket and she picks it up, still running, slipping her arms inside. It is too big for her, I am broader, flapping about her torso. Here, quick. Back over the stile. She retraces her route through the debris, settling beside one of the old minivans, the lesser destroyed of the pair. She tries the handle. It won't budge. You, you do it. I place my foot over the wheel arch and wrench. It opens. My fingers throb with the effort. Well done you. Go on, get in. The front plunges forward with our weight then stops with a clank as it finds the ground. There, it's fine. She removes my jacket and drapes it across the dashboard.

The surreality of her in the driver's seat, the steering wheel missing, her expression expectant. Her hand is outstretched. I put my own hand inside. Fingers motionless against her palm. She doesn't move, doesn't say anything straight away. No, a cigarette, the cigarettes. Of course. I retreat. Pull the packet from my back pocket. Here. Oh

shit, a lighter, we don't have a lighter. I produce that too.
Relieved to feel useful. The sensation of her skin still burns
my fingertips. Ah you're a genius, truly, you think of
everything. She does not mention my hand, where it was
only seconds ago. She is classy, does not want me to feel
ashamed.

She lights the cigarette herself. I would have liked to have
done it for her. Concentrates. A mole at her jaw, another
underneath her ear. Glances at me. I don't look away. The
window on my side is broken. Hers is closed. The cigarette
glows. She does not yet take a drag but instead tries the
window. It won't give. Fuck. Only last minute she smokes.
Long, practised. Her head hits the seat as she exhales. Does
he know you smoke? I don't smoke. She opens one eye.
You're not having one? No thanks. So it's just me. I'm here
for moral support. Crucial, I suppose I couldn't have done
it without you. Did you use to smoke? Obviously. I think
I annoy her. My nightmare, to annoy her. I sit in silence.
She finishes the cigarette and lights another.

I can go, if you want. Why would you go? Is the smoke
bothering you? No, you just seem like you want to be
alone. Well I don't. She bends. Arches her back off the seat
in a catlike stretch. I spend plenty of time alone, and he
does know I smoke, that I used to anyway, the worst thing
about me apparently. You gave up? For him, yes. How long
has it been? What, since I've been married? No, since your
last cigarette. She laughs. Same timeline, though I suppose,
really, twenty years or so, I must have been as young as

you, imagine. Well I'm twenty-two. Said aloud I realize I sound younger, I tie myself in knots. Right, sorry, well let's make this a fair exchange, you tell me something, some bad habit. There's nothing so interesting about me. I don't believe that. Outside, the sound of cars. Non-stop up and down the country road. Everyone urgent in this weather. Unable to deny the unrelenting good fortune. Determined to boil, the desperation to be outside quickly foiled by the heat's reality, they don't care.

I don't talk to my dad. I correct myself, wanting her formality, to measure up. My father, he doesn't talk to me anymore. No? No. The brakes of a lorry release their huge breath. Will you tell me why? He doesn't approve of me. The sound of her smoking fills the silence. Her wrap dress will smell of tobacco. He might guess, Mr S, putting his nose to its shoulder. She will already have an excuse prepared, better than an excuse, a reason. Her husband will choose to believe it. He doesn't approve of you, your father? No, he wants me to be traditional, he's a traditional guy, he likes marriage, women in aprons. And you don't wear an apron? Oh I burn everything. She frowns. I messed up the joke. I try again: I mean I'm a terrible cook, I'm bad in the kitchen. Oh I like cooking, there's pleasure to be had in feeding people.

The mechanic calls out to someone who is too rough with the pump. She freezes as if he is shouting at her. After a second she realizes he is still on the forecourt, nowhere nearby. Her body relaxes. I take the opportunity to laugh.

Very funny, very funny, I used to be much better at breaking the rules. Not me. No? She has got me wrong, has assumed my sexuality, as yet unspoken between us, makes me bold. I correct her. I don't know, if I could, I think I'd be as normal as possible. She smiles. Don't be normal, don't bother. That ease of hers, that ease which makes me jealous, it is born from our precise difference. She looks for a way out, I look for a way in.

Oh I miss it, I miss this. She attempts a smoke ring but fails. Another drag. This time she puckers her mouth in a tighter circle, tension crinkling her lips. The shape appears suddenly, then slowly, expanding, thinning. Soon it is too large for its own density and fades away. She performs three more, each one exact and quickly frail. Impressive. Thank you. Here she is, the reformed rebel. I want to be toyed with. Who taught you to do that? Oh, I can't remember. She does remember but will not say. The packet of cigarettes is picked up and put down again. Her watch looked at. Our time together is over. You need to go? Yes, I'm afraid. There is enough disappointment in her voice to satisfy me. She hands over the packet. Why not hide those here? You think? Yeh, I don't want to be caught with them either, The Nurse would kill me. From the passenger seat I bang open the glovebox. An old can of Coke, dead wasps, the faded wrapper of a chocolate bar. I nestle the cigarettes in between. Our secret.

The Girls wear black lace veils over their faces. Held awkwardly in place by childish hair clips. Pink, blue, green. Discomfort is obvious in the constant movement of their fingers, popping the clips open and closing them again, flinching at the hard snap against their skulls. The drama teacher helps. She walks between the group, adjusting and readjusting the length of each veil, until the fabric is flush with their chins. Stand over there. They move to the back of the room. Not yet on stage but just before it. Let's try again. The Girls, at varying volumes, recite a few lines in what I recognize as Spanish. Six of them. Five I already know from painting the scenery. This evening they are still in uniform. Blue ties slackened, some only in their navy socks, dust collecting under their toes, black shoes lumped against the wall.

No, no, roll the r, roll the rs. The drama teacher sits metres away, in the first row of fold-out chairs used for the audience. Verde, verde, verde. The tip of her tongue quickly flicks each word. It is impressive. Accent executed without embarrassment. The drama teacher has obviously forged some intimate connection to Spain. I imagine a second home in a charming town, near a lesser-known beach, shops fragrant and local. Try, try. The Girls take deep breaths and close their eyes, dropping their foreheads to their navels. An attempt to centre themselves, to arrive at some sort of moment. Most likely a technique learned from the drama teacher. She turns suddenly, calling out to my seat on the last row. And you, do you speak Spanish? Afraid not. Never mind then. She twists back around. Can I see? Of course. Without looking in my direction she holds out a photocopy. I am required to get up, the chair pinging loudly behind me, to retrieve it from her hand. My footsteps fall heavily. The Girls stare impatiently.

The photocopy is not a section of script but a different Lorca poem. Romance Sonámbulo. Both the original Spanish and an English translation fill the page, side by side. Verde que te quiero verde. Green how I want you green. Green, how I want you green. I have the drama teacher's notes. Commas and slashes added for breath. The word green needlessly highlighted at each appearance. Green wind, green branches, green flesh, green hair. The first verse has been circled off, indicating that The Girls will only read the very beginning. Again. She claps her hands. The Girls dramatize the rs. I would laugh were it not for their earnestness. Matching stances, hands knotted behind their backs. Better, better, much better, take five, people. She claps her hands again. The Girls relax. Two hop up on the stage and bang their heels against the wood. They carefully lift the veils to talk, not wanting to dislodge the clips, letting only their mouths move.

The door opens slowly to reveal Mrs S. The Girls pretend not to notice. This is their territory. Even if only for the next hour. I feel it too. Holding the door steady so it does not creak, she moves inside. Don't worry darling, we're taking a minute. The drama teacher reaches out her arms. It's a joy to have you. Oh good. You've arrived at a break-through moment. Wonderful. She sits on the other side of the drama teacher, leaving one seat between them. The theatre is impressive. Small, as if part of some legendary city legacy, the compact design lifted from a famous district of other, similar spaces. Mrs S sees me. She discusses some-thing quietly with the drama teacher. They are friendly, touching arms. Perhaps they are close. Perhaps the drama teacher and her matching husband were the dinner guests.

Right! The drama teacher stands. Mrs S crosses one foot over the other. She is casual. Only a white t-shirt and grey skirt. An outfit I have seen before, except, today, a gold wristwatch. The Girls pull the black veils over their faces. Let's do a scene, shall we? The drama teacher lifts a slim book from her bag. Let's start from the very beginning, a very good place to start. The last line is sung. The tune recognizable although I can't place it. Her voice, too, has the quiver of training, vocal cords disciplined and hefty. Quick quick, set it up. Chairs are dragged across the floor. The theatre's acoustics are buoyed by the large scrape. A space in want of constant noise. Mrs S moves as if to help, then changes her mind, readjusting in her seat, the foot crossed and recrossed. Thick photocopies of the script are retrieved from The Girls' book bags.

The final scene! Position yourselves! The Girls turn to their lines, faces concerned. Each has chosen a different coloured highlighter for her part. They are more nervous than they would like to let on. All I learned about the play was during the painting of the scenery. Daughters oppressed by a mother, a grandmother locked in a room, an unsuitable suitor. The drama teacher is displeased with their positioning. She marches forward and rearranges them, pulling elbows and hips until The Girls are properly cast. Do we keep the veils on for this? Ah no. She wags her finger. Only for the opening, off please. The clips snap in protest, the drama teacher fans herself with the script. And, I shouldn't have to point out, please do remember which is yours. Each veil is put gently to the ground. The Girls pause and commit their placement to memory.

Sitting above Mrs S, I can see her neck, her hands folding in her lap. The wristwatch slipped back and forth. Her hands. Another planet. She decides against the fold, unclasping, instead flexing her fingers into her palms, the softest of fists. Estuaries of neon veins, knuckles rising like moons. Nails short, a practical choice, although this too I happily convert into a concealed lesbianism. Everything is a sign. For the first time I see her bring a finger to her mouth, as if to bite, the movement well known. The finger then released before her teeth can clamp down. Back in her lap. She is more restless than she lets on. I pretend it is my presence. Just one quick fantasy.

The drama teacher sits back down, choosing the seat closest to her. OK, here we go, from Adela's entrance. The Girl playing Adela ruffles her hair in preparation. Another sits in a chair then leaps up. Leave that man alone! The intonation has been hard-learned, her voice slowing and accelerating, man thrown at the ceiling. Hold it right there. The drama teacher on her feet once again. The Girl playing Adela pauses, halfway through her line, embarrassed at the interrupted energy. You, my Aussie. She narrows her eyes with flair. Me? Yes, come come come. She beckons, dragging her forefinger through the air. We need you, darling. I stay sitting. Why? Look at you, in your blue jeans, you're the perfect Pepe el Romano. I'm not much of an actor. You don't have to be, I just need you to pose, it's just about atmosphere, The Girls need the pressure of his gaze. She walks halfway up the stairs to my seat. Don't be shy, we're all friends here. It is not yet clear if she wants to humiliate me on purpose. Either way I have no choice.

She leads me roughly to the side of the scene. Stand here. I stand. Cross your arms. I cross my arms. Tighter! How? Like this. She presses my arms into my chest, her hand at the base of my spine, sending my posture upwards. Marvellous! She is flushed. Now, you watch them. Her fingers flutter at The Girls. Watch them like a hawk, you've been having an affair with Adela, you want her to leave, she wants to leave, you are waiting for her, her mother is completely insane! We've all known a mother like her! The drama teacher walks backwards, squaring off her thumbs around my figure, as if zooming out. Perfect, you look the part, finally, my Pepe! Mrs S is stuck in a half-smile. The Girl playing Adela raises her hand. Yes? Is he, is she, are we supposed to look that way? Is it, is there like a window we're looking through or something? You Girls, always so literal, it is about knowing he is out there, waiting. She stamps the floor. Returns to my side and waves her arms. Imagine this is a thick wall, a thick white wall, Pepe is on the other side, oh he's breathing heavily, he can't hold out much longer! OK. The Girl looks down at her script. OK. You need to feel him, you need to sense him. An ache begins in my calves. I shift my legs closer together. And you, my Aussie charmer, darling, stay still, stay wide. She crouches, brings her palms to my knees and applies pressure, shifting them apart. I shut my eyes at the squeak of my shoes against the varnished floor. It's about being a man! She grips her crotch for sudden effect. The layers of her dress tighten. There it is, the same intonation as The Girl, the word as heavy as a stone. Man, man, man. They, The Girls, are her vessels.

Mrs S reaches across the seat and takes the slim volume. She flicks to the back and searches for the scene. Would you mind showing me where we are? The drama teacher walks back to her side. Here. She turns to the final pages. Thanks, thank you. The ache spreads to my neck. I think of my outfit. I think of The Housemistress's chin, lifting my own at the thought. A hum fades in then out of one ear. From the top! The Girls stretch, swaying their torsos, loosening their diaphragms. Another impersonation, another lesson learned from the drama teacher. Leave that man alone!!! The line is even louder this time. I jump. Mrs S jumps. The drama teacher is ecstatic. See! You're working already, my Pepe, my manly man, with your manly man heart. A new heat emanates from my body. I see Mrs S looking. Not at me but the drama teacher. Her face locked in an expression of forced neutrality, teeth squeezed together, I imagine her tongue riding the roof of her mouth, I sense the effort. She can see, for me, the situation is painful, but cannot decipher why. Against my better judgement I am waiting for her to intervene. I squeeze my own teeth together and feel too conscious of my own tongue, as if I might choke on it.

Hang on, hang on! the drama teacher trills, making her way back towards me in great sideways steps, aiming to fan out the hem of her dress. I need you, I need you to be more, to be more. More? She takes my face and moves my head, putting it in line with The Girl playing Adela. How's that? Without letting go she calls out to The Girls. How's that? What do you think? I'm not sure, I still think we need more, here let me. The Girl playing Adela skids smoothly across the varnished floor, silent in her glossy tights. May I? But of course. The drama teacher steps back. The Girl slips in a circle around my body. You're so tall aren't you, I think he, she, this he-she, should be like this. Bringing her nose close to mine she tilts my head forward, her palm firm at the base of my skull, putting my chin almost at my chest. I am flooded with my own smell. A panicked animal. Smouldering, you need to smoulder. Mrs S looks into her lap. I keep my head low, speak into my own flesh, my voice muffled. Like I said, I'm not sure I'm much of an actor. The Girl removes her hand from my skull. Well you can only do your best. Is that right. She frowns dangerously. That's all any of us can do, you know, our best. A sly smile. The Girls know about humiliation. They trade in it.

I close my eyes against the burn. The theatre, like the rest of the school, has enormous strip lights installed, the kind used for larger architecture, a warehouse maybe, a shopping mall. It is one way to eliminate privacy. No darkened corners, no atmosphere achievable. Hey, you can't close your eyes. The Girl is still at my side. Obviously, you need your eyes open. She has been left in charge. I am forced to think of how I look. My jeans tightening, pressing into my belly, the spill of my belly, my hips. Their eyes. I am surrounded on all sides by mirrors, my own body reflected back to me over and over again. I don't live an exterior life. I avoid my own reflection. I thought, for a long time, everyone did. I was wrong. Most other people study their reflections carefully. Instead I've spent a lifetime focusing on the interior, a place that happens without me, organs passing their intimate thoughts, the chase of blood, valves clenching and releasing. Stunning inevitabilities.

Mrs S stands. The movement, so sudden, makes noise enough to capture the attention of The Girls. Even Adela, hand back on my skull, straightens as Mrs S faces our corner. I think, I think perhaps I could do a better job as Pepe. She is trying to rescue me. I look across at her, confused, embarrassment rising like bile. The Girl, Adela, at my side inhales heavily. Mrs S faces the drama teacher. What do you think? Me as Pepe? She sells it, hands on her hips. The drama teacher spins in my direction. I will not meet her eyes. A pressure builds, is building. All I can hear is air leaving The Girl's lungs. She uses only her mouth. Mrs S strikes a pose, leaning backwards, summoning her masculinity. It is effective. Her thigh muscles soar above her knees. She folds her hands behind her back, shoulders popping through the quiet, through The Girl breathing. The rest of the cast watch. They are unfamiliar with this particular brand of shame. My body's response so predictable. Humming returns to my blood. The hard whistling in my ears. Mrs S uses the drama teacher's first name. Come on, wouldn't it be fun, I've always wanted to act. No one speaks. It is obvious the drama teacher prefers to stretch out moments like this, moments in which she is directly needed to set a tone. Fine, fine! Let's have some fun! Pepe number one you're fired! The Girls relax. A few begin to look excited. This is a new level of intimacy, to have Mrs S a part of their special troupe, to have her as the novice. She moves into position, releasing me by placing her hand gently on my hip.

I sit on the front row. My hands shake. I slide them underneath my legs. The final few lines are directed at Mrs

S. Stilted but poetic, the English sentences missing the Spanish rhythm, moving chaotically through the drama teacher's invisible white wall. The Girl playing Adela ruffles and ruffles her hair, the idea, I think, is to make herself seem sexed, seem unhinged. She seethes her line. I'm his woman, listen, go into the yard and tell him so, he'll rule this whole household, he's there now, breathing like a lion. The Girl playing the mother, curling her hands as if arthritic, mimics lifting and cocking a shotgun. Under its improvised weight she turns heavily, aiming it at Mrs S's head, then lowering it to her chest. She pauses.

What's the problem, go on, shoot! the drama teacher shouts. The Girl hesitates again. What is it, good God? Mrs S replies on her behalf. I don't think she wants to shoot me, because it's me, is that it? The Girl nods, barely moving her head, her imaginary gun still in place. Oh, well, please grant her permission? Mrs S turns to her and smiles carefully. It's fine, it's only acting. She widens her chest, glamorous, expecting her shot. The Girl fires. The drama teacher applauds, proud of her play. Marvellous! Marvellous! Just such a terrible translation! Had I the time I might have done it myself, might have done a better job! The Girls titter in agreement, not necessarily because they agree but because they must appear as if they do. I start to resent my smell. There are no windows, I realize. Not one. Theatres might never have windows, I can't remember. The idea is that, to keep one world intact, you must shut all others out.

Listen, I meant to say, thank you, for the other day. Mrs S makes a sound, a hum, as if to indicate she has no idea what I'm talking about. The rehearsal, you being Pepe. Yes, of course, well it was unfair of her to put you on the spot like that. I don't think she likes me very much. Oh I wouldn't take it personally. So she doesn't like me? Honestly what does it matter, do you like her? No. Well then. She treats me as if I am one of The Girls. I decide to sulk, walking away from her and into the two trees that lean over the wall, their branches low across the path, almost touching the church. Today she flings herself from one mood to the next. I want to be alongside her but cannot find my footing. Perhaps it is because earlier, when I arrived, she touched my side, without thinking at first, then applying more thought, more pressure. Involving herself in my body. Now, embarrassed, even surprised, she must put distance between us. I think back to the cigarettes, to her smoke rings, to her hands on my hip rescuing me from the drama teacher. Perhaps her husband did smell her clothes, demanded that she get on board with their lives here, that she stop acting like the teenagers she has been tasked with protecting. My imagination is so readily confused with intuition. So much of her is not on display, never on display, and yet I still suffer the consequences of whatever she is feeling. I have been drawn in. I suck in my pride like a stomach.

We go back inside the greenhouse. From underneath a flower pot she produces a packet of cigarettes, the same I hid in the van, packet torn with a specific desperation. She returned without me. Brought them here. The lighter lies alongside it. An upturned seashell, left by some former resident, is dusty with ash. She smokes as if it is the most ordinary thing in the world. I don't react, not outwardly. OK, so, what we have to do, if you will help? Sure. Wonderful. The greenhouse fills with her cigarette. She produces a fine paintbrush and a pocketknife, placing them beside each other on the wooden table. These, here, our gear, choose a rose you love and scrape the pollen, well not necessarily a rose you love, but any rose, go by your favourite colour, whatever you want. I pick up the knife. It is rusted at the bottom of the blade. Initials stamped into the red handle. His, relentlessly his. What use would he ever have had for a pocketknife? The passage of boyhood is so easily completed for such men. All they have to do is receive a pocketknife, it need never be put to work.

Where does the pollen go, once I've got it, what do we do after we've got the pollen? We paint it onto the stigma. She articulates almost every letter. Stigma. The word and its double meaning. I touch the paintbrush. Paint? Yes. Good, OK, I can do that. So we must choose a rose, I know, dreadful work for you, the hardest part, you'll have to move past your hatred.

She loops an arm through mine. Uncomfortable and special. I leave my elbow limp against hers. Seconds later I tighten. Let her have some muscle. As we walk an ache begins to grow just before the bone, but I can't let it go slack now. En masse the roses appear weary. The heat, perhaps. From the path each visible head seems lowered, in need of shade, or water. She is not taking care of them. And now she wants to breed them. I can't argue with her, I can't argue with her little tasks, her agency relies on it. Today, we are for the roses.

We walk through the different kinds. Through each new row she announces the varieties she has learned. I think of our time in the water, when she called to me the names of trees, of wild flowers. The roses are different, acute with personality, with ego. Other breeders, making their new flowers. The Smooth Prince, Lady Grey, Peach Cobbler, Sunset Supreme. Sickly-sweet. There is one that has two colours. The petals light pink but rimmed with a darker red, as if just sucked by a lipsticked mouth. This? Good choice. Here, let me show you. She reaches in, pushing back the tight cluster of petals until the centre is revealed. Here, look, this is where all the action takes place. Her thumb and forefinger stretch around the stigma. You scrape the pollen from here, gently. She points at the surrounding, shorter stalks, like clumps of fur. Have you done this before? I laugh. No, definitely not. She doesn't understand the root of my humour. The blatancy of heterosexuality. Her smile is distant, mind elsewhere. I take the knife with its rusty blade and apply it lightly. The pollen falls easily, littering the sharp edge, dusting my hand. She brings her hand to her face. I forgot the things, the things, Christ, wait, wait here. She tears up the path. It is easy to make her happy in this way. I'm beyond happy, I realize, the feeling making me dizzy. Ecstatic, maybe, something dangerous, something with God in it, a sudden ascension into a world in which I do not usually belong. Under the sun, coated in pollen, holding this knife, feeling as though I might suit it. These things of his I like to suit, his knife, his shirt. She needs me to care where she cares, this I can do, this is second nature. Am I being used? Possibly. But maybe to be used like this is not shameful, but heroic.

Here. She returns. Hands me a plastic container, dirty, a Petri dish. Shouldn't we clean it? She mock-rolls her eyes. Spits thickly into the middle and wipes with the corner of her shirt. There, better? Probably not. The sight of her spit leaves a taste in my mouth. I did not expect her to spit. Surely she knows what she is doing to me? I inch closer. Do it, come on. She holds out the Petri dish. I knock the knife tenderly against the edge, the pollen falls, some floating back on the air, the rest trapped. She blows lightly on my hand in an attempt to remove the rest. I try not to appear moved, keeping my face bolted on. Now here's something I prepared earlier, she trills, leading me to another rose, a few rows back. This one is such a pale yellow it is almost white, a dimmed light. These two, these two will mate, they are our parent plants, what do you think, a good combination, we might make a sort of dawn. A dawn? Yes, the colours. For a beat she is embarrassed at her own description. My turn to rescue her. Yeh, I can see that. She tightens her smile, now embarrassed for me, but also relieved. If you say so. She opens up this rose, spreading the petals once again, on this flower they are looser, less romantic. This is called the mother, and this is called emasculating the mother. She rips the petals free, removing each one at speed, until only the rose's naked platform is left. Emasculating, can you even believe. If this is the mother, what is the other called? Guess! The father? Ten points, OK, now cut away everything except the stigma, the stamen, whatever. I take the knife and slit the smaller stems free, leaving the stigma alone, dancing melancholically in the wake of my blade.

She dips her finger into the Petri dish, letting it coat the tip. We're supposed to wait before doing this but who cares. Delicately she brushes her finger over the stigma, side to side, side to side. She returns her fingertip and performs the procedure again. I am always watching. She knows. Doesn't she know? The way she brings her face closer to monitor her technique, the way she closes one eye to bring the miniature procedure into focus. There, that's the mother, emasculated, impregnated. What now? Oh, we wait, I can't remember how long, weeks maybe. But wait for what? I imagine the rose transforming before our eyes, one colour splitting into another, the new rose suffocating the old, shoving its head to one side. She contemplates her work. We wait for the rose hip, like a big pod full of seeds, then we plant those and on it goes, voilà, the world has another rose. That's it? Using the heel of her shoe she squashes the discarded petals. Each one flickers upwards, then dissolves. That's it, we've done all we can for now. She turns to me, offers a cigarette, only remembering last minute I don't smoke. Apologies! She laughs. Lifts up her hands in mock defeat. Oh, she knows what she's doing. Lights the cigarette with her eyes on me. Blows into her words. All the more for me, then.

Is that what you're wearing? Yeh, why? I've chosen a white t-shirt and jeans. You look like fucking Harriet the Spy. The Housemistress is in a dark-navy pinstripe shirt. The same she wears to church. She adds a handsome waistcoat. Gel stiffens her fringe. Not one but two small hoops and a stud I haven't seen before through her cartilage. You don't have anything else? Not really. Let me look, can I look? Fine, sure. She walks up the narrow stairs to my room. My bed is unmade. A notebook is in the middle of the crushed blanket. I didn't know you kept a diary. It's not, I don't keep a diary. My clothes hang on a single rail. Let's see. What about this? She pulls out a dress shirt. Cream, chosen by my mother, the sides curved. No not that.

Or this? She takes out his shirt. No, no. Christ fussy little lesbian aren't you. Maybe. If you have to wear that then at least accessorize. Around her neck is a silver chain, thick. Here, don't lose it, it's my grandad's, it was my grandad's. OK. The weight is reassuring against my neck. And this, these. Using her mouth she pulls one, two rings from her index fingers. Don't lose these either yeh. I won't. Around my own index fingers they are too loose. Wet with her saliva. Then put them on your thumbs. She claps my shoulder. Improved, slightly improved, one last touch. She pulls me forward. Tucks my t-shirt inside my jeans. A belt is whipped from the waistband of her trousers. Smart black leather with its celestial shine. Rather than hand it to me she snakes it directly around my hips. Too tight? No that's good. Alrighty we're ready, look at us. Self-consciously we hug. Chests kept separate at first, arms moving with unexpected force, my head pressed briefly in her neck. There I find her smell, carefully chosen. Orange peel. Wood, woodsmoke, maybe sandalwood. Brine. The whole sea dried to salt behind her ear.

Anything to drink? In the kitchen cupboard is an old bottle of tequila. Left, I assume, by the previous Matron. This? Perfect perfect. Two large shots are poured into tea-stained mugs. For the road. She smacks her lips together. Needs lime but not bad. Here we go, here we go, here we go. She chants absent-mindedly. I rub the rings against my knuckles. The metal worn smooth by three generations of fingers. They look good on you. I double-check the necklace's clasp. This was your grandad's too? Yeh look it's fine don't worry too much, don't be too precious about it or anything, he was a real bastard. Yeh? No interesting story there I'm afraid, just a regular bastard. She pours herself another tequila. More? Sure. Outside, a car horn is hit in quick succession. That's us. We down the drinks in unison.

The last time I was in a car it belonged to her. In his, in the taxi, is a strong smell of peppermint. The Housemistress examines her reflection in the window. By the way there's a rumour going round that we're fucking. She narrows her eyebrows. The same expression The Girls see in lesser moments of discipline. When she says fucking my stomach opens. Us? Yep. Who's saying that? Oh I had a few comments in the staffroom, which means The Girls already think they know it all, and the teachers have been listening in. The day is still bright, too bright for our evening dress code. The taxi driver meets my eyes in the rear-view and winks. But we're not fucking. Correct. She doesn't whisper. What kind of comments then? Nothing obvious don't panic, just the usual, hope YOU have a good WEEKEND. She puts air quotes around certain words. But we're not fucking! You already said that. I know it's just it's not true. Would it be that bad, to be fucking me? The hurt is only half there. A dent in her chin. No, no of course not. Look it's not that surprising, Two Dykes, One Heart, Small School. She imitates the school's Latin motto with her hand against her chest. Written by the dead author's father. The crest designed by him too. In one corner a lamb, the next a heart, the third a snake, the last a lion. Each creature, even the heart, has a demonic goofiness. For dramatic effect a sword penetrates the middle. Or at least, it should penetrate, instead her father, the clergyman, could not fathom the actual plunge. There is just the handle, then the tip of the blade.

Out for the night then ladies? He is in the rear-view mirror again. The peppermint smell comes from the hard sweets he sucks compulsively. Three at least since we left. The Housemistress turns to me. I shake my head, indicating I do not want to be the one to answer. Something like that, yeh. Looking sharp, the two of you. Cheers. Fancy dress, is it? I don't reply but smile instead. It is not easy. It is not easy to stop someone from seeing you. Usually she is better at it than me. On one of her wrists a thick piece of leather has been knotted clumsily into a cuff. Handmade. Every now and again she places her forefinger underneath it and twists. I wait for her to make a joke, a joke as a challenge, about our outfits. Harriet the Spy again. Instead she sits in silence.

The turn out from Devil's Bridge requires his attention. His eyes leave momentarily. Mind putting on the radio mate? Whatever gets you in the mood. Another wink. We drive in the opposite direction from the swimming spot. Two supermarkets, a garden centre. Short rows of matching houses. The same pebbledash. Traffic slows us down. Swallows dart daringly above the cars, sniping the evening insects. The fells fade away, the landscape flattening out into fields. Farm after farm. Grass gone to crisp yellow. The unnerving length of this hot month. I miss rain. I say it aloud. I miss rain. What? She twists and twists the cuff. I miss rain, I miss the rain. I tap the window as if to summon it. You won't be saying that in winter. The taxi driver speaks through the latest mint, pausing it under his tongue, voice wet. I know what you mean. She squeezes my hand. The same ferocity as the hug, the same imperative meeting of bones. I know what you mean. Rain, the rhythm, the chance to disappear.

Signs for the town appear in an intimidating countdown of kilometres. My stomach won't close. I shift around an urge to shit. It's party time! The Housemistress is only excited. Hair fixed, gel wiped discreetly on the underside of the seat. The car turns up a wide cobbled street. He peers at possible numbers. Can't say I know the exact location. You can just let us out here. No, no, I'm a gentleman, I'll get you to the door. Really, it's fine. Both her hands seize the seat in front. Let us out here please. Alright, alright.

I go to get my wallet but am too slow. Cash is produced from her pocket. No wallet. A thick brass clip around the wad of notes. Let me get this, you buy the first round. You sure? Yes. She closes the door and smacks the roof. His face twists, suddenly a boy. Goodbye then. Bye. He doesn't drive away immediately. The engine idles. What he wants is to see where we're heading. A pursuit of knowledge he considers honourable. All he wants, I feel him reasoning through the car window, is to understand. She doesn't move. Her smile breaks through, conspiratorial, slowly picking hairs from the waistcoat, bending to check her laces, neatening the already neat bows. I stand in the shade of a closed shopfront. Her waiting is elegant. I know what it takes. After a few minutes he gives up and leaves. A concession, her minor victory. OK, come on, I'm not entirely sure where it is but we will figure it out. She taps her nose. Lesbian instinct. I still need to shit. Ropes tighten around my guts, my asshole.

You haven't been to this place before? No. We walk up the street. She is careful with her leather shoes. Poising her ankles so as not to scuff them on the cobblestones. The town is bigger than I expected. The cobblestones lead up a steep hill. A cathedral is promised at the end. Generic high-street brands offer sickly coffees, two-for-one pastel polo shirts, meal deals, detailed charm bracelets. Not far away a clock chimes. Just a couple of Cinderellas aren't we? Maybe more like the princes, especially you, in that look. Why thank you. I've embarrassed her. She chews the side of a fingernail. Touches the fly of her trousers. Her body is suddenly too close to the seams. I know the feeling, I say nothing, she doesn't want to be noticed any more than me. She is gracious, grins. Do what we can don't we. I confirm and reconfirm the presence of the necklace and rings. It is hot, of course, hot. Silence and sweat enjoy a mutual grip.

Halfway up the hill she stops. Off the main street, down a narrower alleyway, is a line of bars and restaurants. People smoke cigarettes in large groups. It's around here some-where. I train my eyes, looking for a sign. What's it called? Lips. I laugh, she laughs too. We pass men with ties tucked in their pockets. Some kind of event. A wedding, a race day. Dribbles of beer already stain their shirts. Women put their arms around each other, nuzzling, swapping encouraging sentences. Those shoes will all be off later. She nods at their heels. Plenty of them stare. Only a couple call after us.

Perhaps because I was staring first. Here, in my outfit, the chain now warm as my skin, I am undeniable. Ignore them. She slows down to walk next to me. Bunch of twats. In a bigger city there would be a larger queer geography. But this town has only one bar. Even that is strange. To have a place to go, that is strange.

Here, it's here. The sign is depressing. No sultry neon light. Just a logo. A faded red-lipsticked mouth against a grimy white wall. There is no outdoor seating. A bouncer stands at the entrance, hair tied in a long ponytail. Evening. On you go. Shirt buttons strain across his large chest. At the end of a short corridor we turn down a carpeted staircase. It's still early. Not too busy. A few people sit at tables, intent on seeing the new arrivals. The Housemistress hesitates. In the middle of the room she deliberates between the bar and an empty booth. A heat already on its way to ferocious. The smell of each past encounter like rising damp. Still she deliberates. We are watched carefully. Excitedly. Eyes happening sideways. Come on. I push her softly towards the bar. She dabs her forehead with a red napkin. Music plays. Indiscernible power ballads. In one corner a DJ sets up. Her arms are pure muscle. A quote I can't read is tattooed in cursive across her collarbone.

Without asking for The Housemistress's preference I order two shots of tequila. With lime and salt, I add, looking at her. She chases beads of sweat, the red napkin now twisted around her forefinger. Fuck it's so fucking hot. Here drink this. Good plan, cheers. I fan her with a beer mat. Ah shit me ah fuck that's the stuff. Her bravado lifting. She moves her face into the tiny patch of air I create. Get this too. Her neck is offered to me now. I pick up another beer mat and fan with both hands. Better? Better. Our bodies begin to imprint. Comfortable on our spinning stools. A pathetic fan is flicked on by an employee. Her t-shirt is knotted at the navel, revealing a silver bar. With each of her movements it pulls at the thin fold of her belly-button. Soon the sun will move off the building. For now it thickens through the basement windows. Each pane the size of a brick.

Two more shots yeh? Yeh, maybe pints too. Sure it will get busier later. As she talks she takes in the room. Knees spread wider. Posters on the bar's back wall advertise today's date, the name of the DJ in bold, the outlines of more lips. Purple female gender symbols bounce in the background. Yeh I don't think the night starts really until nine p.m. What is it now? Almost eight. OK, OK, we better pace ourselves, maybe make some friends. She winks and licks the foam from her beer. Anyone you like? Already? Yeh, why not. I glance again at the DJ. A person I assume is the manager talks to her enthusiastically. Christ not her not the DJ what a cliché. Fine then you? Oh oh I think she's fit. She covers a pointing finger with her hand, blocking its direction from the row of tables. In the hat? Yeh, yes. The woman wears a baseball cap tilted up above her fringe. Maroon t-shirt with a logo. A pack of cigarettes tucked in her top pocket is charming enough to be annoying.

More people arrive. I try not to think of her, I try not to think of Mrs S. The bar is busy with elbows. Somebody buys me a drink but I don't know who. The Housemistress is ecstatic. I knew this was a good idea! It doesn't mean anything, maybe it was a mistake, whatever I'll send it back. Seriously what's wrong with you. What, nothing, fine, here. In slow motion I cheers the entire bar and drink. A few people nod back. One wink. The DJ begins. Honest to fuck I could fall in love tonight. She drinks fast. Her voice rises above the music. The woman in the maroon t-shirt has come closer. Her group stands metres away, on the edge of the empty dance floor. Everyone is on the edge of the dance floor. A few people, eager to survey the swelling crowd, now perch on the tables. No one sits, not really. There is a heady elaboration of gesture. Hands flying through the air. Laughter made sexier, drinking made sexier. It seems as though the DJ is looking at me. But this is impossible. I am too far back in the crowd. More and more people arrive. She is looking at all of it, at everyone. I give The Housemistress all my attention. Why don't you talk to her. Who? You know, the new love of your life. I chuck my chin at the woman in the maroon t-shirt. Her hat now on a friend's head. Not yet my innocent friend, not yet. What makes you think I'm innocent? Come on Harriet the Spy. She slaps my thigh. I slap hers back. Not so innocent, actually, not as innocent as you think. The woman in the maroon t-shirt finally approaches. She stands between the two of us. I am cut off. Her smell is citrus. Best seat in the house, this. If you say so. A heavy pause. The Housemistress does not yet offer to buy her a drink. This is just the beginning.

A hangover. Acute. The nail through the forehead. Nausea moving in hiccups. I lie on her floor, one cushion from her sofa under my head. The rug from her sofa is pulled over my body. I register my surroundings one by one. Her snores pass gently through the wall. No, the door, the door to her bedroom is open. Sunday, now it is Sunday. Her snores, tidal, released in waves. The annexe is even smaller than mine. Each section of life squashed into the next. The sofa close to the kitchen, a television close to the window already pumping sun, close to the bedroom which is windowless entirely. Where is the bathroom? There is no bathroom. There is a bathroom, of course, almost inside the kitchen.

Shower pressed against the toilet. I lean my head on the cool edge of the sink. Hopeful that a cool edge will help. I splash water on my face. This will be the cure. Her toothbrush, a little heartbreak, the worn bristles, the man's blue colour. I'm desperate to brush my teeth. This will be the cure, clean teeth. Her toothpaste is the whitening kind, more heartbreak. These improvements we secretly want to make. At the last moment I can't do it and put the toothbrush back in its place. We are not lovers, we have not yet been close enough to each other's tongues. Instead I wipe a minted finger across my teeth. Maybe I will vomit. No, no I won't. I can hold on.

That you up? The snoring has stopped. Her voice already confident. Yes. I sit, defeated, on the floor of the bathroom. She comes to find me. Oh Jesus, ha, you lightweight. Somehow she is fresh. Feeling rough? I nod. Each plate of my skull rubs against its neighbour. She disappears into the kitchen. I can offer two cures, hair of the dog, or hair of the dog. In each hand is a green bottle of beer. What have I got to lose? That's the spirit. You're young, you'll survive. She stands with her back to the window. A warm silhouette. The two green beer bottles come alive. Too alive, the light flung into my eyes, thudding into the hollow behind. You too? Me what? I point weakly at the beer. You'll drink too? She enjoys forcing me to talk. One of those. I slump and lie entirely on the lino in a half-hearted foetal position. Yes, why not, nowhere to be, The Girls aren't here, we're free to fuck about. She leaves me on the floor and returns again with her ring of keys. She uses the largest, oldest one to pop open each bottle. It doesn't happen easily. The serrated lid leaves a cut at the base of her thumb. She doesn't seem to notice. Here, drink.

The first few mouthfuls are almost a disaster. The beer curdles with toothpaste. Come on drink it like you mean it. She sits on the sofa, talking to me as I sip preciously, still lying down, propped up on my elbow. Already she has on the chain she loaned me last night. A black vest, loose across her chest. Tattoos cover her shoulders. Don't tell anyone about these yeh. She winks and touches what I think is the head of a thick snake. No, I say, unable to commit to a sentence. No? No. You're hilarious this morning. She has on boxers. Plaid, baggy. A pair of socks. No. Is that all you can say? No. Using all my energy I open my throat to finish the beer. Don't throw up. I don't throw up. That's it! Fucking hell, OK. In solidarity she finishes hers too. Tequila next? Fuck off. Ah, she lives! Not quite. I close my eyes and turn onto my back. Better? Maybe. Maybe works for me, OK, phase two. Two? Yes, dress, let's go get a bacon sarnie. Where? I know a place. She taps the side of her nose. She wears her clichés so well. The beer is helping.

My clothes from last night have been neatly folded over the arm of the sofa. You're a sweet drunk. She hands me the pile. Even your boxers are folded. Thanks. The light hangs heavy in my head. Opening my eyes is painful. Drawers open and close in her room. My t-shirt smells like cigarette smoke. How did we get home last night? Come on you don't remember? You were such a Chatty Cathy in the taxi. I'm sure it will come back to me. She walks back into the room wearing a smart blue jumper. Her perfume, her cologne, fills the air. Oh come on you look good that's cheating. You never know who you might bump into. Did you get lucky? Get lucky? She laughs. I came home with you mate, what do you think. Still though, she rolls up her sleeve and turns over her arm. Written across her forearm, in blue biro, the colour still sharp, is a telephone number. It wasn't a complete waste of time. For all her talk, she was never going to sleep with anybody, she was never going to get laid. Will you call her? Have you written it down? No, not yet, we'll see, I have until my shower to decide.

You, though, you. She smiles at me and turns her arm back over. Some moves you pulled. What? I can't yet summon a memory. Did I get with anybody? Get with anybody, what are you, fifteen. You know what I mean. Mate I have no idea, you were lost to the dance floor for most of the night. Really? Yeh. She goes back into the bedroom using a cheesy, mock choreography. I follow, slowly. Last night's clothes are piled on the floor. She reaches into the trousers and removes the last of the cash, peeling off what I think is a tenner. How many sandwiches are you planning on buying? Who knows. On the bedside table are three half-finished packets of pills, the foil popped and torn. OK then what was I saying in the taxi then. Oh, your whole life story. But what exactly? She doesn't answer at first. I can't remember, it's not like I was sober. You do remember. Look it was the same life story as mine, homophobic father, avoidant mother. Oh. Don't be embarrassed, we're friends aren't we. Yes, course. Then it doesn't matter what I do or don't know. She goes into the bathroom. Two secs.

She reappears. Are we driving somewhere? No need, it's just up the road. Have I missed some cafe? Don't make me laugh. Outside, the heat has already arrived. A blue so bright it is a knife, slicing. Jesus fuck, I forgot my sunglasses. I feel exposed in last night's outfit. Can I go home and change first? You're fine, not like anyone is here to see. The sun burns my shoulders. Too hot for jeans. Here look. She takes off her jumper to reveal a t-shirt. Now we match, feel better? I nod although I am still self-conscious, still on the lookout for The Girls despite knowing they are away. We go up through the first car park, past the boarding houses for those in their final year. After a second car park the hockey pitches appear on our left. A man mows the grass. The smell of his engine. He is shirtless. Jesus no one needs to see that, she jokes. Still we stop and watch, leaning against the fence, taking a moment to cool. Is it far to walk? No, it's just a van, parks up in a lay-by that way. The man waves to us, then salutes, then jokingly flexes his arm. Jesus fuck. They can't help themselves, see, they just can't help themselves. Her head turns to and fro. Looking up at the fell to our right and back at the man. The snake head glimpsed on every twist of her body, the t-shirt sleeve rising and falling. I would get a tattoo. How happily I borrow from her way of being. The man waves again and she rolls her eyes. She makes the most of masculinity. Not the tattoo, not the t-shirt, but the way she lives in the hinges of her body. The knees, the elbows, the hips. My sweat with its alcohol edge. Her sweat too.

Come on this won't do. She pulls unexpectedly at my hand. Let's eat. We go a way up the narrow road, leaving the pitches behind. In a lay-by is a snack stand. Fried food and hot drinks. What'll it be? Whatever you're having. Your wish is my command. She joins the queue. Another wave of hangover sends me to a squatting position. I am tempted to lie across the tarmac. Instead I find a piece of grass and lean backwards, almost into the hedge. Ahead, beyond the road, is a fuller view of the fell that shoulders the school. I forget the name. It is laid bare. Pinched rock, the great sweep of greens and greys, armpit shadows formed beneath each steep ridge. Here, eat, you're looking pathetic. She sits beside me. The sandwich is good. Great, even. Sauce stings the corners of my mouth. I got you a tea, no idea if you actually drink tea. Thanks. It is sweet. My hands are greasy. I wipe them on the grass and she copies. She finishes her food neatly, determinedly. I close my eyes and think, suddenly, of the fell pressed against my body. Rock biting into my collarbone, pushing me slowly into the grass, into the soil.

Oh shit, here we go. What? Ten o'clock. I don't know what that means. The Housemistress points. She is coming up the road. A short summer dress. Blue. No, green. He, Mr S, is with her, walking a pace ahead, so they form a single file. A car passes too fast and he shakes his head. The Housemistress tugs at her sleeves then remembers her jumper, pulling it on at speed. Fuck I am not in the mood. We have not yet been seen. Even as they arrive in the lay-by neither looks over at us. Fuck, think we could hide in the hedge? She moves backwards, the short sharp branches pulling at her ears. Hardly. She rubs her eyes then pulls them open, pinning back her eyelids, blowing air upwards. Makes me feel like I'm a fucking kid again, how do I look? Fine, me? Knackered mate, you look knackered. Thanks, fuck. I wipe the corners of my mouth. Inexplicably check my nails. They see us. He waves, she smiles. Here we go. The Housemistress stands and I am forced to follow.

Ah the Australian, our Aussie import. I realize he does not remember my name. Mrs S doesn't speak, standing just behind him, reading the short menu. Perhaps pretending to read. I would like her to be pretending. How are you both? Good, good. Enjoying this fine cuisine. He is relentlessly cheerful. Now she speaks, addressing The Housemistress. And what did you have? The usual, a bacon sandwich. A wise choice! We will be having the same! He answers for her. Mrs S drops her sunglasses across her face. It was really good. Your first-ever bacon sarnie? No, not quite. Ah well, hopefully just the best bacon sarnie, we aim to please. We we we. He is, apparently, all of England. Mrs S fades away, placing their order, returning to us slowly. I catch her eye, too briefly.

He rubs his hands together. Nice to see you getting along, don't want to get lonely on these weekends without The Girls. The Housemistress waits for me to say something. Yes, no, it's great. He is well versed in small talk. Have you done much exploring? Me, no. I swallow a smile and instead point at Mrs S. Actually our trip out to a swimming spot is the most travelling I've managed since arriving. For a beat he is silent. Oh, you went swimming, how wonderful, my wife is an excellent host. She is. He is unbothered. My chest swells. She did not tell him. She has not told him. She gives nothing away. Yes, well, I did mention how helpful she was in the garden, it was a thank-you trip of sorts. Her accent sharpens, falling in line with his. The Housemistress steps on the back of my heel. I take from his language. Well it was wonderful, a wonderful day, wonderful to see the fells, or at least a fell, up close. We aim to please, we aim to please. He is distracted, looking hopefully at the van, waiting for his order. I don't look at her.

The sandwiches are called. Mrs S retrieves them. Goes back for tea. She wraps napkins around the takeaway cups. The Housemistress offers up her own polystyrene cup in a bizarre cheers. They reciprocate. He is pleased at the gesture, grinning. What have you got planned for the rest of the weekend? How will you make the most of your freedom? This is as far as we've got. Well look, here's a mad idea, why not join us for supper. Tonight? Yes tonight, why not, it's just the two of us rolling around that house. Mr S grabs Mrs S excitedly. She sips her tea, wincing as it touches her lips too quickly. A professional smile. Yes, a wonderful idea, please do come over, shall we say seven? This is my punishment. I am only sorry for The Housemistress who must now endure it too.

What happened to her? Who? The Girl who punched the boy. He is not surprised so much as forgetful. I wanted him to be shocked by my boldness. Mrs S is in the kitchen. He has a stupid mouth. Lips slack, permanently parted. The Housemistress and I are afraid to look at each other. I know she will agree about the stupid mouth. I will tell her later. She will, I'm guessing, announce that all men have stupid mouths. Nervous, she smooths and resmooths the white tablecloth. Moves the cutlery another split second apart, then, self-conscious, returns it to the original position.

I know the bedroom is just above our heads. Tonight, inside, it looks different, tonight she has lit candles, despite the daylight carrying on outside, the curtains half-drawn. We could have eaten in the back garden, but there is not enough furniture to seat everyone. She was very apologetic. It is warm, sleepy warm, the eyes in each portrait especially menacing, pupils darting with every flicker. Here is my punishment, to sit through this seance, this bizarre invoking of straight lives, of straightened lives. The details of the room are difficult to make out in the low light. Things I did not turn over on my last visit. A few photographs in burnt-silver frames line the top of the piano, obviously rarely played, a stack of books balanced on the stool. Indiscernible faces in the photographs. There are trinkets too, the kind handed down, possibly theirs or possibly belonging to the house.

Ah, That Girl, The Girl, she'll be back to take her exams, I think she's learned her lesson. You don't think, given the same situation, she'd punch him all over again? He drinks his wine. Sucks his teeth. I'm not one for hypothetical questions I'm afraid, can't be bothered with them. It is not just a stupid mouth. Married men have a smugness. I wonder if it evolves or if it is just there after the vows, after the first marital sex. I can hear Mrs S in the kitchen. Noises quick, violent, maybe a blender, a metal bowl. The Housemistress offers to help before I have the chance. You OK in there? Need a hand? Oh I'm fine, in my element, food won't be long now. I suck my own teeth. It's not a hypothetical question, really, is it, isn't the idea to decide whether or not she thought what she did was good or bad? Well she knows it's bad, she's been punished accordingly. That doesn't mean she knows she's been bad. He puts his hands behind his head. Not sure 'been bad' is the phrasing you're after. When he laughs it is irritatingly attractive. Each tooth bright white. His mouth momentarily less stupid. She appears finally. A different summer dress, longer, glancing the backs of her knees. An apron knotted twice around her waist. Her hands are placed lightly on his shoulders. Don't let him wind you up. I would never. He pats her wrist. I for one have never been bad.

The Housemistress doesn't intervene, doesn't offer an opinion. Around him she is temporarily wary. Well we're not here to talk about school. He reaches for the wine bottle and tops up our glasses. No? I wonder what he thinks we have in common. Bacon sandwiches, then? Now there's a subject. She arrives suddenly, The Housemistress, her confidence uncovered. He laughs again. Precisely, yes, wonderful, now there's a topic. Before the wine he mixed martinis. Each movement rehearsed. His whole life pulled from the pages of a novel, the scenes of a film, the lines of a song. His whole life one elongated wink. An inevitable grin when The Housemistress requested that her martini be 'dirty'. My hangover is at least gone. Replaced instead with a detached light-headedness. I look longingly at a leather armchair and think about curling up. Drink more wine. They continue discussing breakfast food. The Housemistress is animated, wanting me to notice when she repeats the word sausage. I don't excuse myself when I stand. It is easy enough to just leave the room.

Mrs S could be angry that I gave her away, that I told him about our swimming trip. It might not have been important enough for her to mention it and now I've made it seem suspicious. She turns her head only slightly at the sound of my body in the doorway. Chin at the top of her shoulder. A ceramic bowl is carefully washed and placed to one side. Jewellery heaped in a little dish on the sill. She could be embarrassed, maybe, too. My presence amongst the domesticity embarrasses her. I am not sure she knows shame. Only this spotlit feeling. The self, her self, suddenly illuminated against her will. Just wanted to see if you needed help. No, I already said, I'm fine, really. Smells good. Oh, nothing complicated, just pasta, spaghetti alle vongole. Another perfect pronunciation, another life revealed, this one taking place in Italy. I see clams in a metal bowl. One hundred set mouths. She pulls the bowl into the sink and removes grit, the tiniest flick of seaweed.

The kitchen is even warmer than the living room, despite the open windows. She finishes cleaning, the clams no longer clattering. I talk so I have something to do. Always a sink designed with a view, why do they do that, give the sink the best view? For the wives, to see something pleasant while they finish their chores. Parsley is rinsed, chopped. Ah yeh, I could've guessed. Cloves of garlic are crushed under the pad of her thumb. Do you feel sorry for me? Still she doesn't turn around. Me? Feel sorry for you? The repetitive thud of the blade. Yes, this, my scene. Each word shared between us is turned over and over. She uses the knife to point at the stove, the window, the dishes piled up on the draining board. This, this, this. As she waves her arms the tip of the knife collides with the tap. She brings it to her fingers to inspect the damage. I come closer. Scene? You know what I mean. She stops. Puts down the knife. I come closer again. I don't know anything.

The sun moves through the final steps of its choreography, striding into the remaining space between us. In the sudden turn I can't see. Her hand finds my wrist and I am pulled towards her. One knee against hers, my hip bone buttoned to her hip bone. In the room behind he keeps laughing. Her cheek, the corner of an eye, eyelashes, the moisture of an eye. I find her throat. My fingers in her mouth first. She tips back her head as if to accept my fist. Her tongue. I touch a sound sent up from her body. A moan, it's there, I stop it from leaving. Wet, I was wet before, as if I knew. The chance she knows me better than anybody. A chair screeches across the dining room floor and we part. At least our bodies part. My fingers remain in her mouth, slipping up over her teeth. The chair moves again. Behind us the scene has continued. She pulls my hand free, closes her lips around each knuckle. A slow exit. Only a pebble of sun remains in the window's corner. Her face is suddenly clear, free from the bright burn behind her head. A trail of saliva runs her chin. Momentarily gold. A piece of jewellery.

The Housemistress wanders the hallway beyond. The bathroom? Her head appears in the kitchen's second entrance. Just down there. Ta. The Housemistress disappears. A door opens and closes. The house breathes a little. She turns back to the preparation of our meal. Garlic is fried in oil. I want to tell her something romantic, something about the buttoning and unbuttoning of our hip bones. She adds parsley to the garlic, green on gold, perfumes colliding. But what is there worth saying. How language suffers compared to smell. The immediacy, a present tense left to distil in the veins, without explanation. I am increasingly dramatic. A pot of water begins to boil. I untie her apron. Put my hand up her dress. Find the small of her back. Her body, momentarily, is built alongside my body. I can't reach her shoulder blades. The house keeps breathing. In the other room he is silent. This silence, his silence, is encouraging. I increase the pressure of my hand. She presses backwards into my palm, taking my body in stages, entering first the crook of my arm, then my pelvis. Our necks are clumsy. Maybe this will be it. Maybe this will be as far as it goes. At the thought I push my knee behind hers, willing her to collapse. Another moan, released. The sound surprises her. She clamps a hand to her mouth.

The throttle of pipes. Footsteps up the hallway, The Housemistress. Our veil is lifted. Nice stained glass you've got in there. Thank you, although, hardly my handiwork. A wasp, sent on by the heat, bumps twice on the window before entering the kitchen. Mrs S is not worried, only looking up once before returning to the bucket of clams, lifting it over the large saucepan. The Housemistress jerks her head as if the wasp has already found her, leaping into the hallway. Hey look listen I don't mess with them. It settles on the windowsill. The slender abdomen throbs. Mrs S pulls a wooden spoon through the shells. A new smell, the smell of sea, brief, a beach in the morning, the sand still gaining warmth. Looks delicious, The

Housemistress calls from the hall. Mrs S calls back. Come in, don't be silly, why don't you just come in, I doubt it wants to sting you. The Housemistress is tentative in the doorway. A foot barely across the threshold. In all honesty I'm allergic, I've been allergic since I was a child. Oh! Well then. I can't tell if The Housemistress is lying. I don't know about her fears.

Mrs S calls out to her husband. I join The Housemistress in the doorway. She grabs my waist and arranges me in front of her. Ah, my bodyguard. Whatever you need. The wasp lifts off from the windowsill and attempts an exit. That abdomen becomes a fingertip against the glass. In the pan I imagine the clams are opening their mouths. I have the sense I might faint and steady myself against the door-frame. How's that hangover treating you? The Housemistress whispers. I feel bloody unstoppable. Yeh right. He makes a leisurely arrival, a record still in his left hand, half out of its sleeve. I was on music duty, what's happening in here, I've been abandoned, have I. She opens a packet of spaghetti with her teeth. There's a wasp, can you get it out? He kisses her not quite on the mouth. Your wish, my command. I did not offer to help and she did not ask. The Housemistress pinches my side, as if we are The Girls let into the staffroom, witnessing some coveted intimacy.

The wasp drifts, then zooms, into the middle of the kitchen. He slides the record back into its sleeve and fans it gently. Can't be good for the vinyl but protecting the masses comes first. He aims his airstreams at the wasp.

There is no particular plan. When the wasp darts chaotically close to his face, the record is put down, a glass taken from a top cupboard. Look, here, this usually works. Isn't that how you trap spiders? Oh it works for all insects. Right. She drops the spaghetti into the boiling pan. Coaxes it underwater with the back of the wooden spoon. We have not yet kissed. I think about kissing her. I think about swallowing her tongue.

Here we go. The wasp lands once again on the window. He leans over the stovetop and brings the glass down over the wasp. Careful. Mrs S shifts his torso with both her hands. You'll set fire to yourself. The wasp is pinned, thrusting back and forth, giving the impression of rage. Mr S doesn't move, turning his stomach concave over the pots, balancing on the balls of his feet. Here, hand me the record, quick. I pass it to him and watch as he slides it awkwardly underneath the glass. Should have just killed you, he murmurs, addressing the wasp directly. What a situation we find ourselves in now.

I heard that when you kill a wasp it releases a pheromone which attracts other wasps. A pheromone? He turns his head a fraction to look at me. A sliver of eye. Yes, well, I don't know if it's a pheromone for sure, but something, some kind of chemical. What and the rest arrive to avenge his death? Not avenge, that wouldn't be very insect behaviour, but maybe make sure the same thing isn't around to kill them too. How logical. Finally he whips around, trying to keep the record tight against the glass. But it is too large a surface. His shirt catches on the stove, threatening a button. The glass smashes against the tiles. The wasp is released. Fuck, fuck, fucking hell. I am too busy looking at the fragments to see the moment he is stung. It is an expensive glass, one of the crystal tumblers, maybe original, maybe belonging to the dead author's father.

Fuck me, fuck, excuse my language, God I haven't been stung before, not even as a boy, fuck that hurts. Mrs S goes to him first. I want to be useful. Shall I grab a broom? Yes, yes, in the hallway cupboard. The wasp is still at large. God it's like a cigarette burn, Christ. She kisses the back of his hand. A bump turns white, then red, then white again. He moves his head away from the injury. Is the stinger still in there? Let me see. Using her mouth she sucks. Not that I can find. His hairstyle has come undone, flopping over his forehead. Where is the bastard, surely killing him would make us even at this stage, don't need to worry about his entourage arriving. It's fine, let me. I take the record from the floor. The wasp has returned to the windowsill. I miss the first time, sending it up the pane. On the second swipe I make contact. It quivers for a moment, hopeful, before the abdomen curls to touch the head. He doesn't thank me. Fuck do you think I'm allergic? The Housemistress returns with the broom. I worry he might start to cry.

Mrs S is graceful with his pain. I no longer exist. He asks again. Do you think I'm allergic? This time it is directed at The Housemistress. She finishes wrapping the fragments of glass in old newspaper found under the sink. Doesn't rush.

Peers at the back of his hand. The wasp has left a pinprick. Yellowing slightly at the centre. It's difficult to tell, how is your breathing? I don't know, fine? His other hand wraps around his neck. Fine I think? Open your mouth. Mrs S steps aside. The Housemistress peers down his gullet. Wider, wider please, I can't quite get a visual, tilt your head up. What The Housemistress needs to see is his tongue, the back of his throat. Look I'm no doctor but all seems normal to me. Good, good. He moves his lips unnaturally, testing them out, searching for an unusual texture, for some indication that he is closer to death.

I mean we can take you up to the sanatorium, to see The Nurse? Me? No, no, I think an, what do you call it, antihistamine and some painkillers will do just fine. His eyelids flutter. Mrs S returns to his side. Why don't you lie down, I'll bring you painkillers. He nods solemnly. The injured hand held limply by the other hand. Perhaps a martini too, while we're self-medicating. He winks weakly. She doesn't respond but smiles at him, putting her fingers to his chin. Such a boy about these things, aren't you. Of course, never had the time to grow up. She kisses his cheek. This is a role she loves. The source of her own embarrassment.

Apologies, everyone. He winces again. This injured soldier needs to take a few minutes. No, no, carry on. I think The Housemistress looks relieved. It will be difficult to respect him after this but we will manage. He will convert it easily into an anecdote. I can already see it. The laugh, his laugh, conjuring the wasp's efficient and powerful body.

Fear will not feature. Anger will not feature. Just an incredulousness that bad things, accidental bad things, can happen, even to men like him. Mrs S adds more white wine to the clams. I offer to help again. Plates, no bowls, if you would. Shouldn't we wait for him? Oh no, I'll bring him a martini, with that and the pill, the antihistamine, you know, he will sleep for days. I resent her composure. Right, we can go home, if that's easier. I try to provoke her. And waste all this food, absolutely not, I hate waste. She works quickly. More parsley, more garlic. No sun, it is vanished by the trees beyond the garden. Each kitchen surface is shadowed. Lights are turned on, adjusted. One bulb pops and disappears. She swears under her breath. What if I am already in love with her. It is not possible. The Housemistress returns to the dining table. Mrs S and I are left alone. We don't talk. I kneel on the floor and check for more shards of the expensive glass. A few are scattered against the wall. Some linger in between the tiles. I press my finger to each piece and collect them in my palm. You don't need to do that, don't do that with your hands. Authoritative. Her voice happens between my legs. It's fine, I don't mind. No, get up, go and sit down. Is she flustered or impatient, I can't tell. I hope his hand swells. I hope his throat closes.

In the dining room's candlelight The Housemistress is a gentleman. All profile. Her nose a perfect shadow on the wall. Wearing the same outfit from last night. When she moves closer to me I smell yesterday's cigarettes. We smoked, I barely remember smoking. Somebody else's packet. The Housemistress turns towards the kitchen and calls. Want us to make the martinis? Yes, that would be wonderful, his should be sweet, ever so slightly sweet, if you could, add a dash more vermouth than usual. The Housemistress rolls her eyes at me. She mixes the drink clumsily. Gin spills onto the floor. Here. Out of sight she takes a swig from the shaker and offers it to me. Fuck it, at this point we may as well commit.

Knives and forks? Forks and spoons, maybe, and these, might be helpful. Mrs S produces a delicate tool I don't recognize. My fingers were in her mouth. I'm unsure where on the table the delicate tools belong. In the end, beside the fork. An empty bowl for the shells. Everything is silver. The atmosphere is well known. One that Mrs S has produced again and again. The white tablecloth. Extra wedges of lemons, extra parsley. Dried chilli flakes. Roses in a vase. She serves the pasta on a large platter, meant for something else I wonder, also silver. The taste of silver is in my mouth. Blood. I have bitten the inside of my cheek. A flap of skin I can flick with my tongue. I change my mind and place the delicate tools beside the spoons. Nobody registers my panic. They are talking now, pleasantly, too pleasantly, about The Girls, something to do with swimming lessons. He is missing. This is what he has done, created something to be missed from. Without him the conversation has lost its centre.

Shall I take him his drink? The pills? No, no, I'll do that. She takes the martini and disappears up the stairs. The

Housemistress puts a finger between my ribs. You OK? Me? Yeh, just fading. Jesus me too, and full disclosure I fucking hate seafood. The Housemistress lifts a clam with her fingers, bringing it in for closer inspection. It just looks inedible. I've never tried. Trust me, you're not missing out, things that come from the sea should just stay in the sea, don't put anything in your mouth that looks like that. A door closes carefully. The Housemistress smiles too wide at Mrs S as she sits down. This all looks lovely. Thank you. We all know by now that the dinner party is a disaster. Mrs S serves us with tongs, adding a twist, a flare, as she places the food onto our plates. Is she changing her mind? Has it already changed? That jewellery, now vanished from her chin. I watch her use the delicate tool. She hooks a clam from the shell and eats it without looking. Is he doing OK? The Housemistress pushes her spaghetti like a child. Oh he'll be fine. Thank you for having us, you know, I'd offer to have you both round in return, but the flat, it's hardly a flat, doesn't have enough room for a table, we could eat on our laps I suppose, I'd have to make something that is able to be eaten from a lap, what can be eaten from a lap? The Housemistress is avoiding her clams. She squeezes lemon over everything.

Do you like it? Mrs S speaks to me. But The Housemistress answers first, nodding, hiding the effort it takes her to swallow. It's delicious, best I've ever had. And you? Mrs S wants my opinion, maybe her mind is not yet changed. I try a clam, texture coughed in from elsewhere, tasting only blood inside my mouth. It's good. There's plenty, please help yourself. Won't he want to eat? The Housemistress points at the ceiling. Oh I've saved him some. How long have you been married? The Housemistress twists spaghetti around her fork and bites half. The rest falls back to the plate. She uses her finger to edge it onto a spoon and swallows without chewing. Hurriedly she drinks wine. Fifteen years. Fifteen years? Solid effort. I suppose it is. The Housemistress eats the rest in enormous mouthfuls. The clams, somehow, have disappeared. I look for them on the floor, under her plate. Nowhere to be seen. She senses my interrogation. Taps her pocket and winks. She has hidden the clams there. Her pocket, a shoreline.

So where did you meet? Oh, university. Eyes across the library floor? Something like that. She touches her throat. I imagine a necklace, some important necklace, once hanging there. The Housemistress puts down her fork. Leans forward. Do I have to keep guessing? No, no, it just isn't particularly interesting, we met through friends, the usual. Mrs S knows small talk too. What about you, is there anyone special? The Housemistress laughs. Brings a fist to the table. Me? Special? No, no, I don't do special. Oh, well. She is unnerved, Mrs S. For once she is unnerved, does not know where to position herself alongside The Housemistress. I want to be asked the same question but she can no longer face me. Who knows, maybe you will one day, these things take time. Sure, there's always time. The Housemistress glances my way. It is not subtle, our conspiracy. She grins. Time aplenty. I spear another clam into my mouth.

I wait for Mrs S to give another piece of herself to me. Nothing. She talks, she chews, every now and again bringing her hand up to cover her chin. Desperation, I try to force it into outrage, something like hurt pride, but it won't shift. What remains of our moment, the pull of her lips over my knuckles. I bend my forefinger, lifting it to my nose. I want her to catch me in the act. He's upstairs simpering, sleeping, the martini gingerly tasted then downed. She thinks of him, I do the same. But don't think of him, look at me instead, I could find her foot under the table and crush it beneath mine, I am too afraid. The Housemistress keeps talking. On the knuckle under my nose, barely a trace of her but enough. A smell that doesn't belong to me. Different chemistry, private, the soft steel of her mouth, her heat carried onto my skin. Then her gaze finally. I have learned its weight, it does not need to be met. I perform for her. My thumb rests under my chin. I pull each knuckle towards me in turn, inhaling, afterwards letting each finger catch my bottom lip. She watches. I'm too much.

A break in The Housemistress's story. I feel for her, she makes herself responsible, wants to recover the evening. Mrs S stands. Excuse me a moment, I might bring the patient some food. I get up, I can't help myself. Bathroom. The Housemistress rattles her pocket. Don't suppose you'd take these with you? The shells. I frown, in my urgency I can't find the funny side. No. Come on, I'd owe you one.

What am I going to do? Flush them? She is taken aback. Guess not, fair point, take your leave then. She waves me away. I check the kitchen, I check the hallway. Find her standing, staring at the front door, steadied against the wall. Planning an escape? She doesn't move, doesn't reply. I don't want to be honourable. What other choice do I have. It's OK, I can go, if you need. She lowers her head. You're always asking me if you should leave. Am I? Yes. Well I can. Shakes her head. I don't know what I'm doing. Yes you do. I use her formal tone, try to project a confidence I'm still learning. It is her now, coming towards me again, she is quick. A pause. Once again we listen to the house, for signs of him, for The Housemistress. Creak of floorboards, the bed shifting as he rolls over, a glass lifted and placed back on the table. She grabs my hand and this time presses it between hers. The force of her fingertips, her palm. It takes her whole body. Her wrists tremble. She presses so hard. I can't speak, surely the shapes of my fingers, my life-lines, are changing in her grip. She lets go. I lean closer, I will put my face in her neck. She stops me gently. Not now, not yet. OK, I agree, I don't ask when. A decision made between heartbeats. I will become whatever she wants.

The Girl who punched the boy has returned to the school. Just like that, she is in the corridor, reading the large blackboard which the teachers use to write their messages. Notes about meetings, PE lessons, changed classrooms. The Girls are not allowed to respond. They can only read and follow whatever instructions have been given. She takes it in, all of it, looking for something, maybe just wanting to appear busy. It is break time. No one speaks to her. The corridor is a river. People rush by, parting around her body. The second they are beyond her back they turn and look, she must be examined, her violence must be somewhere visible. The Girl seems smaller. This violence has rounded her shoulders, has sent her closer to the ground. I tap her lightly and she jumps. All defiance has long since left her. Hello. Hi. Oh hi. How are you? Good, great, happy to be back. A line that has been repeated all day. Were you looking for something? I point at the board. Maybe I can help? No, no, just catching up. Her brightness has a middle-aged falsity. Newly learned, a decoy. I panic. How was home? Home was home, nice to be with family. Right. She looks away, back at the board. Nothing here has changed has it? No, nothing. That's something. I try to see her hands, see her knuckles, but they are jammed inside the pockets of her blazer. So how are you? You already asked me that Miss. I did, yeh. The bell rings and she has an excuse to leave. See you. Yeh, see you. When she doesn't turn around I call again. See you, bye. Halfway up the stairs she pauses as if she might say something else. One hand on the banister. She waits a beat. But whatever it was, she decides against it. I want to call out. Ask her to tell me, to let me prove my worth.

The dead author competed in the same race. Once a year, up the steep hill behind the school, behind the hockey pitch, behind the fields. The last impressive height before the fells. Trees grown in a small circle at its crest. Rumours of witches abound amongst The Girls. Hangings, bodies on fire, familiars alive only in the dark. There was talk of cancellation this year, the teachers concerned about the heatwave. But it cannot be cancelled. It has never been cancelled. Not even during the wars. None remember that time directly but the dates are allowed to linger. Even in wartime, both wars, The Girls raced one another up the hill's sharp summit, required to slap the first ash with flat palms, and descend. The trophy, unpolished, sits in a cabinet in the school's largest corridor. Each winner's name is etched in gold onto the large wooden board that is hung alongside.

The fastest take only ten minutes. The slowest twenty, half an hour, once an hour. I walk past the river bend where I found The Girls drunk. Water still fills the curve but only just. Flint and slate lift their jagged features. Early, the heat is not yet dazzling. A scrim hung over the sun. Pigeons, the hard cackle of squirrels. Underneath the heavier trees a stink comes up off the ground. Active decay, layers of weaker branches, last year's leaves, soil, worms, whatever. The dead author wrote about the race, briefly. She described a tuberculosis outbreak. A few of those girls already buried. Many unable to run. Lungs too sticky. What the dead author liked was the ash, the slapping of it. If you do not remember to slap the ash then you are disqualified. You must have, as the history teacher gleefully explained to me, your wits about you. At the top the dead author pressed both hands to the bark. She took her time, other runners had to reach around her body to touch their own hands to the tree.

All must compete. I see The Nurse already at the base. Two wooden chairs established as the starting line. She wears her outfit. This is her special day. The promise of twisted ankles, heatstroke, nervous vomiting. She lines up jugs of orange squash on a trestle table. I call out to her, knowing it will break her focus. Her body remains clenched, even in a sigh. Is there food for them, for The Girls, too? She rolls her eyes. No, they will eat afterwards, in the dining hall. She has laid old cardboard flat on the ground so no earth will stain her stiff shoes, her white tights. It is a Saturday. This is my life. I pour myself a glass of the squash. She gasps. Grabs my wrist. For a second we both look at the white eyes of her knuckles. I feel her thumb's heartbeat. That, it's not for you. I'm not allowed to drink? You should have brought your own. Right. I peel away her fingers. Hold her briefly by the thumb. Right. I tip the squash back into the jug. Happily ignore The Nurse's horror. More people arrive. She is not yet here. I recognize other teachers. History, English. The head of PE is daring in shorts. She is young for the role. The Girls assume she is having an affair with each male member of staff. I like her enough. She looks good in the shorts. Her top too, sleeveless. A baseball cap low over her forehead.

A few of The Girls emerge from the lower woods. Already dressed to compete. This must happen in uniform. The most ludicrous part of the outfit is the gym knickers. Large, polyester. Navy with a crinkled racing stripe. Underneath is The Girls' own underwear, barely concealed, so they laugh at one another's patterns, frills. It is The Girls well known to the head of PE that have arrived first. They hang shoe bags over their shoulders. Stand with their hands also on their hips. Each of them wants to appear casual. As they speak to her they touch their hair, curling the ends of their ponytails. At the school it is a triumph to be sporty. Inside the shoe bags are light trainers, expensive, each one with its own set of hard spikes that are able to be screwed in and out, helping them grip the hill. The rest of The Girls will not have this same advantage. They will slip, tip backwards, their shoes too ordinary.

More of The Girls arrive. Some will dare to hide. Locked in bathrooms at the boarding houses, wandering out deeper into the woods, rolled under the hedges of the hockey field. They will be found. An enormous roll call is taken. I am beckoned over for it. The Nurse passes me, annoyed at my position. I have a chair. A sign of some importance. Thick wedge of names under my elbows. The whole school, alphabetical. Miss, Miss we're not feeling well, there's something wrong, we're not well. These two plead with me. Younger, maybe eleven. Each touches her stomach to indicate a mysterious pain. On the opposite side to me is one of the school's administrators. Gleeful. Licking the tip of her pencil. She is within earshot. I can only shrug my shoulders. Sorry, I'm sorry, there's nothing I can do. As if you're even sorry, as if. They walk away, keeping their shoulders slumped for my benefit, hands still cradling their bellybuttons. I mark their names off the list. Others stretch in patches of shade. Pulling their gym knickers over their underwear as they bend to touch their toes. Unsure, they try to copy the motions of The Girls who own the better shoes. Their manoeuvres are more complex. Legs twisted under chins and released with deep breaths. A slow circle made with the torso, ankles pulled gently from side to side. They help each other, steadying their bodies, recommending a shifted angle, a better technique.

She arrives. She arrives. Alone but not for long. Out of the woods. A fine white shirt designed to torture me and a sun hat I have not seen before. The brim is wide. Three pearl buttons undone. Already I am inside her mouth. She will have to pass my chair. It is perfect. She waves. I pretend it is not for me and look down at the stack of names. The PE teacher is already at her side. Where is her husband?

Somewhere, undoubtedly. Recovered now from his wasp sting.

The PE teacher might be flirting. I have lost sight of what is straight and what is not straight. She bends to scratch her thigh. Points out the hat, touching the brim. I wouldn't dare. The Girls begin to join them. Mrs S puts her arm around a few. Good luck, I can see the words on her lips, good luck. They are already competitive. Two begin to stretch again for her benefit. Everybody belongs to her. She looks at me again but does not wave. I look back. It is a thrill, to look back, to meet her gaze. Today I wear a t-shirt that skims my arms, the part of my arms I am proud of. I shift forward in my chair. Let my elbows rest on the stack of names. I wish I had The Housemistress's secret tattoos. I would show Mrs S a little of one now, that brief snake head. A queue is forming in front of me. The Girls emerge from the woods in packs. A group of five or six are escorted by the history teacher. Already captured, I assume, after their failed attempts to hide. They puff their chests, talk even louder, refusing to believe they should be in trouble. The history teacher is rough. He grabs the nearest elbows and propels them forward. He would not be afraid to call them his prisoners.

At last Mrs S approaches. Cutting in front of the queue, arriving at my side. She places her palm flat on my stack of names. Busy day? Yes. I give her the word, this yes. Yes. I want her to notice my mouth. Keep up the good work. The Girls call nervously to one another, voices growing larger, sending their fate into the sky, what else is there to receive it. She pauses for a minute. Nothing is said. Her palm remains on my table. We are only inches apart. Mr S, is he OK? Oh he's fine. Here somewhere. She looks out into the crowd. The whole school almost. The history teacher marches up the slight slope towards us. He is bright red, a different red to his alcoholism, a shade of recent protest and pleasure. Tweed waistcoat unbuttoned, blond hair stuck to his temples. Tell no one I was here. She leaves quickly, wanting to avoid him, slipping between The Girls, who smile at her. The history teacher notices her departure and, disappointed, slows his pace. He turns to The Girls that follow him reluctantly. I'll be watching you, no more fussing, do you hear, the race will be over quicker than you think, just get on with it. And there he is. Mr S. A bandage around his hand. I can't believe it. I wonder who has asked him about it. This was his aim, I assume, to be asked about it. Parents have arrived too. This is an historic event. They pay for the history. Over by the hockey fields they will have parked their washed cars, the wives smirking across the grass, the husbands downplaying their own enjoyment, woollen picnic rugs itchy and hot under their arms as they follow the signage through the woods.

Gather round gather round. The tree stump is enormous. Wide, splendid with rings. It has probably always been called from. Behind him, to his right, the hill. A smell emerges as if it is a body also suffering in the heat. Grass burning in the sun, but something wet still lingering at the centre. Yes hello welcome. He waves like a celebrity to the parents. Only the wives wave back. The light flirtation is customary in these circles. Welcome to the, goodness, where are we now, the eighty-first edition of the race, of our special race. People cup their hands over their eyes in order to see him better. The light is brilliant. She stands to one side of the stump, still with the PE teacher. I have to be jealous of everybody. She watches him, smiling.

I know The Girls can't wait to get going. His voice thrown out amongst the masses. He grows more comfortable. Well, most of The Girls can't wait to get going. His audience titters. The starting line is narrow. There are over three hundred of them. Stood in clumps across the field. They will be organized by age. The youngest allowed to begin first, the oldest farther back. I feel bad about the two with the sore bellies. I look for them in the rows of blue but cannot make them out. Ponytail after scraped ponytail. The hill stands just ahead. Enough time, sufficient metres, for those at the back to rush to the front, become leaders of the pack. For this scramble there is only The Nurse, no one else, no ambulance. The sanatorium has only a few beds. She has with her a first aid kit, opening it now, checking its contents, licking her lips.

Somebody hands Mr S a box. He opens it, revealing red silk. A gun in the centre. Perhaps not a gun, what could I possibly know, perhaps something only similar to a gun. It is almost the exact size of his hand, although his hands are large. He uses the one that is not bandaged. An extraordinary thing to see. This man on the tree stump, The Girls below him, eyes alert, ready to follow his fired shot. He puts the megaphone to his mouth. On your marks, get set. The gun goes. Birds, once quiet in the sun, are suddenly alarmed. Pigeons take off clumsily, sprung from themselves, branches turned to elastic. The woods shudder with their departure. Crows too, although more relaxed. Barking into the air only briefly before settling once again. The Girls are ferocious but there is not yet enough room for their ferocity. They push up against one another, shoulder hitting shoulder, elbows gone between ribs. I watch as one vomits from nerves, wipes her mouth, and runs towards the rest. The athletic group are easy to spot. They move quickly, around the outside, cutting back in just as the hill begins. I think I see the spikes catching the light even though they don't in reality. I have been in the heat too long. The sharp, metallic flashes are my own. Parents shout individual names. There is a funnel at the hill's base. The Girls must queue before the ascent. Some run around, trying to find a clever way up, not wanting to appear like everybody else. The hill is less forgiving on its far side. The Girls fade from view until they reappear, grass stains across their chests, having slipped or fallen. The athletes have made it to the front. Now they compete. With a few of the parents I move closer to the action. The sight is irresistible. Six, seven of them, calves rigid with effort, cheeks blown. They climb. Each foot lightly fixed to earth. Nearer to the trees, nearer to the ash, the atmosphere shifts. Heads glance back and forth. Examining the distance of one body to the next. There are three that begin to peel away. A fourth makes a break from behind. Sensing her chase, The Girl just in front jabs her spikes backwards. Her shin is punctured. Blood takes a few seconds to appear. Three holes, red running in steady, thin lines. She looks down, keeps running, reaching out a hand to grab the shirt of The Girl that has injured her but unable to make the distance. The parents standing with me do not react the way I feel they should. A husband and wife only clench their fists with anticipation. Decorum, non-stop decorum. Perhaps one of the athletes belongs to them. It happens again, the trees almost within reach, The Girl barely in second place launches the sole of her shoes, spikes bared like teeth, at The Girl in first. She misses, then finally catches her on the next attempt, ankle left ragged. How is it possible for something to matter this much.

She is nearby. I had not noticed her. A hand inside her shirt, pressed against her collarbone. Her fingers agitated beside her hip. He is not with her. The crowd forms a semicircle around the hill. The finish line is beside the old stone wall. Cheers erupt as The Girls begin to slap the ash. I can hear his voice, Mr S, although I cannot see him. Their arms are tired but they want to make a display, want to have the sound of flesh on bark. The dead author wanted the same. With a final effort they sling forward, the palm making dull contact. The descent is dangerous, the history teacher informed me, the descent is the most dangerous section by far. He slapped his own thighs, others in the staffroom looking our way, the legs give out, you can't grip. I asked if he had tried to climb the hill himself. No, no, no need, all you have to do is watch.

The Girls slip downwards, shuddering. These three do not stumble. The fourth is more tired, more desperate. She does not pick her way sideways as the others do. Her mind is elsewhere, her mind is already at the bottom. At the hill's lip she careens over, at first graceful, but soon the angle is too severe. Knees buckle as if hit from behind. She gives in to the fall. Eyes closed, no sound. Her torso whips and whips. The Girls in front look quickly over their shoulders but do not stop. Finally she is on her stomach, hands clawing at the grass. She looks over her shoulder and sees she is only halfway down. Her fingertips release. A plan to fall to the end. Slowly her body goes, too slowly, she knows it is pathetic. She tries to find speed, rolling, sliding, kicking at the ground. A fifth girl edges past, then a sixth, a seventh. She cannot fall to the bottom.

He is beside Mrs S. An arm around her waist. It is preventative. He does not want her to run to The Girl, whispering in her ear, hoping to soothe, not wanting dramatics. More of The Girls pass by. She refuses to get up. Already the other three are sprinting along the wall. The Nurse will not let them collapse as they cross the finish line. Gold, silver, bronze. She encourages them to walk, to keep their heart rates from falling too quickly. Mr S does not let his wife go. She twists under his arm. Her body is my body.

It is a relief, to be her body. Were it not for her I would not consider this. I am not a brave person. I run towards The Girl, then slow to a walk. Decorum, decorum. My shoes skid. On all fours it is easier to climb the hill's bulk. No longer dignified. I can hear her whimpers.

I can't move. You can, you can get up. I can't. The back of her neck is glazed with sunburn. You should finish. Why. She speaks into the grass. Why should I finish. Her question marks are missing. From this angle I can't see the holes on her shin. Blood not yet dried on her white socks. If I pinched the fabric it would leave a stain on my fingertips. I'll sit here until you get up. I move awkwardly upwards. Brace my legs to hold a position on the slope. Below a small crowd has turned towards us. The Nurse already at the bottom, shouting, waving, wanting everyone to notice the spectacle I have created. Mrs S has been released. She has moved away from him, standing slightly in front. His arms crossed against his chest. The bandaged hand held slightly aloft. I could get in trouble. The rules for the race are written down on some old piece of paper, carefully preserved behind glass, kept in the headmaster's study. I haven't read them. Intervention, though, intervention is surely cheating. I try to be tough. You can't just sit there. She turns her head. There are no tears, I am surprised, if I was her I would be crying. You can't just lie there. The Girls come down the hill in spates. The last of them. Most go slower now, carefully. A few call out her name, the one lying beside me. Not enough breath left for a full sentence. I try talking to her a final time. Your friends want you to finish. They're not my friends.

The crowd loses interest in us. Most walk towards the finish line to celebrate the winners. Even The Nurse gives up. As she leaves she casts her head over her shoulder again and again. She wants me to know it is not over. I've broken a rule. Only Mrs S remains. I can't see her face. Her hat, the stupid, wonderful hat. Is she proud of me? She is unbearably still. Her hand no longer inside her shirt. Maybe I was wrong. Perhaps she did not want to rescue The Girl. But it is her thing, to rescue them. That is all she has, to rescue them. There is nothing I can do now but sit. The Girls have stopped coming down the hill. It is over. At the finish line The Nurse hands out her orange squash. Somewhere The Housemistress, the PE teacher, the history teacher mingle. Mrs S should be with them. Momentarily she allows herself to be forgotten.

How long do you think you'll lie there for? I don't care. Are you injured? Can you walk? Of course I can walk, I could run if I wanted. A blade of grass is caught between her teeth. With a loud suck of her tongue she sets it free, spitting it back onto the ground. Well I don't want to sit here all day. Then don't. The Girl rolls over. She licks the flat of her palm and wipes at the holes in her shin. Gross, no? Now a question mark, her tone invigorated. Tiny chunks of skin loosen. Dint after dint. Drying blood comes off in crumbs. She antagonizes one hole enough that fresh blood begins again. Somebody should clean that properly for you. Whatever it doesn't hurt. She notices Mrs S, has noticed Mrs S, perhaps that is why she rolled over. There's always next year. I don't plan on being here next year. Right.

Do you two need help getting down, what's the hold-up? Mrs S looks at us. We are both pleased. We're fine. She walks towards the hill's base, her hat now flapping in one hand. It is good to see her eyes. If you don't come down I shall have to climb up and it will be a sight. Her foot scrapes the earth. A sight. The Girl laughs. A real laugh. She gets up and offers me her hand, as if I am the one in need. I refuse it. She shrugs and begins to balance downwards, moving her feet with expertise, at speed. I try to follow. The hill betrays my shape, my stance. It doesn't believe I can make it down. I can't. I slip. The Girl is already at the bottom. She releases her long hair then ties it up again, smoothing her temples, scraping her fingers across her crown. Go sideways, she calls up to me, turns her body in an example. Lift your knees, go sideways. I don't listen. I stand, twist my neck as if it is on purpose, that I had to stand, that I had to stop moving for some great reason. They watch in silence. I want to tell them to stop watching. Behind me, behind the hill, the fells doze. A single bird of prey calls, breaking through the sound of the crowd still ecstatic at the finish line. I make this bird my great reason. I look for it. It angles over the next field. I know nothing about birds.

Mrs S crouches and looks at The Girl's injuries. One hand on the back of her calf. The Girl balances by placing a palm on her back. They share an easy femininity, a peculiar safety in one another's presence. The hat lies on the ground beside them. I begin to move again. Encouraged by their distraction. I make it to the bottom unscathed. They are deep in conversation. The Girl's chin juts. Now she is close to tears, holding back, it takes her whole chest. Mrs S soothes. You should go and see The Nurse, get those war wounds taken care of. I can't just go over there. You can, you will, look at those, very impressive. Mrs S reaches out towards the cut on her face. The Girl considers this for a moment. They are aren't they, they're pretty impressive, war wounds. She looks down at her legs. Hairless, she already shaves. Her age is difficult to pinpoint. She is taller than I realized. Mrs S rubs her back. Go on. Reluctantly The Girl makes her way across the field. She does not turn around to look at us again. A limp is added to her walk.

Hello. We have not been alone since her hallway. Hello. At the finish line he is on his megaphone again. Performing a ceremony of cheap medals that The Girls are allowed to keep. They come from the larger supermarket, on the edge of town, metal only from a distance, plastic up close. Even The Girl in first place will not be allowed to touch the real trophy. The crowd stands in its semicircle, backs to us. It was good of you, to go up there. I'm not sure. No, it was. I wanted to, I wanted to go myself. I saw. You did? Of course. The bird of prey calls again. Broken, a note snapped in two, thrown back up the fells. I pretend again to search for it. Its large wings are nowhere to be seen. My gaze returns to her face. She puts a finger to her lip and pauses. Holds it there. One second, two seconds, three seconds. With fast violence her finger moves, pushing into her mouth, a glimpse of teeth, back and forth. At last she bites down. Releases. We are in public. Unable to take me in her mouth, she imitates my finger, our kitchen scene. This is what it is to be wanted. Loving her will be impossible. There is nothing I can do to stop it.

A note in my cubbyhole. Both the drama teacher and the maths teacher separately informed me. They were gleeful. I rarely have anything in my cubbyhole. An enormous set of shelves, kept in the staffroom, used between the adults only. The others share books, jumpers, wrapped presents on birthdays, inside jokes, food made at home. A piece of paper, torn. Requesting my help at the church at one. Already it is twelve forty-five. I do not recognize the hand-writing. Each letter careful, perhaps a revised draft, other versions fluttering to the floor.

Anything exciting? The history teacher looms. Nothing like that. Like what? He thinks he is charming. Nothing friendly, no gifts, not a gift voucher. His chest is only inches from my chest. I am taller than he is, even as he stretches up his calves. I can almost see the top of his head. Right you are, shame, maybe next time eh. Yeh maybe next time. I push open the door and read the note again in the corridor. Come to the church for 1 p.m. That's it, that's all.

In the bathroom I look at my face. It has been a while. There I am, never as I expect. My hair greasy at my temples. Jaw belonging to my father, to my grandfather. Masculine legacies. I am not proud of my father but I am proud of his jaw. Unbreakable. His brow too. Chin, eyes, both my mother's. Although something else has happened to my eyes. They can no longer be placed. The colour a light brown, some depth, then a limit. People mistake me for cold. I don't know what it means when it is said to me, to be cold. That I am not able to be immediately understood, to be read one way or another. My nose, once broken, is no longer anybody's, not even mine. A car crash years ago. A scar across my cheekbone. Two more below my ear. This landscape, my landscape. I rub my eyes with water.

Two of The Girls enter and join me at the mirrors. Hi Miss. In unison. There must be some boys due to visit from the other school. They apply lip gloss, checking one another's. Little licks of mascara. More lip gloss, a fingertip to the corner of the mouth, adjusting a smear. They take steps back and forward. Contemplating each other from a distance. More make-up is added. Pinkish eyeshadow is applied with the curved sweep of a thumb. A brush is dusted with bronzer, pale concealer dabbed under their eyes. They clasp hands then release. Their belief in each other is genuine, their beauty unstoppable. Every inch of the present tense lived. Even as they piss, separated by stalls, they chat. Once re-emerged they are back to the mirror again, turning, bringing their chins up and down. One last look. See you Miss. Yeh see you Miss.

I wait a few minutes until they will be clear of the corridor. Through the front door and out onto the path. It is twelve fifty-five. I walk slowly, only a few minutes from the church. Twelve fifty-seven. If it isn't her in the church I might die. Flowers on the bushes have bloomed yellow. Above, the sky is a bruise. Sped-up, faster than flesh, darkening at the centre. Maybe a storm, finally a storm. The first church gate. I don't go inside immediately. I've made it to twelve fifty-nine. It would be better to be late, to seem as though I could have been elsewhere. A roll of thunder, no rain. Lightning. The dead author did not write through summer. She needed the damp. Slick rock faces, feet sinking into sodden grasses, longer, darker nights. The hairs on my arms rise, hopeful, in anticipation of rain. My watch will not make it to one. The door to the church is closed. She must already be inside. Still no rain. I look up, the sky bulges. I am trapped under a glass. The air hot as my breath. I step inside. Hello, hello. My voice is good in the church, it has body, it takes possession. Up the aisles are roses in buckets. Pink, red, peach. Stems long. Some are not in buckets but jars, the roses leaning hard, about to tip. Hello. She waves. It is her, waving. At the broken window, layers of black plastic billow. Still no repair.

Aha, you got my note. Yes. I tap my pocket. Well we're flower-arranging. She is in the shorts again. A shirt too, although different, not one I have seen before. The cotton rougher. We greet each other as we always have. At a distance. I want to move closer to her but don't. Here, so the plan is, arrange these in the larger ones, you see. Along the far walls of the church, underneath the stained-glass windows, are large brass vases. What is it for? A wedding, there will be a wedding, tomorrow. Who? Who is getting married? Oh somebody, I don't know, the vicar asked if I would sort the flowers, we have flowers in excess, I underestimated the job of course and thought you'd be able to help. I play dumb and fold my arms. You know this isn't my skillset. Oh I know. A flicker across her face, she reaches into my ribs. They give her these jobs to ensure she feels important. She knows it, I know it. No doubt her husband's idea, delivered to her by the vicar.

It won't take much arranging. I reach out and touch a rose now, peach, perhaps the variety the history teacher obsessed over. How so? Well they're all roses, won't they all just look fine together, doesn't matter how we arrange them. That's not quite true, there's a certain art. Is this the author's? To avoid the thorns I hook my fingers under the rose's head and lift it free. That? No, I'm not sure I'd want her rose growing in my garden. Why not? I don't know, it's named after her skin, only men abide that sort of morbidity, or worse, think it's romantic. She walks towards a pew and sits. I look closely at the colour of the rose between my fingers. I find it vaguely horrible, as all roses are vaguely horrible, love's caricatures. I'm with you. Lightning. Thunder goes again. We are quiet underneath it.

Moody out there. It's nice. You like a storm? I don't think it's quite a storm, not yet, no rain. No wind either. A bloated stillness. The stained glass is stern in the failing light. The eyes of the saints cannot be seen. It is encouraging. I don't mind a storm, I hope the weather doesn't change, this weather has been a blessing. A blessing? Oh you know what I mean, if not, I mean it does change, this wedding will be a wash-out. She gets up again, wiping the backs of her thighs, moving towards me. They asked for roses? No but they will get what they're given. I've not seen roses in church before. She doesn't answer, perhaps she didn't hear, she lifts two buckets then places them both back down again. You know, we need more light, I wonder where the light switches are. I follow her towards the back, near the room where The Girls ring the bells. She runs her hand along the wall.

Perhaps in here. Beside the bell room is another door. She explains as she moves. The vestry, this is the vestry, where the vicar sweats it out. A desk. Two sets of robes on wire hangers. One embellished, red and gold. At his desk are two Bibles, bright Post-its growing out of each like weeds. There are handwritten notes. Sentences aggressively underlined. Two empty plastic bottles of water. Three dirty coffee mugs. Ah, here. She flicks each switch. Bulbs flare above the pews, brighter nearer the organ. Each archway has its own spotlight, a heavenly slight, as if the congregation might only be inches away from ascending.

I stand next to her. She darts away, suddenly remembering my question, suddenly remembering my body. Roses aren't so strange in churches, it's associated with miracle, with miracles, it could be a miracle, the rose. How so? Oh I can't recall the precise details, from memory I think various people slipped bread to starving Christians and when they were caught the stolen bread turned into roses. Handy. Yes, handy, and there was a saint, I can't remember her name, you wouldn't find her on stained glass, her dead body apparently smelled like roses when the tombstone was lifted. What were they doing lifting her tombstone? Hoping for a miracle, of course. Makes sense, what else could smell like death but roses. She smiles. I think of eating a rose, whole, a bud. Biting through the clutched petals as if it were a loaf's heel.

Do you believe in God? What a question! I lift one of the Bibles from the vicar's desk. Do you? No, but I get it, I get why God works for some people. I try to read the vicar's notes. His handwriting is minuscule, littered with exclamation marks. Why, what do you get, what is it about God that you get? You haven't answered the question. I haven't, have I. She sighs. No, yes, no, who cares, I rather like the look of God, well Jesus anyway, he has a charming aesthetic, that's the whole idea, isn't it? You know I'm not sure that's yours to read. She nods at the Bible. I don't put it down. Aren't you interested? To see how a man of God thinks? I want to seem coy, intellectual. We know how he thinks, we listen to him three times a week. She reaches up and tries to loosen the Bible from my fist. It is playful, she is forced closer. Both of us have been looking for a way in. She does not let go, leans forward first, or we lean forward together, my memory has no chance, later I will be desperate to remember. It will fail me.

She brings her hand to my throat, sliding up my neck, gripping below my jaw. Soft, but she threatens to tighten. The pressure of our mouths is not enough. Her desire is equal to mine, she shocks me. I thought I was alone, that I had lured her in, mistakenly assumed a passivity. Instead it is me she takes, in the half-light, the bright robes catching the edge of my vision. Her fingers at the base of my skull, pushing me harder, the full expression of her want. I stumble backwards. She moves with me. Her tongue so close to mine I almost choke. She whimpers. I open my mouth wider. Let her flex in and out, she starts her fucking here. Wraps a leg around mine and squeezes, my knee buckles. There is still enough storm outside. Static, peals of thunder. How she shocks me, stealing my breath. Her hand moves from my throat. She pulls back and forth between my legs. I did not think it would be so easy to submit. I did not know it was something I wanted. My body positions itself gratefully. For once I move before I think. Knees apart. Wrap my hand around her forearm. I release her, crack my chest, spread my arms wide across the desk, not yet touching her. Hips tilted, shoulders rolled back. She is encouraged. Comes to me. The electricity of a zipper undone.

At first I can't translate her whispers. Then I hear: yes yes yes. Not only said to me, but to herself, she creates a chorus. An expertise to her movements. She pushes inside me. More, I want more, it is not like me to want more. My hand back around her forearm. I hold harder. The widening ache of her fingers. More, I say again, more. I feel the bump of her knuckles. I take her other hand and push it flat against my chest. She wants my clothes off. I can't, not now. The binder is a protective layer. Her palm flattens against me and moves across the fabric like water. She lets me keep it on, keep on the t-shirt. Doesn't yet ask why I won't undress. I know the questions will come, I am able to savour this moment, to live in the time before. Her fingers can't move as deep as she wants. Move, get on the floor. I don't respond quick enough. Please, get on the floor. Please. I shift downwards. On my knees I lean back, pause, try to adjust the rise of my jeans, she doesn't let me, forcing me flat, guiding the back of my head so it does not collide with stone. Returns her hand to my chest. Her stroke, the pressure of a river. She comforts me as she thrusts, arching her back with each movement, her heat against my stomach. Is this OK? Yes. The size and shape of her. Three fingers, four.

I am close, I don't know how to come like this, I will learn. I pull her hand free and finish myself. She watches. Eyes circling my throat. Now I happen through her gaze. A heap of knuckles. I reach up and lick the sweat from her neck, behind her ear. All I have is the arch of her back. I try not to overthink her pleasure. Her finger against my lips. Silence has such a violent quality. This is what she wants, the violent quality. I steady my breath. The church hums, desperate for noise, for our noise. She presses her hips into mine. The humming lifts an octave, it becomes high-pitched, frustrated at our pinched breath, the hairs on end, the prickling skin. I lift her up, we switch, she opens to me. My tongue between her legs now, honeyed, large. I fuck her like this, with my tongue, until I am dizzy. Mouth swollen, muscles swollen. Hold her thighs. My knees purpling against the stone floor. She tightens around me. The silence has ended. I wait on all fours. She wipes my chin, my nose, with her thumb. Places her thumb in her mouth.

Standing, she warms my hands between hers. My mind gone weak. I don't want to return to it, my thinking. She speaks, her breath still heavy. Did you know? I can't answer. There is a chance I will cry, what I suspected but had not yet experienced, that sex can transform faster, harder, than anything else, the sensation still moving through my body. The moment I start to think, the moment I answer her, I will abandon the transformation. I don't understand how to hold on to it, how to carry it forward. My reaction will frighten her. I gather myself. Swallow. Did I know what? She pinches me. Don't be facetious, I mean before, before the kitchen, did you know how I felt? No, I didn't, I mean I thought about it, but I didn't know if you were thinking about me, I didn't think anything would ever actually happen. Why? Come on. What? You're married, very much to a man, it didn't matter what there was between us. So you wanted me. I don't stand to meet her. She bends, runs two fingers down my ear as if it is her own. You wanted me too. Her nail digs into my earlobe. I want you too. Lightning, we wait for the thunder. She rolls her eyes. Calls into the rafters, as if addressing Him directly.

God, how clichéd, to have a storm, unbearable. The turn of her watch. I'll leave first OK. OK. Her sentence is almost a question, lifting before the last word, then flattening out into an instruction. I prefer it. She turns back once. I can't see her face. The door closes heavily behind her. I feel its weight bang against my chest.

The drama teacher wants to appear on the verge of tears but cannot actually cry. She addresses The Girls before the first dress rehearsal. Hands clasped and resting over her heart. Her voice manages to waver, as she intends, but the tears will not come. She blinks, hopeful, but her face remains dry. The Girls seem awkward, left out of the emotion she is desperate to include them in. They watch their shoes. A few glances swiped at The Girl closest, wanting to make sure the awkward feeling is shared. I am here early. Not by request but by error. I thought the performance started half an hour sooner. I wait once again in the theatre's back seats.

The Girls' costumes are simple. Black tops, black skirts, black heels. All have dark-red lipstick. It has been applied carefully, in dense layers, making them afraid to move their mouths. The black lace veils are already in place. A few clutch copies of their lines, running fingers over their high-lighted sections, last-minute checks. My darlings I'm so proud of you all, very proud, you've worked terribly hard. They nod. I wait for her, for Mrs S. She asked that I come, that I watch the dress rehearsal with her. It is not so odd for us to be together here. I was Pepe, she was Pepe. At last the door creaks open. She wears jeans, she is romantic. The jeans have been carefully chosen, an echo, me into her, the suggestion we are alike. She doesn't wave at me. How long have I wanted her wave? I see her palm lift, the fingers almost flex, paused mid-thigh. Oh you're here, how wonderful. The drama teacher grabs her hand. Wouldn't miss the big debut, well almost debut. Mrs S places her other hand on top of their knot and squeezes. You're very kind. The drama teacher rumples her face. Still no tears. It pleases me, to have noticed her malfunction.

The Girls are agitated. If Mrs S is here things are deadly serious. This is the person to impress, more than their parents, more than their friends. Their lips twitch, expressions heavy under the make-up. Hello. Most greet her. The Girl playing Adela does not. She remains the largest personality. Her black skirt is cut on a bias, separating her from the rest. She bends her visible leg, tilts her hip. Behind the stage the enormous Guernica has been installed. Hanging from the ceiling, rippling slightly, moved by the opening and closing of the large doors. It has enough menace. Tenderness accidental, found in places where the paint has thickened or where one stroke has run over a boundary. I search for the parts I completed but can no longer remember what I did. Oh! Mrs S looks towards it. Oh! It doesn't look half bad! The Girls agree through pursed lips. Yes! Not bad.

The drama teacher has not yet undone the knot of their hands. She moves it up and down. It is marvellous, marvel-

lous, oh you did a marvellous job. Thank you. Mrs S steps
to the side, trying to pull herself free. The drama teacher
lets go but quickly takes her by the shoulder instead. The
Girls have been working so hard, we've had our ups and
downs, but we're there, we're practically there. Mrs S
addresses the group. That's good, I'm looking forward to it.
Yes, yes. Finally she is free to come to me. I have barely
taken a breath. I do now, hard, becoming an unintentional
gasp. Before she can sit down she is forced to re-engage.
The drama teacher claps. No! No, we don't start here, we
start out there. She points at the door. Come, come. The
Girls move to the side of the room and collect objects from
the floor.

I walk behind Mrs S, I did not see her shoulder blades,
next time we fuck I will turn her around. Outside, The
Girls wait at the top of the corridor. It is late but not yet
dark. Black paper has been applied to the few windows.
Mrs S brushes my side. Nothing is accidental anymore. I
jolt. She does it again. The drama teacher snaps a lighter. I
see what The Girls collected from the floor. Their fingers
looped through matching candleholders, old-fashioned, the
metal winking. She walks along and lights each wick in
turn. The Girls are not relaxed. They hold the fire
cautiously, as far from their chests as is possible, while also
wanting to seem unafraid.

We stand to one side, Mrs S and I. Behind us is the beginning of a staircase. Below our feet is the library reserved for
the sixth-formers. There is nobody else around. At an

extravagant nod from the drama teacher The Girls begin to process. Single-file, heads bowed. Rather than lift their feet they shuffle, keeping time with one another. The drama teacher is desperate to make eye contact with us, to make sure we are having an experience, that we are involved in her atmosphere. I avoid it. I look at the red tiles, moving sideways ever so slightly to be able to see Mrs S's foot. She wears sandals. The sweet pile of bones, its hesitation. She crosses one leg over the other. The hem of her jeans rides up. Her shin, like a mast, oh God. She does make eye contact with the drama teacher. It is her duty. She is encouraging, not smiling, but bunching her bottom lip so she appears moved. Perhaps it is genuine. I don't know.

The Girls' fear of the flames is distracting. They don't dare look anywhere else for fear of setting fire to The Girl just ahead. Before the turn into the theatre they stop dead. The Girl at the front howls. It is impressive. She plays the tyrant of a mother. This procession is a funeral, or is at least funereal. The father has died, The Girls forced into years of mourning. Without sex. She howls once more. It manages to be paralysing. Even the drama teacher flinches, shocked, as if she doubted The Girl could ever find such a sound. The theatre doors are propped open. They go inside, processing, and gratefully blow out their candles, setting the holders on the floor. The task does not look easy. They have been required to do it in character, crouching, trying to maintain the tension from the corridor. We follow, the drama teacher sitting beside us, sighing loudly. The Girls

line up, evenly spaced, and begin to recite the Lorca poem
in Spanish. They have learned to roll their rs. It would have
been better had they not, the effect is pretentious, their
mouths flaking lipstick as they perform each syllable. The
drama teacher sighs again and closes her eyes. She wants us,
she needs us, to know every wave of sentiment that rolls
through her body. Mrs S crosses her legs then uncrosses
them. She knows I am watching. She spreads them wider.
Puts her hands on her thighs and squeezes. The drama
teacher sits right beside her, sighing, carrying on. She turns
and whispers loudly. You won't believe how long it took to
get them here, I mean really, well you know, don't you, you
saw them before. Mrs S nods appreciatively. Her legs still
wide. I hope she is only herself around me. That the rest,
this nod, is not another version of her, but a farce. I wonder
if we will fuck later, I am already wet, she could fit her
whole hand inside me. Church stones at my knees. I will
know her better than anyone.

The Girls finish the poem. Verde que te quiero verde.
The Guernica no longer ripples. It has been lit clumsily so
only the horse can really be seen. They move to the sides of
the stage and pull chairs across in a learned arrangement.
Obviously we'll have help, we'll have backstage people, on
the actual night. The drama teacher's whisper grows even
louder. This isn't done to include me, she speaks only to
Mrs S, she doesn't care who hears, and so here I am, forced
to listen. She sits half-slumped in her seat, hips thrust
forward, more of that awful sentiment rippling down her

stomach. Mrs S is required to nod again. I want to grab her chin and hold it tight, hold it still. The Girls move on to their dialogue. They cave into the chairs, each opening a fan, bodies languid in the phantom heat of Spain. The drama teacher sighs again. I could hit her. The feeling is strong enough that I clench my fist.

I wait a moment before crossing the road. She is arriving at the church. Confident, her posture betrays nothing, unlike mine. Summer does not afford us much cover. A car passes and she does not flinch. I do. Even as she unlocks the huge doors, planting her feet on the ground and pulling them open with force, she does not look over her shoulder. Has she done this before? Our time together is rare. I want it to be perfect, to always say the right thing, to be more like her. I watch until she has gone inside. Another car, beeping furiously. I stand still on the tarmac, the driver staring at me in the rear-view. The gravestones glow orange. Soon I will be between her legs. All day I have been anticipating what I will do. I know she likes my tongue not on her clit but stiffened inside her, moving quickly back and forth, my face ready to disappear. Afterwards she will lift me free. Tease me with one finger, or tease herself, until she cannot resist, fucking me with her whole hand. All of her. I will have it.

I understand why The Girls need the trees, need the wood-lands. Pigeons growl softly from a beech's canopy. Maybe to match the river. All throat, I feel it. There is no one else here. The Girls have lessons. I walk out to meet Mrs S. Following in their footsteps, The Girls. The dead author too. Supposedly her second most famous novel was written beneath a particular oak. Which one was it? I look around. There are three in my immediate vision. I test one out. No way of telling if it is a celebrity or not. All trees have a celebrity quality, anyway. I sit on the ground. The temperature is cooler, damper. I feel the hot rash at my cheeks fade. I will be handsome for her. Footsteps? No. My listening does not work here, under these leaves. Afraid that if I call out something else will call back. That is what The Girls like, I suppose. We agreed to meet, she is already late. Always held up. In my hand is the stained glass. Wrapped and wrapped in plastic bags. I wish I had made a more glamorous effort. I want her to be moved. The most painful desire of all, surely, to want somebody to be moved, to want to be so significant. I could bury it in the ground rather than give it to her. I won't, obviously I won't. This

time there are definitely footsteps. I choose a position.
Decide to stay sitting beneath the oak. I breathe through
my sexuality. The knot at the centre of me loosed. I am
handsome. Legs folded. Unfolded. It is not footsteps, no,
some other noise.

At last she appears. Searching for me without calling out.
Her head swivels. Running the trees, the space between, the
slope to the river. Me, waiting to be found. She walks
slowly. Says nothing, not until she is close. I am hunted,
turns out I love to be hunted, each day she reveals a new
fact about me, about my body. Sits, knee heavy against my
own. She executes these small things. Knows herself.
Lovely spot, although rather melancholic don't you think.
Why? All these trees, the darkness, the damp. I don't think
so. No? No. I pick up her hand and put it around my
throat. She waits a second, an entire heartbeat, before
squeezing. I want to be fucked here. She doesn't respond at
first. Hand tightening. Lets my mouth fail, pushing against
her, leaving hers only slightly open. That hand. Ice of her
fingertips. Have you been good? I don't know where her
language comes from. Yes. Said like a piece of muscle, voice
changed by her grip. There is a right answer. She kneels and
winces. Ground sharp. Skirt splayed. Tree trunk against my
skull. Whispers now, she is so easily kind. Are you alright?
Is this alright? Yes. Her hand moves underneath my shorts.
Rubs, has learned I like this too. Have you been good? A
flash of nerves before her face changes. This time I don't
answer. Let my body beg instead. It does a better job, she

can taste it. Her tongue is not part of the deal. I pinch the hand around my throat. Not that, not now, fuck me, please, fuck me. There is the force I want. Her desire, made known. A whole chest behind each movement. Folded into me, head butting my collarbone, she needs to grunt. I did not think I could love her more. Sent backwards into the tree, what could be better?

Afterwards she makes herself into an offering. Weak, straddling my lap. Asks for nothing, needs me to decide. I shift forward, let her ankles close behind me. Enough knowledge, now, between us. The ghost of my hand already there. She anticipates it. Rides, calling out to my hand, calling out to the ghost of my hand, all the times we have fucked before. Afterwards we wipe our mouths. She stays across me. Our smell. The leaf stuck to the side of her thigh. I pick it free. She shivers. She is already becoming absent-minded, switching gears as she does, thinking outside of the woods. If I'm going to give her the stained glass it has to be now. She has either ignored or failed to notice the package beside me. I reach for it. Here, I have something for you. You do? She frowns at me, does not like to be surprised, to feel out of control. Behind us sheep bleat, only just grown out of being lambs, voices still have that despair. What is it? Come on you're about to see. I watch her fingers struggle with the plastic bags, handles tied around hands. She works at it faster. Getting closer. I realize she could cut herself and panic. Hang on, let me. I retrace my pattern. Impatient, are we. Not that. I pull the fragment free carefully. There.

What? What have you done? She takes it from me. Handles it the same way I first did. Entranced, fearful. What kind of rebellion is she capable of, I wonder. She stands, finds the light fallen through the branches, holds it up. You've stolen it? I guess so. You just took it, just like that? Yes. It suits her, as I knew it would. The white of the snake-woman's face turned warm by the fabric of her dress. The green foliage brief across her cheek as she lifts it closer, investigating that eyelid, the gentle persuasion. I'm shocked, I can't quite believe you've done it. Why not? I don't know, won't he notice once the window repairs begin, that this part is missing? Of course he'll notice. And I'm supposed to keep it? Yes. She is at odds with herself. Impressed, I hope, by my audacity. Envious, even. That I still have such will.

She tuts. It will drive him insane. Which him? Don't be like that, you know who I mean. The men in her life. She is talking about the vicar. He'll recover, they just make a replacement for it. And you know that for sure, do you? Yes, that's what he said himself, in case we couldn't find each bit, or something had shattered into too many pieces. Right, right. Yet there remains part of my gesture she doesn't understand. Would have been better to give it to her in the middle of our fucking, her hand still around my throat. Then she would see right through me – why not have a piece of the architecture, a piece of the building, our only witness it will dawn on her later, when she is alone, maybe. I think she is also frightened. And yet. She does not ask me to take it back, does not ask me to return it, which she could, it would be easy. Nor can she figure out how to say thank you. Oh, here she is, caught between her worlds.

Straight in the pocket my friend, tell me that's not sapphic, clams in the pocket, fucking clams. As we walk past the bus stop The Housemistress drops suddenly onto the plastic bench. We are listless after the pub. Still sweating. Tonight she is in shorts, the weather too warm for anything but. We have matching damp hairlines. I sit beside her. Legs sticky. Do buses even come here? I try and make out the faded schedule, see lumps of chewing gum, tooth-marks intact. I've never seen one. Look, there's the Big Dipper. The Housemistress points upwards at the famous series of stars. Yeh I know that one. She is easily distracted, drunker than I am. Through the plastic shelter the moon is almost full, lending a theatrical light, changing her profile as she looks upwards. So what did you do with the clams? What? The Housemistress squints at the moon, fastening shut one eye and then the other. Next she touches the tip of her forefinger to her thumb and tries to fit the moon inside, making a circle of knuckle and muscle and skin, zooming in and out. What did you do with the clams, once we'd left? Oh fuck I can't remember, threw them in the river I think, back where they belong, ugly little things.

I think of The Housemistress balancing on the slippery stones, emptying the pockets of her suit, those small shells with their dead tongues floating downstream. I smile. She once again makes the circle with her thumb and forefinger. Whispers in mock conspiracy: The moon is so a lesbian. A grandiose sigh. How's that? Just look at it. She offers me her thumb and forefinger and I peer through. Her skin smells of earth, then something stale and sugary, maybe beer. Hemmed in by her hand like this, the moon becomes more pronounced, a trick. Of course it is no bigger but suddenly it seems to advance. I blink and it remains, a sequin rolled into my eye socket. Come on. She is excited by her own drunken theory. Just look at it, it controls the sea, summoning the tides, what could be more butch. At this she flexes one arm. Biceps lovely.

The possible scale of lesbian qualities pleases me. That it could be lesbian to control the sea, to beam into households on summer nights. That anything could be lesbian, all you have to do is announce it. I squeeze her biceps when it is offered to me. To play her game I would have to think of something else, something huge and non-human, some-thing that has this matching, inexpressible lesbianism. I clap my hands. Then the ocean too, surely that's a lesbian, so close to the moon, you know, under its command. Yes! Yes, you've got it, I wonder if it's the whole ocean, or particular seas, something like the Atlantic, now that's pure dyke, all huge waves and cold temperatures. She slides onto her back. Legs propped up on one another. God I wish there was somewhere else to get a drink around here, the end of the world, we've already fucking found it, it's here, right fucking here. I've still got that tequila at mine? Ooft, tequila could be a bit harsh on the old system. She pats her stomach. So that's a no then? Calm down, didn't disagree did I, got to take what I can where I can. I get to my feet. Come on then. She stands and salutes the moon, here's to you faithful leader.

She sings a song I don't recognize. The word lovesick on repeat. Enjoying each other, we take the longer route, looping up towards the church. In the moonlight each tombstone happens twice. Upright and then in shadows laid out on the ground. Suddenly she stops and puts a finger to her lips. In a stage whisper, breath full of booze. Listen, what's that? At first I hear nothing. Slowly it comes to me. The sound of The Girls, somewhere nearby. Hushed and hushing, a giggle uncoiling every few seconds. Neither of us wants to find the scene and be responsible for it. For a few seconds we stand still. The Housemistress swallows loudly, perhaps willing herself to sober up. It is late. The Girls should not be out of bed. Should not be anywhere near the church. Last time she, we, let them off easy. The Housemistress pinches one of her cheeks, then the other. Better go and deal with this, right? Yeh, right, let's go see.

Around the far side of the church, opposite Mrs S's house, is the other graveyard, the one filled with the dead author's schoolmates. The Girls are here, a larger group, maybe ten or so. Each beside a different tombstone. Tea lights burn in lines. I feel a wave of fear. Here things are less recognizable. There are no bottles of alcohol that I can see. The Girls don't even register our arrival. The Housemistress marches straight to the gate, calling out to them once she stands at the top of the stone steps. Oi, oi. Shock in her voice. An inability to think of the right word upon which to enter the situation, their attention too far away. The Girls react slowly, turning their heads, necks unnaturally soft. The Housemistress doesn't bother to whisper. What the fuck, are they on drugs, fuck. The Girl closest to the path laughs. It is a solid, frightening sound, a tumbling rock.

OK, OK, enough, what have you taken. The Housemistress strides between the tombstones. It's very important you tell me what you've taken. Don't worry, it's organic. More giggles fire into the air. She's a ceremony, don't you see. The Girl spins. The Housemistress walks quickly, peering at the ground, kneeling at certain spots. She finds no evidence. Panicking she grabs the hands of The Girl nearest to her and tries to prise open her fingers. Get off me, you're not allowed to touch me, you fucking dyke. What have you taken? It's important you tell me. The Housemistress does not let go of her hand. Tell me, you have to tell me. I don't have to tell you anything. Still, there is a fragility to The Girl's resistance. Her pupils snap. Every word requires an additional ounce of energy.

Yeh don't ruin our trip, another pipes up, just as weakly. The Girl furthest away. Slouched against the wall, feet pressed against the front of a tombstone. It is The Girl who punched the boy, her features hardened into silver. Your trip? The Housemistress turns to look at me. Will you be helping at all or just fucking standing there? Glares at me. She is not yet sober although she wants to be. I try to only raise my voice, but cannot find the right volume, instead I shout. No one can leave, OK, no one can leave until you tell us the truth, what you've taken, OK? The Housemistress is disappointed in me. I don't think they're planning on leaving anytime soon, do you? The Girls begin to lose interest in us. A few lie on the ground, bodies posed over the graves, eyelids fluttering. None wear their shoes. I see them now, lined up beside the gate, socks tucked dutifully inside. Narrative, there is a narrative at play, one that has been organized into ritual. I imagine that they have been in careful planning for weeks. Covert meetings, only this select few allowed in, the rest of The Girls, the lessers, left wondering. An aim to honour these dead girls as the school doesn't.

We just want to connect. The Girl who punched the boy speaks up again. She flexes her toes against the tombstone. The night is still enough that I can hear the friction of her skin. We want to connect and let them know we're thinking. The sentence remains unfinished. Her features slacken. Chin floats towards chest. Shit, oh shit. The Housemistress is agile. I follow. The Girl has fainted. Her mouth remains parted. The Housemistress taps her arm lightly. Come on, come on love. When The Girl does not respond, her body falling further forward, The Housemistress begins to shout.

Hey, wake up, wake up, wake up. Stop, stop it, she's out cold. I put my fingers to her neck like I know what I'm doing. A pulse is not so easy to find, how ridiculous. I check for my own, searching across my neck. For fucksake. The Housemistress is standing, looking around at the others, making sure all are still conscious. There, there's the pulse, the thick artery below the hinge of my jaw. I replicate the spot on The Girl's neck. It is there, hard, certain. I hover the back of my hand over her mouth and feel her breath. She's fine, it's OK. We need to call an ambulance, fuck. The Housemistress looks up at the old vicarage. Lights off in every front-facing room. Mrs S most likely fast asleep.

Go, will you, just ring the doorbell. We need to call an ambulance. I can't move. I don't move. The Housemistress pushes my back. Go, what the fuck are you waiting for. She crouches and cradles The Girl. I run out of the gate and up the driveway, slowing down once out of sight, my chest tight. There are certain things I am not supposed to do. Calling on her in the middle of the night like this. The scent of roses. At the door I knock too quietly at first. Nothing happens. The house does not make a sound. I knock again, this time with both fists. I step back so I can see into the windows. Finally a light is turned on, their bedroom. He answers the door. I forget him, I forget he would of course answer the door. What? What is it? He is sweet with sleep. Skin around his eyes crushed like silk. It's, it's, there's a problem, we need to call an ambulance, can I use your phone. I wonder if he can smell beer on me. We are not standing close enough together, I think, for him to realize. He wears a dark-blue dressing gown. I notice his legs, his calves, their sudden and sensual shape. He has everything. In the darkness he moves to the wall and flicks a light switch, blinking as the bulb brightens. What is it? He is firmer. The Girls, I think they've taken something. Right, where? The graveyard. He tries not to show panic.

I lift the receiver and dial. As I begin to speak to the operator she appears on the stairs. A matching dark-blue dressing gown. She doesn't smile at me. Her face strains. I can't recognize her. I cover the mouthpiece with my hand so I can explain. There's been an emergency. She looks at him and he lifts his hands in the air in dramatized confusion, jutting out his bottom lip. Did she think I was here to confess? To let the world know? She tightens the cord of her dressing gown. The operator asks me for details and I give them, trying to slow my speech, wanting to seem calm. They listen in, the pair of them now side by side, she has gone to him at the doorway, elbows touching. Oh God, she mutters, oh God. She turns and starts to walk quickly, trying not to break into a run, stumbling on the steps, heading down the driveway. He shouts after her, using a nickname, then her first name. She does not turn around. I lose sight of her but hear the graveyard gate swing open.

Christ, what am I supposed to do. He speaks as if I am not here. Just, just wait. I watch him run up the stairs, taking two at a time, his boyishness irresistible to me. I hate myself. I am not sure what to do. I have to wait for him. I keep my hands in my pockets, practising a pose, wanting to find my boyishness in return. My cheeks are flushed. I am thinking about The Girl but not enough. Her face finally pulls into focus, the transparency of her skin, how she disappeared behind her eyelids. A tide pulls at the edges of my stomach. I hear a door close and seconds later he is back in my field of vision, coming down the stairs. He has dressed as if going to morning assembly, except he has not put on his tie. The top buttons of his shirt are undone. His trousers, too, are wrinkled as if lifted from the back of a chair, not taken from the wardrobe. Yesterday's clothes. Once beside me he touches my shoulder. Tell me, then, what's happened, while we walk. He guides me outside. We were going past, up there, The Housemistress and I, and we heard voices, we followed them to the graveyard and just found them. He frowns. We were at the pub, we were just heading home, taking the long route, the night was too lovely, you know. The word lovely. He pauses at it, at my use of such a word, roaming my face, trying to uncover what I mean. He would not understand, anyway, about the moonlight, the way it made The Housemistress and I feel possible.

He nods, distracted. I see Mrs S inside the churchyard, hunched over. There are voices. The Girls are now more attentive, standing closer. As we enter he says nothing. The Girls bow their heads. The Housemistress hovers, her hand moving through and through her hair. The Girl who punched the boy has come to. She doesn't speak but looks steadily at Mrs S. What have we here, what has gone on.

Disbelief in his voice. This won't do. He addresses The Girls. This won't do, you know that. His voice rising. Not now. Mrs S wraps her hand around his leg, his knee. Not now. He turns his back. Two of The Girls move as if to leave, grabbing the gate, not stopping to collect their shoes. They have no chance. His job, as he understands it, is to see everything. No, no, stay here, do you hear me, stay right here. He speaks to The Housemistress. Do you know what it is they've taken? Have they taken something? No, I mean yes they have taken something, but they won't say. Is that right. He paces between The Girls. Do you realize you could die? That your friend might die? It isn't true, what he's saying, death does not feel close, it is only the unknown, the way their eyes roll around in their heads, set loose. I think of his bandaged hand, the wasp sting. Under his feet, under his brown leather shoes, tea light after tea light is smothered, the thin metal crushed. At this loss of control, he only asserts more control. Fire hazards, these are fire hazards. He walks along, now lifting his shoes higher to have more of an impact, to make clear the sound of destruction, to make clear the possibility of his power. All that can be heard is the river, the slamming of his foot into the ground. I will stay here all night, unless you tell me what you've taken. Briefly I wonder if The Girls have taken anything at all. I know the unofficial history of femininity, stories of mass hysteria, mass fainting, mass illness. The speed at which symptoms can move between bodies. Perhaps their ritual, the anticipation of it, the execution of it, has been powerful enough. Maybe they have been drawn out by the heat.

Where is that ambulance? Mrs S looks to me. I don't know, they said they'd be here as fast as they can. The Housemistress checks her watch. Nearest hospital, the bigger one anyway, is at least a half an hour drive. Should we call The Nurse? No, no, I don't think there would be much more she would know. The Nurse is a gossip, it is well known. The Girl who punched the boy closes her eyes. Don't do that, come on now. Mrs S redirects her attention, stroking her hairline. Stay with me, stay awake, you must keep looking at me. The Girl opens her eyes again, a faint smile forming. She moves her lips to speak and Mrs S lowers her head to receive it. Her dressing gown parts at the chest. Mr S does not notice their exchange. With no tea lights left to put out, he instead walks to each of The Girls in turn, bending his face underneath their bowed heads, forcing them into eye contact. What has gone on, then, he mutters, his tone lowered. What has gone on. Two of The Girls giggle again, helplessly. He clasps his hands behind his back in restraint. Funny, is it? You think this is funny?

Whatever The Girl who punched the boy has told Mrs S is kept secret. The Housemistress points at the road. The ambulance, there. From the church's raised position it is possible to see all the way to the first bend in the road, beside the garage. The sound of sirens strengthening. Mr S smacks his hands together. It's about to get very real, do you understand. He walks over to the section of the wall where The Housemistress stands. Jesus, this time of night, did they really need to use the sirens, all the bloody pomp, it will wake the whole school, the whole village. Blue and red. It rounds the corner finally. The Housemistress runs down to the crossing to wave them in, sending them half into the driveway of the old vicarage. The ambulance parks awkwardly, almost hitting the grand iron gate. With less emergency than I would have thought, two paramedics emerge. They are confused, unable to locate the problem, The Housemistress is still rounding the back end of the vehicle. She appears and waves again. Here, up here. They pull surgical gloves over their hands. Bags slung heavily around their shoulders. One woman and one man. What's the issue? Where am I looking? Mr S touches a hand to the back of the man, guiding him towards The Girl who punched the boy.

Hello love. The man is kind. He kneels beside her. The woman stands just behind his shoulder. She takes in the rest of The Girls and speaks quietly to Mr S, asking if she ought to check them out too. Yes, he responds, please. Hello love, can you hear me? The Girl nods delicately. Gently lifting her eyelid, he points a miniature torch at her pupil, moving it from side to side. Mrs S grips his forearm. It's mushrooms, she told me, they've all taken mushrooms, is that OK, will it be OK, apparently they grow in the woods or somewhere, I don't know. Right. If the information is shocking it does not show on his face. The Girl begins to cry, soundlessly, tears rolling the edge of her lip. He clicks off his torch and pats her shoulder. I know it's all a bit over-whelming isn't it, listen to me, everything is fine, you're fine. He takes her blood pressure. She winces as the strap tightens. Afterwards he checks the inside of her mouth with his index finger. Do you feel sick at all love? No, she shakes her head. Any pain anywhere? She shakes her head again. Not here? He places his hand on her abdomen. No. She whispers, coughing her voice free. It returns, firmer. No. Alright, good job.

He stands. Here, can you take her. Mrs S motions at me. Of course. I move down beside her. Slowly she inches The Girl from her arms and places her into mine. Her head is heavy. The Girl holds my t-shirt in a great handful. Listen. The man speaks to Mrs S as if she is the one in charge. Mr S is forced to join her from the other side of the graveyard. She's fine more or less, I don't know what time they took anything but it could last up to eight hours, the effects, keep an eye on them, if there's any vomiting, stomach cramps, anything, get us out here again immediately. And what, exactly, are we supposed to do in the meantime? It is hard to know what Mr S expected. That the paramedics might take all of The Girls with them, leading each one to the ambulance, clearing space amongst the gurney, the machin-ery, for them to sit. Drive them far away from here. At the hospital they would no longer be disobedient, but patients. The man waits a few seconds before replying. He looks Mr S up and down, it is old-fashioned, purposeful. That, I'm afraid, is up to you boss.

So you're just going to leave them here, drugged up, high on God knows what, picked from God knows where. For a moment the man hesitates. He looks back down at The Girl who punched the boy. Look there's no vomiting, no stomach cramps, there's no good reason to bring her in, she's fine, needs to eat probably. She fainted, isn't that something? Could be panic, or stress, it's hard to know, that can happen, on psychedelics. As he speaks Mrs S listens intently, as if he might impart some piece of advice that could be essential to The Girl's well-being, to how she might be able to take care of her. The woman paramedic joins her colleague, her hands in her pockets. This lot are fine too, high as kites, but healthy. I watch her eyes flit towards The Housemistress. One, two seconds, perhaps taking in the pockets on her shorts, her legs wide apart. The woman paramedic looks away, then returns, pulled in, as the moon draws the tide. The Housemistress misses it. She is too preoccupied with what the man is saying.

For now, for now they're healthy. Mrs S takes his hand, not looking at me. These are the experts, they've said she's fine. She addresses the man and the woman with authority. We'll be fine, thank you, thank you so much. Alright, not a problem. Synchronized the man and woman make their way back through The Girls, the headstones. They wave cheerfully before pulling away. I wave back. Mrs S comes close. I smell her sleep, the place her body was only an hour ago. She touches The Girl's forehead. You're looking better. All night she has not looked at me. I try not to care, I try not to wait for her. Are you OK holding her like that? Yes, it's fine. She notices The Girl's fist, full of the fabric of my t-shirt. I try to remember if it is the same fist with which The Girl punched the boy. Left or right? Her other hand is tucked underneath her side. There is no scarring, swelling long gone. I try to remember details of the day, the aftermath. All I can see is the gym. The pair of us, absorbed into it. I can no longer conjure the smell of the blood, the bleach. There's only the weak light through the windows, the sound of The Girls' laughter as they passed below.

Can you get up? Mrs S puts a light hand at the base of The Girl's skull. I can try, everything is spinning. The Girl keeps her voice small. Blinks quickly. She could be partially faking it. Embarrassed at the fuss, now looking to retreat. Midges have begun to dance over our heads. To loosen The Girl's fist from my t-shirt I stroke the tops of her knuckles. Slowly we, Mrs S and I, lift her until she is standing. She sways one way and then another. At the last second she stumbles. Mrs S catches her waist and holds her steady. Where are we going? Mr S has begun to move The Girls out of the graveyard. The Housemistress helps, meekly. She stands at the back of the slow group and speaks to them encouragingly. Off you go, shoes on, that's it. Shall I take them back to their dorms? she calls out to Mr S who stands on the path. I suppose so, yes, good idea.

Three of The Girls lift their shoes and laugh, turning them over, playing with the laces. No one knows what to do with the laughter. The Housemistress tries to ignore them. One of The Girls throws one of her shoes over the stone wall. It lands on the road below. Another follows suit, the shoe landing somewhere unknown, caught in a hedge, a verge, or lost to the river. The third presses her own pair to her chest. I want to laugh with them. Laughter is an expanding balloon in my stomach. Mr S is shocked. He will not retrieve the shoe. It languishes in the road. Ready to be crushed or flung by the next car. The Housemistress is forced to act. She draws closer to the little group. Each of their bodies boneless with laughter. They slip and shift, flopping forward, unable to be contained. Here, let me. The Housemistress hitches her shorts, then drops to her haunches. With difficulty she aims each shoe onto a soft foot. After a few seconds of her effort, calm spreads through The Girls. Laughter turns to heavy breath. They wonder what they were laughing about. She is their true mother. More than their own mothers, more than Mrs S. No one else would say it except for me.

The Girl pulls herself free from Mrs S. She walks forward, wanting her shoes, wanting to be with the others. They float down the steps. Cluster around Mr S. Their heads bob up and down, calling out at the stars. Eyes large as windows. Without warning Mrs S places her head on my shoulder. I turn slightly. The top of her head, ready to be kissed. Mr S is busy with The Girls on the pavement. She wanted to laugh too. I sense her throat tight with sound. What we have is rare, I'm sure of it, here is a reason why. To laugh at the same thing. Confirming my suspicions, she whispers,

I'll have whatever they're having. The fear has passed. The Girls are only high, allowed to be ridiculous. They will survive, they cannot be punished tonight. Do you think, do you think I ought to have them stay at our, my, house? They could all sleep in the living room, I could keep an eye on them, just in case, these things can turn so quickly, what do you think? Could I stay too? I already know the answer. She does not reply. Her head stays on my shoulder. I feel the slight lift of nerves, that he might see, veins broadening.

The Housemistress is almost at the gate, her arm around The Girl who punched the boy. Last minute, she looks our way. Mrs S jolts upwards. For her sake The Housemistress pretends to see nothing. A few odd socks have been left behind. She already holds the single shoe, now she returns to retrieve the rest. To prove a point, Mrs S takes off ahead of me. I smile at The Housemistress, at the sight of her cradling the socks. She smiles back. She has discovered something. The smile is not for me but for this new, uncovered fact. It is extraordinary to think of Mrs S and I as a fact. Later I will mention the woman paramedic, the flirt lost across the graveyard. This will please her. For a moment The Housemistress expects me to join her, perhaps she is hopeful, eager to discuss what she's seen. She is forced to go with Mrs S, who stops to say something to her. I wonder if it is a denial, perhaps a lie about a headache, a crick in the neck. Too late, I think, too late. I have given us away.

Mr S has The Girls standing in a circle. He is in the centre, wanting to be their leader. Even in their ordinary clothes, shorts, jumpers, it remains a cultish apparition. Mrs S pulls him free. She speaks to him in the driveway. He paces, touches his head, paces again. The last thing he wants is The Girls in his house. But he will do what she wants. She knows him well. Better than he will ever know her. After less than a minute of persuasion, he relents. Left in the graveyard I scoop up the tea lights. I have not tried mushrooms before. It seems to me that Mrs S has. In her other life, the one I'm waiting to uncover. I look for signs of leftovers but don't know what to look for, the type of mushroom that can be used in this way. I slink through the headstones, trying not to read the ages of the dead girls. Alone I am more afraid. Even worried their ritual has worked. Each headstone has its own platitude written below the name. Angels, God's children, flowers. Words that rhyme: thine, shine, glory, story. I realize it does not matter whether I read the headstones or not. I already know the details of each almost by heart. Too many times I have walked past and gone over, almost carelessly, these final, vague lines of their lives.

A folded piece of paper flickers against the wall. It is a poem, written by the dead author. Not one that I immediately know. One of The Girls has copied it out for the occasion. The handwriting is very fine, precise. There is finally a slight chill in the air. Mystery, blown in. My legs tremble. I am, I realize, exhausted. The poem is thinly veiled, about the school. A river running black, then brightening again, the moon making crystals of its surface. Frost too, the sloping fields, all speaking in crystal. Lichen described as the last light across the graveyard, kissing as it moves the south-facing stone. I fold it up. Put it in my pocket. Did they read it aloud? Perhaps the ringleader, in her confident voice. Ghosts were not expected, but already here. That is how they saw things. The Girls moved amongst ghosts of other girls. Epilogue after epilogue.

Mrs S calls to me. She stands in the driveway, the path below, her house glimpsed from the graveyard. Clothes on, new clothes, the dressing gown at last gone. When I don't answer she begins to wave. The tea lights sit in the scoop of my t-shirt. I am slow through the gate. She comes to help. Just leave those there, what are you doing bringing them. Trying to be helpful. I get a look, I think it's loving. Fine, The Girls are all staying, we're setting up in there, no rest for the wicked. I can help? This time, she glances over her shoulder, she answers. You can't really stay, I don't think it's a good idea. Why? She slips her hand between my legs. Keeps it still. Increases the pressure of her fingers. Pressing first against the tilt, then shifting until she is at my entrance. You know why. She puts her lips a moment away from mine. I turn to water. Fast as the river. You know why.

The weekend passes. By Monday Mr S is away. An annual gathering of headmasters from the country's finest schools. Assembly happens without him, led instead by the deputy head. Another man in a suit, this one slightly cheaper, his belly rounder. He reads aloud the weekend's sports results. His heels twist on the gym floor, leaving a squeak in between every other word. The Girls who were at the graveyard have not yet been disciplined. It hangs over them. Since the event I notice them everywhere. They move together, huddling in doorways, petering down the corridor. Protective of one another, or afraid to be alone. From my chair at the side of the gym I can see them all, sitting cross-legged in a line. Uniforms extra-neat. Buttons done all the way to the throat, jumpers around their shoulders, not tied around their waists. They wait. It is crueller, to have them wait. Mr S knows this. The Housemistress, too, is smarter than usual, making an effort. She wears her suit, ignores the heat. Slumped. I try to catch her eye but she is avoiding me. There is too much one look could say.

Mrs S is not here this morning. She does as she pleases. Despite her usual attendance, assembly is not an obligation for her. Perhaps she drove Mr S to the station. Him, rehearsing a speech in the car, knowing he does not need to rehearse, he does it to show off. She listens, loving him but thinking of me, she drifts, she cannot help it. My taste, she loves my taste. Pushing her tongue against her teeth. My taste. The excitement of Saturday night has vanished. It is like that, here. To move forward difficult things must quickly disappear, how else can a legacy remain intact. In my pocket is the dead author's poem. I have an idea to give it back to The Girls, that it might be bad luck to keep it. In memory, the entire night has become embellished, as if I had seen the whites of their rolling eyes, choreographed movements, heads unified under the moon.

The assembly finishes on a final squeak of the deputy head's shoes. He is swivelling, encouraging a round of applause for some achievement, I don't know what. I clap as commanded. After assembly I am supposed to help moderate examinations. I will have to sit with another teacher, only useful once she leaves for her toilet break and I am left alone to survey the single desks in their rows. They have asked that I keep an eye on The Girls. I must watch out for their tricks, make sure they don't cheat, many will, I have been assured, write answers on their forearms. It was an entire meeting. Forty-five minutes long. The history teacher demonstrated the sly manoeuvre, how The Girls steal glances, that you can't take your eyes off them even for a moment.

The Girls file out of the room, the little group sticking together. The Housemistress waits for me outside. Sitting on the steps that lead to the art block. I lift up my arm and tap my watch, as if I have somewhere to be. She leaps up and jogs towards me. Her suit jacket folded over her arm. Pink shirt loosened at the neck, sleeves pushed up, cheeks reddened. Don't think you'd get away that easily. Wouldn't dare. So. So. She holds my arm. You've got some talking to do, it would seem. Do I? Ah playing it all fucking coy, that's your thing is it. I stop, letting The Girls pass. I can't exactly talk about it here. Where do you have to be? Back in the gym in ten, invigilating some exam. Plenty of time then. She spins me at my waist, changing our direction. We walk in silence past the art block, heading out towards the stables. In the bright sun the building looks worse for wear. A few wooden boards missing from the roof. The school has two horses. There used to be more. The pair graze in the field behind, surrounded by jumps that are barely used, equipment lumped about in once-organized piles.

Here we can talk, just you, me and the horses. The larger of the two comes towards us. Eyelashes lovely. The Housemistress yanks a handful of long grass, able to grow tall on this side of the fence, where the horses cannot reach. There you go. She hands it to him in her fist. I close my hand around hers. Not like that, he might bite. What would you know about horses? Some, there were horses where I grew up. Posher than I thought then. Not like that, there were just horses, in the town, not my horses. I smooth out her fingers. Arrange the grass in her flattened palm. Watch your thumb. What do you mean? I press it inwards, tucking it away. They're not picky about what they put in their mouths. Unlike some people. She roars with laughter at her joke, frightening the horse, who dips his head. She leaps backwards. Fuck, shit. It's fine. I catch him by his nose and soothe the elegant bone. There, try now. Tentatively she puts out her hand again. He eats. She relaxes slightly, cooing at him, but her body hangs back, still unsettled. Fucking horse whisperer too, so much I don't know about you. I don't reply. She is whispering, afraid of the horse, but angry at me. I want to reach out and put my fingers to her jaw, set hard, determined. We are friends, I have lied. It is our sexuality, our conspiracy. I have let someone else in without her knowledge. A kind of humiliation.

Listen it's no big deal. The horse has finished his meal. She wipes her palm against her suit trousers without thinking. Wet glistens against the dark fabric. I mean it is, you're, I assume anyway, fucking the headmaster's wife, I'll say it aloud so you don't have to. Don't talk like that. Like what? Like it's only fucking. Oh for Christssake, it's a relationship, is that it? Girlfriend and girlfriend? Have you even fucked yet? Or is it all just, the tantalizing, the forbidden fruit. I smile, I want to calm her down. Don't be jealous. Fuck off, I'm not jealous, you cunt. She smiles back. Returned to me.

I have, we have slept together, we are sleeping together. Flies dive for the moisture of our eyes and lips. The Housemistress huffs, hoping to displace them with her breath. Jesus. Yes. Is it, I don't know, good? Yes. Jesus. You think, I mean, is she gay? I don't know, haven't really had to ask so far. God they, the two of them, just seemed so fucking straight, like. She shakes her head. I know, well, she's not that, she's definitely not straight. In the pause between us she bends to pick more grass, then changes her mind. Do you know what you're doing? Her mothering look. Eyebrows raised, set stern. Nostrils flared. But her eyes give away her core. Kind, fearful. No, I don't. Do you need me to tell you to stop? What difference would that make. She sighs dramatically, wags her finger. You should stop, there, now I've said it, it would stand up in court, with these horses as my witness. A shirtsleeve unravels, she pushes it back up. I don't talk about you, I haven't said anything. She puts her hands on the fence. Looks upwards. Said anything about what? She knows what I mean, that I haven't outed her, that I would never. Just us, that's all, our friendship. Why would I worry about that? I'm just saying, you don't need to worry. Sure you're not doing much talking at all.

The larger horse stands by the fence. He waits for more grass. The Housemistress offers him her empty palm. She flinches slightly as his lips rub against her skin but does not pull away her hand. Realizing it is empty, he snorts, walks purposefully towards the centre of the field. You should have given him something. Oh I'll be sure to bring him an apple next time to make up for it. A bell rings, in the near distance, perhaps the one at the art block. Shit. I check my watch. Shit, I'm late, are we OK? Of course we are, you don't have to keep this stuff from me, who are you going to tell if it's not me. I know. Do you? Yeh. The Housemistress stops to watch the other horse, the one further away, drop to the ground to roll, his great weight of muscle and bone twisting in the dried earth. His body soon obscured by dust.

I show Mrs S around my room like a child, pointing out this and that. There is not much to see. The clumsy ceramic mug made by an ex, my only long-term ex, a love heart carved as a signature on the bottom. She turns this over. Runs her fingertip over the heart. Someone loved you. They did, might still do. Is that right? Her face a new mood, one only just revealed. Lips folded in. For once she needs to know more. Maybe I will oblige. We broke up when I left, when I was coming here for the job. Recent, then. Sort of. Do you miss her? No. I lower my eyes for effect, so she might think I am lying. Of course the truth is I have not thought about my ex, not on purpose, her face appearing only as I masturbate, when my imagination fails me.

She touches my books, one by one. Reading the summaries, opening each at random and holding a sentence in her mouth. Clever, aren't you. Not really. A big fan of hers then? She lifts my old edition of the dead author's novel. Of course, aren't you? Sure, I was at school at least, although maybe now I might not be able to read her work in the same way. She turns the book to the opening chapter. Because of being here, because of the school, now you've seen it? Yes, it changes things, makes it too, I don't know, too close, it's all too close, tragic, really. For a moment I think she might read the dead author aloud. An intake of breath, she has found some pertinent line. But the book is closed suddenly. Instead she sits on my bed, smooths a hand across the centre. So this is where you lie and think of me. Yes.

I am shy. The room becomes pathetic. The bed slopes slightly, the mattress pings. I see the dust, the past damage to the walls, the old poster of a Victorian steam train I never bothered to remove. Green carriages cutting through greener fells, a perfect holiday promised in a happy, yellow font. In her half of the building The Nurse puts on one of her tapes. As if on cue. It is her favourite, played a few times a week, an entire album of piano covers, wordless versions of famous songs from famous films. Mrs S listens in, tapping out the familiar tune on my bedspread. She laughs and I put my finger to my lips. Oh, The Nurse would die to know about us. She laughs again when the next track begins. I go to her and put my own finger to her lips. She takes me quickly in her mouth, grazing my skin with her teeth, before forcing my finger deeper, reaching a choke. I feel her throat constrict. Yes. Mrs S kisses me. A new habit, before our lips touch, I echo her yes. What's mine is hers. Yes, yes, yes. I stand above her. It feels good, to have her look up at me. Yes, yes, yes. I make her wait, undoing the button of my jeans, putting my own hand inside, fucking myself. She reaches out for my knees, to show me what she needs, to be

inside me, or for me to touch her. I grab her chin and turn
her head from side to side. No. She needs to be quiet, I tell
her. Be quiet. Please. She stays sitting, tries to take my forearms, to stop my fucking. Please. Her voice breaks. Please.
I don't stop.

Instead she interrupts me, she breaks my focus. Do you
have anything we could use? This is how she will win. What
do you mean? You know. I don't. Her game, to never name
anything, as if she can slip so easily from her own reality.
You do know. She grabs my crotch. What she is asking for
is my cock. Yes, she will win. I go to the laundry basket and
pull out what I have. You're in luck. She holds them one by
one, feeling their weight, rolling them up and down her
inner thigh. Before making her final choice she begins to
undress. What do you want? I hope to sound authoritative,
hardening my voice. All of it. Flesh-coloured, her lips
around the tip, stare unbroken. I have made her wait long
enough. I sit on the bed. She opens her legs. Fuck me. Puts
a hand on her breast, moving the nipple between her thumb
and forefinger. Fuck me.

I hold the cock at my clit. Go towards her on my knees.
Around her, when I am around her, there is no choice but
to like myself. Even love, right now, I love myself. I love
myself. I spit on my palms and slick the tip. She watches.
How she watches. Bared to me, her legs still open, I am
only inches away. Press my cock lightly against her. She
moves, only slightly. I adjust, sliding up then down, she
can't have me yet. Please, please. She moves to accept me

once more, her hips urgent, until she finds a new pleasure. Her voice travels from octave to octave. I hush her, I cannot hold out any longer.

You. Her new habit. She announces me to myself. I fall into place. You. It is as if she has always been waiting for this arrival, of me into my body. You. I don't have a name. Isn't it so much better, to not have a name, to be dropped straight from the clouds? Today we meet in full daylight. Wild garlic, the smell somehow reminiscent of our fucking, the sweetened damp of the interior. She pulls me in the direction of my annexe, my room. No. I stand still, feet firmly planted. Let's go to your house. Mine? I have shocked her. Yes. We shouldn't, we can't. Mr S, his trip extended to see family. We can, he's away, it's not like I've not been to your house before, no one would suspect anything. I don't know. She is caught off guard, unable to find a reason to deny me, I like to see part of her give way under my gaze. I want to fuck among her things. I want to leave a trace, to be lodged in her memory, to have her see their bed and think of me. She bites the flesh around her fingers. It is unrefined, gorgeous, part of the pressure of my gaze. You really want to? More than anything. Don't be dramatic. Come on, he's away, surely now is our only chance. I kiss her neck, I think of it as cheesy, to kiss someone's neck, like a thing from the films, a thing that other people do, a thing that he might do. But today I want to be like other people. I keep going, I kiss the mound behind her ear. She wriggles out of my grip, shuddering, the touch too much. Stop it, stop it, OK, we can go. I smile. She offers me her neck again.

Mrs S laughs at things that surprise me. The sudden slipping of the cock, today it is her cock, from between my legs. The hard catch of muscle and skin, my gasp. She didn't mean to. It is her first time fucking somebody else. I understand from this that she has fucked herself. This intimate knowledge, her private routine, she shares with me. When she turns me over I ask her to hit the gentle rise of my cheeks. She does. Again and again, she lifts her hand, hovers for a second, my breath breaking in the pause, bringing it down until she finds the right sound, wet and ripe. Whispers can I take it, I say yes. Abandons the cock and uses her fingers. More questions, she widens her palm, does it hurt, am I the only one who has touched you like this. Yes. Trust, this kind, I did not expect. My body hands itself over, I give her my pain, even the possibility of my pain, I grow bigger. Grab her hand and push it deeper. I sob into the pillow. Not wanting her to see, not realizing the sound that leaves me, a wail I only hear after my mouth has already closed. Oh God, I have, I've hurt you, I'm sorry. No, no, you haven't, I'm fine, really. She withdraws her fingers slowly. Understanding, I hope, that in these moments she makes me feel like myself. I want her skin. Lift off my t-shirt, then binder. She has not seen me like this. I start to loosen it, to peel it from my chest. Other questions are forming in her mouth, the kind that take the air from the room. In doing this, by revealing myself, I know I will have to answer them.

I pull over the covers. She finds me underneath. Raises my arm and strokes my armpit. I let her. Hand travelling down my side, the places nobody touches, only my second skin of elastic and cotton. Ribs shocked by the sudden space. I allow myself extra breath. Under her fingertips are the worn grooves, the raw creases. Creep of blisters. Scars. Here, this part of me, is patterned stone. What she can trace I don't know. Her nails trip a raw piece of skin. A livewire. Nerves spill over and subside. Summer has worn me away. My tolerance of pain, I realize, it was already there.

Her hand reaches around, towards my tits. I catch her fingers. Don't, not there. She tries to be soft. I find you beautiful. I shake my head. It's not that, that's not the point. She curls her torso away. A signal. I have begun to owe her something, now we have to talk. I know the moment. We are hermetically sealed. You don't trust me to see you naked? No, that isn't it either. There is no explaining, I do trust her and also trust is not the word here, not for this, how do I tell her I need to control perception, her perception, in order to stay intact. I do, I do trust you, of course I do. Then what is it? You mean what is this? I roll over, pick up the binder. I thought it was some kind of sports bra, I thought perhaps you were shy. It's different, it's. I can't remember how to finish the sentence. What have I said before? She moves closer. You can tell me. Her empathy is working overtime, she prides herself on an instinct for those that struggle. It's hard to explain. Please try, do try. I use it to flatten my chest. I let her do the rest. Flatten it? Yes. What, so, to be more like a man? Here is another word that doesn't work. Man. The priority she affords it. I want to correct her. I don't know if it's 'like a man', it's more about masculinity. Same thing. I don't think it is.

She inhales. OK, I'm not sure I follow you, is it about feeling manly, how about that. She needs more detail. I don't know, I never know, how to provide it. To talk it through, to use language as it is already known, requires how I feel to be a fixed state. It isn't. A self always on the move. I give in to a simplicity I don't believe in. I guess, yeh, it lets me feel more manly. She seems satisfied. Takes the binder. Slips her hands inside and pulls it taut. It must hurt. It does, I don't notice it so much anymore. Tough, aren't you. Guess so. She kisses me, reaches for the cock, turns it over in her hand. I think I can understand it. She puts the cock between her legs, held against her pubic bone, where it was only moments ago. It does feel good, powerful, to be manly. But she doesn't understand. And yet understanding is everything to her, she cannot see the ego in it, her need to grasp it all, rather than accept what she does not know. It's fine, I reassure myself. At least the question is over. I don't want to push. My heart rate levels, the certain self-loathing that comes with this relief. I should have more pride. There are too many things I want.

Afterwards I get up and begin to dress. Boxers, jeans. I pick up the binder and pull it with difficulty over my head. Think of the shape of her hands inside it. My shirt lies close to the doorway. Crumpled, arched. Still a little muscle in the fabric. I wash our cock in their sink. All dildos are eventually an artwork. Especially now, rude and proud against the porcelain. Sex and its afterwards; full of procedures. She gets up, gives me one look, then resumes a sort of busyness. Our rhythms are smoothed out of the sheets, the curtains pulled apart, window opened. The afternoon returns. That powerful sun rearranges the room. As if our conversation never happened. Later I know she will wash the sheets. Get rid of my smell. For now she places the pillows over the duvet, tugs at their corners. A glass of water is handed to me. I have to exit quickly. That is the unspoken rule. There's no time to be leisurely. Today I am grateful for it.

I'd like to leave the cock to dry on her sink. For a moment I admire it beside the his-and-hers toothbrushes. Pink, blue, silicone skin. I laugh quietly. A devastation so mild. How long before he would notice? It would catch his eye as he pissed, maybe. If not, if he was too long enjoying the sight of his back garden through the window behind the toilet, he might graze it with his hand as he reached for his green mouthwash. I carry the cock out of the bathroom and put it inside my tote bag. She sits, half-naked, on the bed opposite the window. Today the church bells are rehearsed, clumsy, a tune starts and then falters, chords hang in my teeth. Last minute I kiss each of her knees. See you soon. Yes, soon.

There is a swift surge of panic as I exit the bedroom. I leave myself behind, I've given too much of myself away. Outside, I try not to look up at her window, to need her reassurance, she will not be waiting to look for me. The smell of sex hangs between my nose and mouth. The faint drone of my pelvic bone, the lasting pressure of the cock. Weak legs. I haven't eaten since yesterday. Out of sight of the house I lean against the last curve in the churchyard's stone wall. I should not have shown her, I should not have kissed her knees. The surge again. Why did I kiss her knees. Not thinking I walk back up towards the school. I have an idea to visit the larger library, to try and find the particular book of poems by the dead author. The idea is to be alone, but not completely.

The cock lends the tote bag a comical, bouncing weight. It spins and bangs against my hip. All I want to do now is talk to her. Everything is too quiet. The day deflates. The Girls are leisurely. Two or three nod in false solemnity as they pass me on my way up the grand staircase. Some lounge on the grass. I avoid the front entrance. Sex is still warm on my fingertips too. Four Girls play messy doubles on the tennis court. A small audience has gathered, music comes from a radio. One Girl waves but I can't see her face through the sun. Vague haloes attach to each head, each racket, each tree.

I wave back. The muscles of my forearm ache. Play a game Miss? The Girl stands up. Other heads turn. Not today. She shrugs and sits back down. I imagine sitting with them, the cock rolling out of the tote bag and down the hill, coming to an unsteady stop against the net. The Girl's shoulders are pink. Sun cream! My voice cracks halfway through the command. Put some sun cream on! No one responds. I pretend to reach into the tote bag and feel only silicone. Somebody, one of The Girls, laughs. Then another. I kissed her knees because I didn't know what else to do.

My birthday, out of nowhere. I check the post, those great lumpy sacks hung each morning in the corridor. Nothing. What did I expect? She forgets things, my mother. I am old enough now, she might say, I no longer need a card, the stuff of childhood. I can't help but call her. Prompt her memory. She is vague, busy, reading a magazine while she talks. Sections offered aloud to me. A marriage, royal, he is very sexy, very handsome, he's a real man, a good wedding is in the details. At the end I say I love you. A minute's silence. She is always grieving me. Yeh I know. Her standard reply. She can't end it there, gives me some parting gossip, an aunty's broken ankle, God knows how much Baileys, at least a bottle. Bye, I say, goodbye, as if it could be forever. But she cannot locate the drama in my voice. Speak soon, enjoy the weather.

The Housemistress finds me. Phone receiver still in my hand, her long gone. Fancy seeing you here. I look up. Jesus who died? She panics. Oh God did somebody actually die? No, no. Fucking phewf. Rumbles her top lip. You had me going there. Grips the back of my plastic chair. It bends slightly under her strength. Sorry. Everything OK? Yeh, no. I decide whether or not to tell her. What? What is it? She doesn't give me a choice. It's my birthday, actually. What the fuck, happy birthday! Thanks. I'd take you straight to the pub but I'm on bloody duty. That's OK, don't worry, it's not your responsibility. Responsibility? Birthdays are supposed to be fun, a good thing, you know. Scratches her chin. Have you told your lover? Gross, don't call her that. That's what she is though. A challenge, I can barely rise to it. My lover, no, I haven't told her. You should, she'd probably give you something good, silver-ware, a fat cheque inside a card. Piss off.

Seriously though, you should tell her, I'm sure she'd want to know. Thanks, not sure about that to be honest, it's hardly an event, looks like my own mother doesn't remem-ber. Fuck, fucking parents. A pause, she roams her own archives, finds something for me. Well at least she isn't pretending, my mum. She trails off. Her smile more of a wince. A shared pain does not need to be turned over. The same? Oh, worse. She tips the chair backwards. Balances her face over mine. We'll do something later in the week, personally I'm very pleased you were born. Thanks. Don't mention it, take it slow yeh, have a drink, go for a walk, reflect, maybe not in that order. Sounds more like New Year's. Whatever, it is your new year anyway. Ah aren't you sweet. She checks the time. Her big wristwatch. Leather strap. She takes good care of it. The motion of her forearm as she looks at the face, polished-steel rim, fingers tucked against her palm, tilted towards her eyes. Ways of being I didn't know existed. I guess a walk might help. Yeh, usually does, and plenty of them around here, don't go getting lost on the fells please, it's expensive to call out mountain rescue. I'll do my best. She looks hard at me. I mean it, we will celebrate. I know, I know you mean it.

The Housemistress leaves and I feel emptier than before. At least I have a plan. A walk. Outside, I follow the road away from the school. Pressing into the hedge with every passing car. Dogs bark, grey snouts appearing under a black metal gate. Stench of silage, a word recently learned, smell it too long and I might pass out, The Girls teased. The road offers a footpath. Through a slit in the stone wall. Designed to squeeze and scrape thighs. I lift up, take in the power of my forearms, swing my hips through. A field, fells rise on either side, like walking through a cupped palm. Ahead is another enclosure. Cows work the grass. They call out, what is the word, bray? No, it's something else, I can't remember. I stand and listen.

Organized patches of green. Those intimate stone walls. Built by men with big hands, carefully selecting their slates, splitting them in half. A piece of farm equipment, giant, still, blades painted a cheerful red. Abandoned buildings, straw bales paused on slopes. In the past I dealt with beauty by assuming it was too good for me. Now, who knows. I walk up, not quite the fell but the hill before, panting. The path runs out. Below me is the school. Laid out like the dead author's novel. The plot suddenly small enough to fit between my fingers. Mrs S's house obscured by the pine trees that grow on its large border, by the scoop of road. You can buy a postcard of this view. I have seen the image in the bookshop. Torn clouds. A bird of prey's needling cry. A cliché, here I am reflecting by mistake, this is my new year after all. The Housemistress is right. I will tell Mrs S about my birthday. Don't I already know what it is to have something to lose?

We will sit outside. His return scheduled for later today. Mrs S pours coffee into dainty cups. Porcelain. In the kitchen I watch her panic over biscuits, bringing the packet out then putting it away again. She struggles to know what kind of guest I am. Biscuits would be nice. I encourage her. She laughs, a high pitch. Sorry, I'm nervous, suddenly you make me nervous. She senses it now. To her I have new size, new mystery. My chest broader. Is it my birthday? Is that it? She shrugs. Could be. Did you get me anything? A smile, purposefully shy. Of course. I take a biscuit straight from the plate. She replaces it. Nothing big though, I'd have liked more time to think about it. Sorry, I don't usually do birth-days. No? No, it's too much pressure, too much of the spotlight. I think I understand, I can't say I look forward to them much now either, although when I was your age I was very pro-birthday, I rather enjoyed them. A silver tray, belonging to the house. Milk goes into a fine blue jug. When's yours? Now that I won't disclose. Usual, in her circles, to leave such things unsaid. Her exact age almost impossible to master. That posture. I'm left guessing, piecing together the fact of her from what she's let slip, forty, maybe older.

251

She asks me to move the table into the shade of a willow, closer to the river, away, I realize, from the house. We will see him before he sees us. She sets down the cups. I follow with the chairs. The furniture heavy, impractical. We sip the coffee. I watch the workings of her throat. What? Nothing. The day leans in to us. I want you. Not here. Underneath the table I glimpse the movement of her thighs, suddenly pressed together, trying to dam the feeling. She wants me too. I lay my palm, half-open, across the table. Make my fingers explicit. Don't, not here. But already she is in the game. I circle my thumb against the tip of my forefinger. Move on to the next, touching each one gently, the sound of my skin turned to insects' wings. Her eyes bounce off the house. She keeps an eye out for him. Back to me. Inches her legs apart. Slides her own hand up her thigh. From a distance we would only be sitting, talking, ordinary. Only I know the moment she enters herself. She lets it be known. A tear in her breath.

The Girls pass by on the road beside the church. We are disturbed by their gossip, sound travelling around the house, they cannot see us. Mrs S turns her head but does not immediately remove her hand. Instead she presses her legs tighter. Takes the most, whatever she can, from the moment. A shudder, designed for me. I don't turn my head to follow the sound of The Girls as she does. Surprised by my own confidence. Today he will return to our life, our lives. He might ask to join us for coffee, stuffing biscuits into his mouth. Maybe I want to be caught, to let this new self be known, to show what our fucking has given me. Did you like that? Yes. Now she is genuinely shy. Swept up by our impulse. Quickly puts her fingers in mine. I bow to them, take one in my mouth, find her taste. Stop that, no. You can't do that then just expect me to sit here. Can't I? Was that my present then? Consider it one of them, wait here. She rises, tilts slightly, affected by her fucking. I laugh. Enough. She is playful, stern. Halfway to the house she removes both her heels and walks across the grass barefoot. Looks over her shoulder to make sure I have noticed. So easily wild in her domesticity.

I could touch myself. But the garden already has that after-fuck peace. With only me as a witness, a robin calls cockily from a low-lying bush. The river. On the other side of the house, the roses. From here you cannot see the fells. Instead I am surrounded by a high brick wall, other flowers, hers too, also half-heartedly taken care of. Most allowed to become too large, they risk choking out their neighbours, in desperation they have grown forwards. Only one cloud above. Travelling fast. I close my eyes and do not notice her until she is at my side, her form only a sensation. She slides a hand over mine, prises it open. Places something heavy inside. Happy birthday, it's the best I could do. Rolled in layers of gold tissue paper, recycled from some other gift. A large grey pebble. Is this, is it from the church? The broken window? That vulnerability, when it appears, collapses her face. The fine features muddled. No, goodness no. For a moment she thinks of me, of the things I might want. Would you have preferred that? No, maybe, I don't know. Quietly I consider it. It would have been a kind of exchange, the piece of stained glass, the damage, for her. The stone for me. As if I had been the hand that threw it. Well. She wants to brighten the mood. Well then, there's always next year, or Christmas, if you're very good. I grin, weakly.

She points at her pebble. Turn it over. Underneath she has taped a tiny, handwritten note in blue pen. The name of the fell, the river where we swam, and the date. The stone as smooth as a trout's belly. I would make it wet, rinse it under the tap, find the shine I remembered. You took this? That day? I did. Where did you keep it? She frowns. I have forgotten to say thank you. So you like it? Yes. I struggle for another word. Something as tangible as the pebble. Yes. She is upset. I love it, I do, I think it's the nicest thing anyone has ever given me. Too much and not enough. Nice, wrong, nicest, especially wrong. Embarrassment begins to take her body. She rounds her shoulders, clears her throat, resorts to the safety of an average joke. Then you must not have had many decent gifts, it's just a pebble, plenty of them in the world. Waves her hand. To let me know I am momentarily dismissed. The lone cloud long since sprinted, we are swallowed by blue.

I want to know where you kept it, can you tell me. Why? She drinks her coffee again, even though it is cold. Because, I want to challenge her, to say because it is a piece of you, of us, isn't it, that's what this is. I don't, choosing instead to agree with her. We sit in our silence: it's just a pebble. She won't tell me where she kept it. I allow myself to guess, imagining it nestled in her underwear drawer, rolling heavily each time she pulls it open. Either way it is in her bedroom, on her bedside table, touched every now and again with her assertive fingers, or observed suddenly, mid-conversation, mid-contemplation. He doesn't notice its arrival.

She is ready to recover. More coffee? I am permitted to stay longer. Rubs her arms. Suggests we move back into the heat. I know I won't last long, but right now I'm cold. Another smile, larger. I place the pebble in my pocket. Enjoy the manly weight. That is her word, I realize, manly. She directs her limbs into the sun. Like one of her roses. That's better. I feel the familiar kiss of sweat. Her body always able to reveal itself. Still barefoot. In poor imitation I roll up my t-shirt sleeves, give away my knees, the sun hits my skin as if I am made from wax. Feels good, doesn't it, so what else have you done for your birthday? This is it so far. Have your parents called? Not yet, Mum will, though, my mother, she usually does. I lie. Too late she remembers my father, that I don't speak to him. Opening her eyes, offering her empathy. Is it difficult, on your birthday? Not really, not more than any other day. Both my parents are dead. An announcement, no-nonsense, she does not need my empathy though I will offer it anyway. I'm sorry. Oh I'm used to it by now. She moves her foot across mine. But you, you're too young, you shouldn't be used to it, can't you call him, your father? It's not that easy. I'm not saying it is. She has to offer her advice. All I mean is, you ought to try, I'm sure he misses you. Doubt that. How can you know if you don't try? Irritation moves like an itch across my cheeks. Trust me, he doesn't want to hear from me, not unless I've magically changed. And have you, changed? I realize she can't understand what I'm referring to. That she has assumed my father and I have fallen out over some petty, solvable difference. Well I haven't stopped being a lesbian, if that's what you mean. She tries not to appear shocked. My heart has also grown larger, bolder, it's true, to fit inside this chest. That isn't, it's not what I meant. This word, lesbian, finally between us. Its bruising success. I look at her. Perhaps it isn't shock she tries to hide but fear.

She fidgets with the cup. Wipes a finger around the rim. Can I ask you something? Yes. Did you always know? Know what? This time I will have her say it. That you were, you know, that you were a lesbian? I leave the word suspended. She'd like me to scoop it from her mouth, to take responsibility for its meaning. It's not possible, to always know, that directly, I mean I knew I felt differently, that I thought differently, but when I was a kid, it could have meant anything. She is cautious, choosing her next question delicately. Was there a specific moment, then, that you can remember? Her foot is still across mine, its presence suddenly at the forefront of my mind, the high curve of her arch, the shoes still in the middle of the lawn. Well, there are moments, more than one. I sense that she is not asking to get to know me, but to understand herself, to use my history to search for some crucial indicator in hers. You won't tell me? I don't know, I'm just thinking, I'm trying to think. In order to explain I'd have to recreate an inexplicable context. The things I began to fall in love with. A schoolfriend's handwriting, the time I accidentally wrote her name instead of mine on the cover of an exercise book. What else? The bus driver, her hands around the wheel, an English teacher buttoning a cardigan. Obsessions, tangible, like a pebble in the pocket.

In the end, she is generous. Does not wait for an answer. Offers herself up instead. You know, you're not my first. I suspected it, the way she fucks, but did not think I would ever hear a confession. No? No, there was somebody else. Just one? She can't help herself, she picks up my hand and bites the skin between forefinger and thumb. Just one. When? She decides how to tell me. Bottom lip pinned between her teeth. University, when else. Who was she? A friend of a friend, I found her beautiful, the moment I met her, and there was nothing I could do. To resist, you mean? Yes. She was irresistible? Yes. I'm jealous. I can see that. Tell me everything. You know I've never spoken to anyone about it before. No? I move from my chair and sit at her feet, leaning my back against her legs. It is a dangerous thing, to fold into her, to risk being seen. She allows it. At the sound of his footsteps up the drive I will scramble away. No, it wasn't, you understand, it was even worse back then. I nod, letting her feel it, my cheek grazing her calf. She is quiet, the images of her past slowly redrawn. Impatient, I prompt her. So she was irresistible. Yes, sorry. I'd like her to say irresistible like you. She does not, she moves backwards, I am reduced to a witness.

I suppose I was your age, maybe younger actually, I was younger, twenty. OK, I say, OK. Really. She sighs. Really the story isn't as interesting as you're hoping, we met at a party, there was too much to drink. I cut her off, I must have my details. What did you drink? What do you mean, does it matter? Her patience tested but not yet broken. Matters to me. Fine, you strange thing. She looks around her garden. Takes stock of her desperate flowers, the new paths they have been forced to make. Most likely we were drinking cheap champagne, it was a birthday party, in fact it might have been good champagne. She nudges me at the mention of a birthday. What were you wearing? Oh now, come on, I have no idea. Yes, you do. She does not know how much I want her memory. I turn and put my face to her thigh. Run up my lips. Increasing voltage. A gasp. Alright, alright, it was the seventies, I had this blue dress, short, these sleeves that fanned out. Good, and her? Polka dots, a blouse, we both had boyfriends, dreadful boyfriends.

Was it him? Goodness no, although, I would meet him not long after. I let my stomach sink. The usual, we talked, we couldn't talk close enough, at some point we left, walked along the green, she asked if she could kiss me, I agreed. Where? I said. On the green. What green? The university green, it's just a big lawn, I've already explained, honestly, you're too much. She denies me the last part. The inexplicable context. Perhaps this she understands. The thing that is known first in the body. What happened afterwards? We started seeing each other, in secret of course, she had her own place, made it easier. For how long? Months, three months. She sighs again. Pins my arms. That's enough questions, birthday or not. Sorry. You don't need to be sorry. I'm being greedy. Yes, you are.

Footsteps, the front door. He is back earlier than planned. I stand up, rush into the chair. Check my pocket for the pebble. It is still there, safe. She smooths her dress as if I have creased it. Wipes her thumbs under her eyes, she hasn't cried, she is worried about the crumpled look of sex, of sexuality. A piece of her given over. Now, in his presence, she needs it back. Perhaps her guilt will acquire new size. Before he appears, in person, or at the kitchen window, she grabs my hand. Crushes the knuckles together. It hurts. Happy birthday, she whispers, as if even my birthday might give us away. His voice, across the lawn, searching for her. When he comes into view I see he has loosened his tie. He notices me. His hand fusses the collar of his shirt, considering doing it back up, wanting to maintain the aesthetic of authority. Good afternoon. Hi. Hello darling. She moves to him. Before, I think, before he sees her shoes. Still abandoned in the grass.

The pebble is too large to fit underneath my tongue. I try, I am an idiot. I forget her label. Remove it carefully, stuck to the sink, place the pebble back under my tongue. When it doesn't work I look in the mirror and try again, keeping my focus on my mouth. The pebble's texture, rough against my tongue, causes a wave of nausea. I have not seen her in days. As is our rhythm. I should be more accustomed to it by now. My cheeks flood with spit, my body wants me to swallow. Love won't leave. Is that how you know it is love? My recurring thought is the woman in the polka-dot shirt, the smell of grass, perhaps she taught her how to make that perfect smoke ring. Before I fall asleep, to gain some sort of agency, I kiss her instead. Mrs S forced to watch. Now her memory belongs to me. Shouldn't I take what I can? Self-preservation, perfect in its simplicity. There is no explanation for my love except that I want to say it. I don't remember thinking it through before it appeared, I love you, a brand-new reality. The spit, the sweat, the veins riding closer to the skin. Such things the heart cannot help but translate.

I ask her to turn around. I want her shoulder blades. In flight, as I remember them. She moves lightly. Bends her neck towards the sheets. This is how he likes to fuck. Unwittingly I have created his context. She moves her hips, expectant. Makes a noise I don't recognize. Her submission different, rehearsed. Still she finds pleasure in it. Flicks her head around, impatient. She sways on all fours. It works. My need opens, thighs bearing forward. I grip the cock at its base. I want to be like him. I weigh a hand in the small of her back. She tilts upwards. Reaches her arms forward. Shoulder blades drawn. The swim of her muscle. Pooling like water around the bone. Strong, rarely does she use her strength. Other people do things for her. Me, I am one of them. You want it, don't you? Yes, yes. The language of sex. Sincere because it does not have to be. Only speaks to what is already in motion, sentences swallowed by their own action. She spreads her legs wider. Shows herself to me. I want to be better than him. I hold myself still, she senses my skin, the way it will not touch hers. That noise again. Not belonging to us, but her other life, I am taking it from her. She reaches around and grabs my cock. This is what he

261

would need. I let her. That hand, its rhythm. She has me. Wants to guide me inside. I resist, I reposition her, my hands holding her hips. Enter her slowly. Pull her onto me. She wants to move deeper. Then comes a sound I recognize, a pleading, cracked, from the dark of her lungs.

There is no shade. The Girls line up in the car park between the sixth-form houses. In the heat the glue from their straw boaters begins to melt, sticking the lining to their foreheads. Hymn books, hymn books. The Housemistress walks the line, calling out, checking. Each of The Girls smacks a thick red tome in response. A fine if they forget, worse if it is lost. For church I must wear a suit. I suffer with the only one I have, purchased by my mother, a woman's suit, the blazer tailored to create a phantom pinched waist. A shirt designed to be undone to reveal the collarbone. The Housemistress's suit is handsome. The sleeves a little long, stopping only at her mount of Venus, her thumb half-visible. She does not dare wear a tie even though the suit would take it. It would be too masculine, an affront to the rest, to the other, lesser men in their own suits. She catches me staring and winks. I wink back but too slowly, she misses it, marching past. A few of The Girls giggle. I don't know if it's at me. I keep my arms pinned to my sides so they will not see me sweat.

The Housemistress offers me a bottle of whisky. Happy day of birth, sorry I didn't have time to wrap it. I lift it to the light, see a couple of glassfuls have already been drunk. You shouldn't have. I didn't. She winks. Best I could do, next time I'll know in advance, I've put the date in the mind palace. She taps her temple. I read the label. Pretend to know what I'm looking at, to understand a good whisky from a bad one. Don't worry, it's nice enough, I should know I've already sampled it. Thanks. Pour us a glass then. Back in my kitchen. Broad in the limited space. T-shirt and shorts, declared to be too hot for anything else. Got any ice? She pushes past me and opens the freezer. Finds an empty ice tray and drops it, disappointed, into the sink. Lukewarm it is, then. I pour some into two mugs. Seriously? She stands behind me and grabs the bottle, lifting it higher, doubling the amount. It's for your fucking birthday. Cheers. We hug. She holds me very tight, then releases. Salt and skin, the last note of her perfume.

So what did she get you then? Who? I know she means Mrs S. She likes to wind me up. I rise to it lightly. Who? Very funny, don't tell me she didn't bother. No, she did.

I'm imagining the card, handmade, a dedication done in calligraphy, I bet it rhymed. Fuck off. Couldn't possibly. She downs her whisky and winces. That good? Yep. I can't yet meet her in her drinking. I sip it. Pussy, you're such a pussy, or is it that she's been teaching you manners. Her mouth makes an excessive pout, pinkie finger held out, fluttering. No, it's just too early. She covers the face of her watch. Makes up the time. It's three minutes past five, you're fine, so come on, stop dodging the question, what'd she get you? I take a larger sip. Try not to let the sour burn show. Fuck, what, was it a dildo?! No, you wish. I do actually. She gave me a pebble. A pebble? A pebble. OK. The Housemistress is high-energy. Unable to stand still, her hips impatient. I look into my mug to avoid her eyes. She turns gentler. Well as long as a pebble is exactly what you wanted. It is, it was, very high on the wish list. She waits for me to finish. Tops us both up. I drink faster, more accustomed to the taste, beginning to enjoy it, my mouth cleansed. Look, not to show up your fancy lover, or whatever she is, but I also thought you might like this. Her hand scrambles in the pocket of her shorts. Produces something small and slippery. Here. I am afraid, suddenly, of her love, the quality of it. Between my fingers I roll the thick silver chain. Her grandfather's, the not-nice man, the one I wore to the bar. Happy birthday, again. You sure? I'm sure. She is matter-of-fact, she won't let me fuss. It looked good on you, besides, I'm taking whatever's left of the whisky home, so.

I put it around my neck. She finishes the fastening. Fingertips like breath, efficient, learned. Care is second nature to her. Pats my cheek affectionately. See? Suits you better. You reckon? Now it can begin a new legacy, you can pass it on to the next impressionable young dyke you come across. Is that me? An impressionable young dyke? She laughs. No, not anymore, I guess not, I mean I should be taking tips from you really, you're the one fucking the headmaster's wife. She wants to talk about it but is unsure how to ask. It is me, it is my fault, the sense of duty Mrs S has imparted, our world idealized by its privacy. I don't mean to take the piss. She removes an imaginary fleck from her t-shirt. It's just bizarro, you don't bring it up, it's like this whole other side to you. I know I'm sorry. When I don't know what to say I apologize. This habit suddenly glaring. I'm not offended, I guess, if you don't want to talk about it I can respect that and maybe I don't want to know anyway, I have to look her in the eyes most days, maybe I can't handle whatever kinky shit you get up to.

I reach out to The Housemistress. Squeeze her shoulder. Hard as a Greek god, I imagine her bones, an entire skeleton, made of beautiful marble. I guess I haven't been in this situation before, I just don't know who I owe what. You don't owe anyone anything. She is clear-eyed. Stands still long enough for me to take her seriously. You know that don't you? You don't owe anyone anything, you've got to take care of yourself. I know. Did I know that, though? How The Housemistress said it, my hand still on her marble shoulder, getting warmer, the flesh coming real. I hope you do. Gently she mocks my position, placing her own hand on my shoulder, applying a matching pressure. I seem too small under her grip. People like us, we've got to take care of ourselves, we've got to take care of each other. Her earnestness, unexpected, makes me awkward. I laugh anxiously. It's good, it's just fun. Impossible, lesbians rarely have any fun. She raises a special eyebrow. I will have to learn how to do the same. Practise in front of the mirror. Honestly, it is. Remember, yeh, don't go falling in love with her or anything ridiculous like that. Deal. It's not too late, is it? No, I lie. It's definitely not too late.

Movement behind a curtain. Two of The Girls, kissing on the large windowsill. They wrap around each other. The kiss finishing, a shocked laugh pressed into a neck. The windowsill cramped, dusty. Library books abandoned and stacked along the glass. A space now entirely rewritten. Neither registers me until it is too late. I stall. Miss, Miss, it's just a dare OK. One of them is quickly tearful. Don't tell. Where they have chosen is barely private. Perhaps, inside, behind the old fabric, they made their own distance from the world. An impulse so urgent it had to be here, halfway down the stairs. It's a quiet evening. Supper only just finished. My own history rises in my throat. Rare to be confronted by the past, by anything reminiscent of how my own life began. Blood marches back to the voids. I would never have been so brave. Miss? I have made an audience of them. Listen, back to your dorms, OK. But Miss, will you tell? Just go back to your dorms. They hesitate. Afraid of me for the first time. When it is clear I won't give an answer, they shuffle forward, slide off the windowsill. No more eye contact. Side by side down the corridor. Without touching, although their hands swing close, fingertips can't help their hopefulness.

She stays longer than usual. I want to hold her but can't make the request. Inches away, her head on the crook of her arm, looking at me. Love felt, I think, in the slowed current that passes between us after fucking, now separated, required once again to find the edges of our own bodies. Flush of her orgasm running up her neck. She doesn't mind that I see it. Puts her palm against it to register its temperature. Incredible, no idea why that happens, what a thing. Lets me think only I can do it to her. Bring her whole self to the surface. I stay flat on my back. Her hand goes to my chest, I am naked apart from my binder, touching it as she did the first time we fucked. Except now she is lighter, more careful. Rhythm of water faded. Thinks she is caring in her new caution. I place my hand over hers and press it down.

So far she has not mentioned leaving. Her eyes close, as if she might sleep. I have never seen her sleep. I want it. Any chance to catch her vulnerable. Mouth half-open, maybe, a soft snore. Could be she never sleeps. Or only in bursts, when she is certain of her solitude, that no one will find her unguarded. I reach across and touch her eyelids with my thumbs. Saintly treatment, as in, I confirm her sainthood, those parts of herself she cannot name, but I have devoted myself to. I move underneath her eyes and sweep the fragile skin. What're you doing? she whispers. My thumbs continue making their map. I don't want to leave her body just yet, I don't want to return to mine. Cheekbones, nose. At her lips she shudders, biting down after I have moved on, resetting the sensation. Her chin. Along the wave of her jaw. Surprised at the undulations, the bone not smooth as glass, instead I find the surface of the sea. Disturbances. Muscle, tendons, whatever else lives there. Her ears, then behind her ears, around the base of her skull, a thinking route, I imagine her as a collection of synapses, arching under my stroke. I take my hands away. She doesn't speak. Not even a whisper. You OK? She nods. Reaches out and takes my wrist. Pulls me on top of her. I concentrate my weight on her chest, my head underneath her chin. We lie like this in silence. For seconds, for minutes. At her request, a gentle tapping on my back, I lift off her body. She breathes deeply. Kisses me. It is time for her to go.

She dresses. Takes her underwear and tucks it under my pillow. Keep them, that way I'm not really leaving. Except that she is. A uselessness rises in my chest. Shame, it finds me everywhere, I give in to its resourcefulness. She pulls her dress straight, a side zipper, patterned. Checks her earrings, still in place. My cracked, crappy mirror. I take her underwear and drape them across my face. What are you doing, don't do that. She sits on the bed. I pull at the elastic, hold them tighter. Stop it, come on. She fights me now, fingers prying mine open. Her own shame, internalized, authoritative. Will sit on my face, but decides there's a time and a place for such things, to inhale her like this, in this moment, the moment afterwards, she disapproves.

I forgot to tell you. What? She snatches the underwear from me. Tucks them back underneath the pillow. You won't believe it, I saw two of The Girls kissing. What? Voice like a struck match. She stands again. I had not anticipated this reaction. Stupid, it dawns on me, how stupid. What do you mean? I mean I saw two of The Girls kissing. I don't understand, where? On the windowsill, the one going up the first flight of stairs, above the long corridor. She doesn't want to believe me. Shakes her head. I don't understand. What is there to understand? It was sweet, romantic, they seem to like each other. I won't explain that twinge of pain, although I had planned to, her reaction no longer deserving of my honesty. I don't think so. She turns her back to me. Crouches, finishes the buckle that waits at her heel. The shoes a delicate summer sandal. Beige. You don't think so? No, all I mean is, they ought not to, it's not encouraged, it would be the same if it was a boy, if you'd seen one of The Girls kissing a boy and told me. Would it? Yes! She is incredulous. So am I. But, I mean, you have those discos, dances, whatever, don't those encourage it? Encourage what? Come on, heterosexuality, girls kissing boys, girls growing up to marry boys, fuck, it even means girls punching boys. You're dramatizing something that doesn't need to be dramatized. Heterosexuality, she parrots me, throwing air quotes around my word, mocking the way I used it, lingering at my bedroom door. No, I just, I'm trying to understand why this is different. Goodness it isn't that complicated, it's just the rules. There's an actual rule? Yes, of course, it would be difficult, to have romance amongst The Girls, the idea is they can focus here, in a same-sex environment, they can become the best version of themselves. I laugh. Unless that version is a lesbian, of course. Why do you have to do that? Do what? Dramatize it, Christ, make this political, it will be a slapped wrist, two slapped wrists, I'll handle it myself. What does that mean? She holds her answer. There's no torture chamber, Christ, don't fret. She puts her forehead to the doorframe. Closes her eyes. I've exhausted her. Why is it always you? Her voice smaller. Me? You, always you, finding The Girls in these positions, the drugs, now this. I stare at the ceiling. The skylight bright enough to collapse my vision. Cursed, I guess. The word enters the space between us, cursed. In her presence, her eyes averted, I believe it. My body, turning other bodies bad. She thinks, even if only for a second, that what I have is contagious.

Her face takes on a neutrality I cannot trust. Almost naked, I am aware of my legs, my hips, sun cutting out shapes of skin. I see it, her distaste, the mobility of her eyes, lips, how quickly they rearrange. She sighs, I sigh back. Fine, deal with it, do it your way. She returns to the bed. Calmer. I don't have a choice, they can't, it's for their own good, whatever they do after school, when they've left, that's a different matter, clearly I'm not against any of that. I let her hold my hand. Any of that, her words, hardening in my gut. I see The Girls, their brushing fingertips, let the pain return like a dropped glass.

I don't sit up, speak only to the skylight. Sure, yeh, I get it. You do? Sure. Alright, that's good. She pauses, not wanting to ask me the next question, which I already know is coming. This time I am ready, this time I know who I am dealing with. Which of The Girls was it, that you saw? I look at her now. Scrunch my face in faux-thinking. I can't remember. You can't remember? No, I'm sorry, if it comes back to me I'll let you know. She takes her hand away. Alright, good, well you just let me know then. I will. She kisses me lightly. The lie between us known and sealed. She rises, gives an awkward wave, as if suddenly finding me at a great distance. The bedroom door closes behind her. I hear her pause, only for a second, on the landing. Expect her to return. She does not.

Rain, without warning. I think of my teenage note in the margins of the dead author's novel, PATHETIC FALLACY, written excitedly, as if no one else had ever spotted it, her dark mood reflected in sky. I lie in bed but don't reach for the book. Choose to picture my handwriting instead. Each letter carefully carved out. My very best blue biro. Hopeful that someone might look across at my desk and see it, might see the beauty of my discovery. Nobody did, I don't think, I can't remember. This is no ordinary rain. Water thumps the skylight like knuckles, thumps the ancient slate roof. My eyelids close. I am made from weather. I try to see myself at fourteen, at thirteen, at fifteen. Already living in my knees. Shoulders rolled forward, hunched, why are you always hunched, my mother asking me. She did not know I was protecting the core of myself. Her hands forcing my shoulders straight. Muscle coiled, recoiled. I heaved back into place. That is what we learn to do. Above me the rain thickens. Turns to a wet veil, pulled down the glass. I imagine The Housemistress in the tiny flat. Watching the rain as I am, her window opened a crack to let the sound in. She'll start on her sofa, then, not close enough, she'll lie for a minute right underneath the sill. My first kiss. What to do with a memory like that. There was a way it was supposed to be. The Girls kissing behind the curtain. I think of them every minute, I want to explain all of this to them. Truth or dare, my brother's friends already knew I was different, the way only teenagers can. The smell of fireworks set off. Months of drought, land that could burn for days, weeks. We drank tins of beer. Rolled tight cigarettes. Boys singed each other's forearms, I offered mine up, it thrilled them. Truth, dare. Dare. Truth didn't have a chance. It was demanded I kiss a girl, didn't matter which, the nearest one to me would do. We protested, she and I. Our heads forced together by other hands. Teeth, skin. I bit my own tongue to stop it from touching hers.

In his office I see the portrait of the dead author. Her skin is apricot, as described by the history teacher. She is demure, what else. Men did not know how to paint any other expression on a woman. Her apricot skin. More rose than skin, she is one large petal, pinned into place. It hangs precisely behind his desk. Fine isn't it? Mr S points at the gilded frame, turning in his seat. I nod. How are you? Well, I hope? There are two more portraits, both of the dead author's father, the school's founder. In one he is youthful, daring, a leg up on a rock, the mountain setting moody. Rarely is there a painting on a sunny day, I think. The other shows him older, not entirely old, but wiser at least, eyebrows appropriately thickened, at a desk with a quill in his hand. I want to laugh. The desk in the portrait is the same one Mr S sits behind, waiting for my response.

Fine, thanks. Good, that's good, excuse me, please, while I get myself sorted. He unpacks a briefcase, wears a light linen suit. He seems always to walk on air. There is no way he could know, I decided on the way to his office. No way, she is too careful, besides, he wouldn't believe such a thing could be real. Unless Mrs S told him directly, it would never cross his mind. A weak imagination keeps him safe. So. He sits, checking his cufflinks, tucking loose papers under a glass paperweight. Curved like a lens. The sun, on the right angle, could set fire to his desk. My panic renews. Maybe she did give us away, late night, after some romantic gesture of his, she had to confess. The guilt too much to bear, she dropped to her knees, begged for his forgiveness. I try to read his face, to look for a clue, anything. He buries whatever he feels. My teeth want to chatter. I clamp my mouth shut. He clears his throat. So, this isn't, well, this won't be an easy conversation. He puts the end of his tie between his fingers and snakes it through. OK, I mutter, the tremor goes to my jaw. His expression is pitying, his smile takes effort. I spoke to The Girls, I have been speaking to The Girls, The Girls who were there, that night at the graveyard, as you know.

Two large windows are either side of the moody portrait. They look out on the sloping lawn below, so named The Headmaster's Lawn. A few of The Girls arrive, spreading out textbooks, wanting to revise in the sunshine. Willows bowed and touching their arms to the ground. The view, as framed by the window, creates an almost identical image to the one on the front cover of the school's prospectus. Unless The Girls have been inside his office, they might not realize the clarity with which they can be seen. I have tried looking in from the outside. It is not possible, the direction of the light, the way it bounces off the old glass.

He is still speaking. She has told him nothing. I haven't been listening. He knows this, his face now following my gaze out of the window. I know this is hard to hear, The Girls told me, they mentioned that you and The Housemistress had caught some of the others drinking a few weeks back, they were upset as that group did not get in much trouble, whereas they are facing larger disciplines. On the lawn The Girls flip onto their stomachs, flicking through pages. I had to pretend to know what they were talking about, it wasn't ideal, as you can imagine, for me not to know such a thing. He waits for me to be sorry. Instead I say nothing. What is there to say? He knows he is right, I am only here to bear witness to his display of morality. So I'm forced to ask, did it happen? Did you catch some of The Girls drinking? I've been fucking your wife, I want to say, I've fucked her in your house, in your bed.

There are hardly any lines around his eyes. He sleeps well. I did, yes, I found them, down by the river. You did? Yes. You should have informed me, immediately, that is the obvious protocol. I didn't know that. Yes, well, if you didn't know, The Housemistress would have known. He leans back, puts his tie through his fingers again, fabric whipping his skin. The Housemistress, an apparition, I see her suit, her ring of keys, the hole in her dressing gown. The way she treats The Girls, their mother. He gets up, sits on the edge of the desk, folds his arms. Oh I asked her not to say anything. Why? On the spot I can't think of a good enough lie, one that might protect us both, The Housemistress and I. She didn't know they'd been drinking. No? No. It wasn't obvious? No, and, it was me, I bought them the alcohol, they'd promised to be sensible, The Housemistress didn't know that either, she just thought they'd been caught out of bed, I brought them back. I am clumsy, stumbling over the words. That's why I didn't want her to tell anyone.

His shock enlivens me. You bought it for them? Yes. What did you buy? Beers. They claim it was vodka. Well they might, I suppose, to make the whole thing seem more dramatic. He considers me half-heartedly, coasting over the features of my face. Men stare at me from all sides. Mr S, the portraits. I realize this is the desired effect. To have the person sitting in this chair squirming under their weight. I remember in fast slides the posters he chose for Mrs S's office, a million miles away. The Georgia O'Keeffe. Her role, her feminine role, as he sees it, to weaken The Girls before he throws the final blow. The Girls moving, constantly, from premeditated space to premeditated space. And now me.

I stand up, I will get ahead of him. I think I ought to leave, to quit, I'm not sure it's the right fit for me here. He stands too. Hides his relief well. I have saved him paperwork. Offers me his hand. A terrible shame, but perhaps yes, for the best. I look over his head at the dead author. She does not look back. Her eyes are aimed at the front of the room, the front of every room in which she is hung. I pause in the doorway. She almost finds me here, the dead author, her gaze skimming the top of my head. The Girls, what will you do with them? Do with them? He slides the papers out from underneath the paperweight. How will they be punished? We try not to use words like punish. He reads, or he pretends to read, the first page. You won't tell me? It's still under consideration. I linger, hopeful. He will not look up. Please, do close the door behind you. He is still polite, despite how much he wants me gone. By tomorrow he won't think of me at all.

I can't catch my breath, I go to see her. Her driveway. The scent of pines, almost healing. Then their voices, his and hers. He shouts excitedly. I wait in a shadow, cradled by a tree, opposite the house. A ladder positioned under an eave. Gloves, a spray, can red and yellow. Shirt cuffs tightened with elastic bands. Trousers too. She appears. Places a hat on his head. Lovingly. The solid drone of wasps. He plans to kill them all with one can of spray. To arrest their nervous systems. Up the ladder. He leans forward with fear, keeps his face away, the first wasps emerge. They sense him. He climbs down again, rattled. She provides him with a pep talk. Calls out. Be quick, darling, just be quick. I see her hands. Spread against her thighs. I want to find evidence I know her better. That she is alarmed, that she is disgusted. No, instead she is at his side, rubbing, soothing, he climbs back up. Darling, just do it, go on, be quick. He holds the can and sprays. Looks away. The wasps change their tone, grow heavier with fury. He jumps from the ladder. They watch from a distance, holding each other's shoulders. Proud of their project. Wasps begin to drop. Some will carry the poison back inside the nest, accidentally killing their queen. This is the aim. The pair of them grow bored, laughing over something else, they turn and make their way deeper into the garden, the back of the house. Out of sight.

I walk up to the hockey pitch. After school The Housemistress takes The Girls for rounders. At the gate I pause and watch. The distant purr of a lawnmower, the slow rustle of wind. Noises that seduce. Summer. Time pulled thin by pleasure. The Girls cry out in disappointment, in joy, at the satisfying knock of the ball against their wooden bat. They want each other to run harder, to hit faster. I try to put together a sentence. To at least know what I will tell The Housemistress before I face her. I'd like to say aloud what she means to me. She would hate this, maybe. I consider writing a letter, leaving it on her bedside table, slipping it under her door, but she would hate that even more. What would I say, anyway?

She wears a vest, long shorts, clapping her big hands together. It is glorious, to see her almost unleashed. The huge snake winking across her arm. The Girls do not fuss about her tattoos, out there, beside the fells. They call out, beckoning for her to stand at the mound and take a turn, they want to see her power, they want to be inspired. She steps up, resisting only lightly, putting her body into position. The Girl closest hands her the bat. She jokes around, lifting one leg and then the other, stretch after farcical stretch, The Girls scream with laughter. She nods at The Girl bowling, who throws a decent ball. Their eyes follow her happily. They see her strength. A perfect hit, the ball travelling half the field. Four, five of them scramble across the grass in chase. The Housemistress does not run around the posts but walks, they love this even more, she rests the bat on her shoulder casually, whistling, she has all the time in the world. The Girls flock around her, jumping at her shoulders, throwing their arms around her waist. I wave, she waves back.

There's love, what I feel for her, but that's not all. Love, so tight-lipped, so belonging to other people. Not us. It's more, that shared mineral under the skin. Maybe I am a coward, to not try and speak. Or is it enough, to say good-bye with our bodies, The Housemistress and I, those loaded hinges of our wrists, elbows, fingers? To exchange our masculinity, the places it lives. I wave again. She pauses a little longer, beckons me over. I shake my head, tap my forearm like a watch, like her watch, as if I have somewhere to be. Next time, I shout. She can't hear me, she raises her thumb in acknowledgement. Next time.

Sun returns. Rain only a smell across the tarmac. The theatre is too hot. One of The Girls, in her unpaid job as an usher, props open the doors. We wait for air to arrive but none does. A few of the women, the mothers, fan themselves with flimsy programmes. Water is sucked from plastic cups. People try to muffle the smack and pop of their mouths. The Housemistress will see the play tomorrow night, we were supposed to go together. Mrs S is not here. I can't leave, trapped now until the end, the drama teacher has already recognized me, winking as I watched the corridor procession. She has managed an atmosphere of sorts. Two green lights hit the Guernica, obscuring the centre, leaving only the chaotic edges on display. The Girls use the chairs with an exaggerated expertise. Sitting, standing, glaring. On the front row the drama teacher has settled in, her own features polished. She wants to be without expression, hopeful that she too is being watched, that she will be witnessed taking in her play intimately, profoundly.

The scene on stage develops, bringing with it an awkward silence, initiated by the presence of the parents.

Lorca describes an image of sex sold to the men who work the fields. The Girls carry themselves with an attitude that, I imagine, must be unrecognizable to their mothers and fathers. They walk with a different gait, as if their hips have widened. Adela has her new pout. She uses it, lips arching over every word. Another of The Girls, tall, flustered through her black veil. To be born a woman is the great crime. Not even our eyes are our own. The rest nod in agreement. Offstage a tape is clicked on. Through the tinny speakers suspended above the seats plays a recording of men singing, of men chattering, of men walking. There is the heavy swish of their trousers. Boots hitting a dusty track. Metal dangling, clanking, tools attached to belts, not in use but about to be. The volume is turned up, their voices melodic. It cuts. The Girls turn their heads to the audience and begin to chant. The reapers are leaving, they're off to the reaping, and with them the hearts, of all the girls watching.

A bright white light fires down the centre. A parody of sunlight. The audience shifts, I feel their discomfort. The chanting halts. Adela reaches a hand around her own throat and squeezes, rolling back her eyes. The rest of The Girls turn to watch her in unison. Into the centre of their semicircle walks Bernarda. The mother, the tyrant, her hips closed off. The Girl strides, back hunched. In her hand is a walking stick. It is too high for her. She moves through The Girls, past Adela. In front, close to the audience, she slams her walking stick into the ground. Behind her The Girls lower their heads. An audience member gasps, then laughs nervously.

Intermission. In darkness The Girls leave the stage. My cheeks flare. In desperation I look once more for Mrs S, hoping she somehow slipped past me, that perhaps I will find her shoulder blades in the crowds of people. They are concerned. I overhear their muttering. There are permanently raised eyebrows, they wait for their outrage to be acknowledged, the play is not appropriate for their daughters. For other daughters, maybe, but not their daughters. I can't see her, what if I never see her again.

A hand is around my forearm. I look up. It is the drama teacher. Her eyes wide. Pepe! My Pepe. There is a pause. She waits for me to talk about the play. I consider saying nothing, telling her I have to be elsewhere, but I am not that brave. It's going well, are you happy? Her eyes grow even wider, an explosion of red veins, she drinks, she is stressed. Darling there is an energy tonight, you know? Surprising even to me. I think it's good. You do? Bracelets slide up and down her wrist. Thank you, oh that means so much, it's not easy, to do something different in this place. She doesn't know I am leaving, that my opinion means nothing. I could say anything.

In the corridor a trestle table has been set up with red and white wine. The Girls in charge pour out precise measures. Those chosen for the task are careful, serious. Each bottle meticulously accounted for. White napkins draped over their arms. They say, repeatedly, white wine? Red wine? The parents hold out their hands and take glass after glass, some already have purple-stained teeth. Others ask for beer, or coffee, or water, or juice. There is none. The Girls shake their heads gravely, they are very sorry, very very sorry. I drink one white wine, then another, unsure of what to do. The interval will last only fifteen minutes. I walk away, down the corridor, aiming for her office. The door is locked. The chatter of the parents is at my back, the noise, the tang of wine, the bitterness. I rattle her door. Turn the handle. Bang once on the white-painted wood. At the end of the corridor I heave open the exit and stand outside. Ahead of me is the shoddy bookshop, behind the art centre. There is nobody else. Only me.

I hear the hand-held bell ring, indicating it is time to go back inside for the second half. I could run back to her house. I could run, follow the road down from the book-shop, I could run. It is my favourite time of day. Swallows dive from the building's corners. Light turning to pink, as if leaned against skin, the world held in a fist. He has proba-bly told her. Mr S making his eyes sorrowful, he had no choice, that is the thing, he will shrug, what else was he to do. She will listen, face stony, planning her reaction, to care just enough but not too much. She knows and she has not come for me. Perhaps she believes him, is shocked that I would do such a thing, now I am forever changed to her, she can never forgive me.

The corridor is quiet. A few parents down the last of the drinks, cringing at the final swish of wine, used to something superior. They look at each other as if going into battle. This is the British way, to not complain until later, to enter the room anyway. I walk in behind these last parents, feeling their disapproval. My seat is still empty. I must cross over laps to reach it. Excuse me, excuse me, excuse me. They do not excuse me. Their legs barely move.

I watch and watch. The play does not end. At last I recognize the final scenes. The Girl playing Adela finds a new pitch. She pulls off her veil, ripping the pins from her hair. If she feels pain it does not register. She leaves the stage and returns, straw through her hair, tucked down the front of her shirt. An accusation. She has been having sex with Pepe in the barn. A stallion kicks the wall of the house. He waits, he wants, to be delivered to the mares. True to the script, every few lines there is a drum banged offstage, supposedly brutish hooves.

I have always known I would have to live without her. But the how, how I might do that, has not crossed my mind until now. To face myself, alone. The hooves hit the wall again, louder. The men either side of me jump. This time there is no nervous laughter. I know what will happen next. Bernarda will get her gun and pretend to shoot Pepe. Bang. The horse, the drum. Bang. I am distracted by the door slowly opening. The men next to me swivel slightly to see. Somebody is too late, the play is about to finish. They love a petty drama, the possible failure of other parents. The noise of the door affects the crescendo happening before us.

An entire audience trying not to look. The Girls on stage do not seem to notice. Bang. This time it is the gunshot, the drum hit with finality, even louder. The Girls, the daughters, wail, dropping to their knees.

Mrs S appears. Her face twisted around the door. An apparition, walking straight out of my chest. Her eyes over the crowd. She is looking for me. I don't know what to do, I can't stand, I can't wave. I wait instead for her eyes. She is afraid. Here I am, I want to shout, here I am. She looks to the back of the room, up the seats, now she comes back down the other side. Almost, almost. The men next to me are watching her too. They recognize her, perhaps. Finally, she finds me. Her mouth opens, she beckons, the door closes. Applause begins. The play has ended. Others are too slow to get up. I scramble back across those laps, hitting each knee I can. The applause fades away, then increases, The Girls walk back on stage to complete their bowing. I see more mannerisms of the drama teacher, they put their hands over their hearts, they do not know gratitude, only an impersonation of it. Adela seems close to tears. I am at the door. Just as I push it open, the drama teacher makes brief, vicious eye contact before she too enters the stage, to take her bows. She points to The Girls, The Girls point to her.

Mrs S wears one of her summer dresses. I notice the buttons have been done haphazardly, as if she changed clothes in a hurry. She does not yet speak to me. As I walk towards her she turns, moving quickly to the main doors, opening them. I follow. She stops only once we have reached the gate, the church in front of us, her house only seconds away. We are in the shade of a bay tree, two bay trees, enormous together. I rub a leaf between my thumb and forefinger, waiting for her to talk. I realize she does not know what to say but that, like me, she needed to be together. In the end she is blunt. So you'll leave? Yes. Just like that? What else am I supposed to do? She chews her fingers, no longer tries not to, teeth pulling at pieces of skin, the edges of her nails raw. I don't know, I don't know. She looks behind me, her eyes finding the church. Is it even true? She stands a few feet away. Even for ordinary people, for friends, this would be too large a distance. The places our hands have been, now hung at our sides. Voices like stage whispers. Her question not so easy to answer. What did he tell you? That you bought them alcohol, that you caught them drinking. It's only half-true, I didn't buy them any booze, I wouldn't do that.

You lied, I don't understand. I had to. What, for her? She means The Housemistress. I didn't plan anything, it just didn't seem fair, for her to be fired, she cares about The Girls. She can't care about them that much if she's not acting in their best interests. Best interests? Don't. Her hand flies to her forehead and she holds it there. I didn't realize you two were so close. She is hurt and wants me to know, speech cold. I didn't realize. Not like that. I lose my knees, I steady myself on the gate. It swings away, I pull it back. Like what then? What is it like? I pick at a patch of rust. I'd like to slam the gate shut. I can't. Still I stay loyal to our subtlety.

What does it matter? You're still married. She searches for an answer. She has the posture of a married woman. At once self-satisfied and disappointed, the body giving itself away in certain places: the downturn of her eyes, those chewed fingers. I see her wedding ring, her engagement ring. She has not worn either around me recently. Removed for gardening, for fucking, for cooking, slipped off before I arrive, or before meeting me, left in the little dish. Even now, residual heat between my legs. Haven't I spent a lifetime separating my body from my mind? That is how I've survived. I should not be surprised it acts without me. I love you. She deploys it, said for the first time. This is love as it is already known, the translation that already exists, well used, it's in the tone of her voice. Working to justify, used to plead. It turns me on to hear it. Being like everyone else is so difficult to resist. To love, just like that.

She knows. Steps closer. Says it again. I love you. Looks towards the school. Reaches for my fingertips. I find her rings. I touch the gold band. The other is flashier, those sapphires, maybe his family heirloom. It is clichéd, to see it now, but it rescues me, as clichés can, that enormous swipe of inherited knowledge. I know you love me too. Her confidence is worn, this is not what she knows, she does not know how to be sure. Licks her lips. Waits for my confirmation. For me to submit. Heterosexuality, I remember her fingers moving around the word, making air quotes, like bird claws. She is and she isn't, one self is for private and one is for public. Would you leave him? I've never asked before, I didn't need to. I've learned to like our privacy. Maybe I relied on it. The safety of it, untested. That's not fair, that's not what we're talking about. Aren't you asking me to stay? My fingertips radiate. Of course, of course I want you to stay, it's complicated, I know, but if you stay, there'd be more time.

Behind us a few parents begin to exit the main doors. Making their way to the cars hurriedly parked on the road, unable to find space in the car park. I swear under my breath. Go to move, away from the gate, away from the path. Wait, don't, please wait. She dares to grab my arm. I have awakened something in her too. They walk towards us. A group of six. The Girls, their daughters, trail behind. All of them will have dinner together, drive to the best restaurant in the big town. The Girls looked at surreptitiously across the table, the concerned parents checking for new pouts, for new whispers, shocked by the play. We stand to one side. She greets them as they pass. One mother is thrilled to have caught her, they must catch up, it has been too long, how long has it been. Her eyes narrow, what an interesting evening it has been. The Girls recognize me. Hi Miss, they smile like cats. Do they already know? What do they know? A father hurries them along, the booking is soon, they'd best not be late. She watches the cars pull out, crawling down the thin road, honking their horns. Waves.

Laughs as if they can hear her. Her expression only changing once they are out of sight.

Sorry, I'm sorry about that, horrible timing, I know, it's not. The sentence has no ending. Unknots her hands. She can't think of what to say. Her fingers back in her mouth. I saw you. What? I saw you, with the wasp's nest. The strain of my binder. A dam. My body rises behind it, a wave about to break. She bunches her fingers in frustration. Almost a fist. What are you talking about, what wasps? You and him, getting rid of it, the nest. You came to the house? To find you. You shouldn't have done that. I wanted to see you. I know, I understand, but you shouldn't, you can't, you can't just show up. She misses the point. Does not think twice about what I saw. How the scene settled in my stomach. The way the world turns without me. Her heterosexuality, public-facing. Its cosy violence. Who does she want to be? If I ask her that, she might fall apart. If I ask her that, I must be willing to live through the answer. Ahead of me, in the thinning light, the church grows smaller. Oh, I enjoy cliché after cliché. The church, our church, grows smaller before my eyes. Without her, without clichés, there is not enough self to get me through. I rely on metaphor, I rely on signs. I forgive myself.

She waits for me to speak. To hear that I love her. I can't say it. My body wants to, that residual heat, the wetness, the ache where her hand has been. It will not give up so easily, my body. For a second I am weak. She sees the crack appear, the line starting at my mouth, she says it again, her voice lowered to a whisper. I know you love me too. Reaches out as if to touch my chest. Palm floating. To put the feeling in my mind. Her hand back and forth, the river she has sent me down. But she can only work the air, to touch me now would give us away. Our inescapable audience, the cars that drive along the road, the voices that carry from the school. If she did, if right now she gave me her hand, placed it against me, she might change my mind. She can't.

Our loneliness is not the same. It has been easier to pretend that it is. Fucking each other into being. She is trying to be two people, I am not. Maybe I was. Not anymore. Her ring flashing, her hand across her forehead. She cannot bear the silence. The waiting softens her, it always does. Listen to me, it's going to be fine, just tell him you didn't do it, he'd give you your job back, I know he would, I said I'd speak with you, that I didn't believe that was the truth. You did? Yes, of course, what do you think of me? She thinks language is this easy. I allowed myself to think the same, didn't it seem a nicer way to live, to believe in her language, the way she possesses it. When she is not around, I invent her. When she is around, I invent her. It is not her fault. Hasn't she made me feel this deserving? Please. Her please, riding her breath, its power. Please. I love you. The ring, that dead eye. I take her hand, the hand with its ring, and kiss it gently. She will not change, it is not her fault. I am changing, I have always been changing. This is not a state she can understand. She moves only towards what she has already seen. I could hit my own chest. Not me, not me. I will have a different life. Yes. I will leave. Her eyes. Oh, I will leave and she does not know it yet.